PENGUIN BO

Head over Heels

Head Over Heels

RAIN MITCHELL

PENGUIN BOOKS

PENGUIN BOOKS

Published by the Penguin Group
Penguin Books Ltd, 80 Strand, London WC2R 0RL, England
Penguin Group (USA) Inc., 375 Hudson Street, New York, New York 10014, USA
Penguin Group (Canada), 90 Eglinton Avenue East, Suite 700, Toronto, Ontario, Canada M4P 2Y3
(a division of Pearson Penguin Canada Inc.)
Penguin Ireland, 25 St Stephen's Green, Dublin 2, Ireland (a division of Penguin Books Ltd)
Penguin Group (Australia), 707 Collins Street, Melbourne, Victoria 3008, Australia
(a division of Pearson Australia Group Pty Ltd)
Penguin Books India Pvt Ltd, 11 Community Centre, Panchsheel Park, New Delhi – 110 017, India
Penguin Group (NZ), 67 Apollo Drive, Rosedale, Auckland 0632, New Zealand
(a division of Pearson New Zealand Ltd)
Penguin Books (South Africa) (Pty) Ltd, Block D, Rosebank Office Park, 181 Jan Smuts Avenue,
Parktown North, Gauteng 2193, South Africa

Penguin Books Ltd, Registered Offices: 80 Strand, London WC2R 0RL, England

www.penguin.com

First published in the United States of America by Plume,
a member of Penguin Group (USA) Inc., 2012
Fist published in Great Britain in Penguin Books 2012

001

Copyright © Penguin Group (USA) Inc., 2012
All rights reserved

The moral right of the author has been asserted

This is a work of fiction. Names, characters, places and incidents are either the product of the
author's imagination or are used fictitiously, and any resemblance to actual persons,
living or dead, business establishments, events or locales, is entirely coincidental.

Typeset by Palimpsest Book Production Ltd, Falkirk, Stirlingshire
Printed in Great Britain by Clays Ltd, St Ives plc

ISBN: 978–0–241–95367–9

www.greenpenguin.co.uk

Penguin Books is committed to a sustainable
future for our business, our readers and our planet.
This book is made from Forest Stewardship
Council™ certified paper.

ALWAYS LEARNING   **PEARSON**

To P. H. Thanks for getting the ball rolling and bending over backward to keep it moving.

PART ONE

It's a hot May morning, and Lee is sitting on her mat in a small yoga studio a few blocks from the beach in Santa Monica. There's a window open on one side of the room, but the sultry breeze blowing in is doing little to disperse the heavy smell of Nag Champa incense that's hanging in the air like a toxic cloud. It makes Lee happy that she stopped burning incense at Edendale, the studio she owns in Silver Lake — not for health reasons, but because it seems like such a tired cliché.

The studio is packed, as she suspected it would be, and buzzing with excitement. The teacher, David Todd, is someone she's been hearing about off and on for months now but has been too busy to take a class with. He's an itinerant, under-the-radar teacher with a loyal following but no home studio. He freelances all over town and has a reputation for being fiercely independent and somewhat eccentric, qualities that Lee usually approves of in a teacher, provided they don't lurch into diva-dom. He's famously antiestablishment and against the commercialization of yoga that's going on all over these days, a fact that, oddly enough, makes him more commercially valuable and sought after by the establishment. To add to his status as master teacher, yoga is only one of the things he does. From what she's heard, David Todd (DT to his followers) teaches martial arts to troubled teens in the public schools and is an accomplished sculptor.

Lee read about today's class on a yoga blog called Asana Junkie. Lainey, the new assistant Lee hired to help her out at Edendale, has been insisting she read at least three of the infinite number of yoga blogs out there every morning, with an eye to getting herself and the studio mentioned in a few. Six months ago, Lee took out a lease on a former bookstore next to her studio, and the new and expanded version of Edendale is set to open in a month or so. They'll need all the new business they can get to keep the bills paid.

DT is going to be in SM tomorrow morning, the blog read, *and unless I'm in the ER or Johnny Depp finally returns my call, I am going to be there, Manduka eKO mat in hand. And as long as you don't take my spot, you should be there, too.*

Lee clicked on the link and signed up for two spots. Unfortunately, Katherine, her friend and the masseuse at her studio, canceled without explanation at the last minute. It took a long time to get from Silver Lake to Santa Monica this morning, but hopefully it will be worth the drive. It's been ages since Lee had a morning to herself to go to a studio and be a student again.

Even though she arrived early, the room was already jammed. It's an unassuming place, not much bigger than the current studio at Edendale. Since she's in the process of decorating the new space and sprucing up the old, Lee pays special attention to the appearance of the place. The walls here are a washed-out blue, and there are a few posters scattered around in a random fashion of lotus blossoms and water imagery and unspecified purple deities. Lee has devoted her life to yoga and is thankful, on a daily basis, for her teachers and guides, but she has to admit that, on the whole, the yoga aesthetic on display in most studios is pretty discouraging.

Lee recognized a few familiar faces from conferences and could tell from the buzz in the air and overheard scraps of conversation that more than two-thirds of the people in the class are teachers themselves. There was all the nervous excitement about more new studios opening, the complaints about finding reliable volunteer studio assistants, and the usual discussions of enrollment figures in teacher-training programs. Lee, who has been resisting the idea of offering training programs herself, is officially tired of this particular topic.

'I'm holding three teacher trainings this year. The demand is so high, I could probably hold ten if there were enough weeks in the year.'

'We're going to offer a full-day session at the end of our training program about how to use the training to get non-yoga-related jobs.'

'That's a great idea. A friend of mine is a consultant who works with teacher-training graduates, to help them transition back into the fields they quit in order to take the training programs. I'm sure she'd come talk.'

'I tried to get Kyra Monroe to do a guest teaching spot at our training, but she gets a flat fee *and* seventy-five percent of the profits for that day.'

'Well, her husband used to be a film agent, so –'

'I heard they broke up.'

'Someone told me she calls herself Priestess Kyra on her website.'

'No surprise, given her looks.'

'I heard she never even went to a teacher-training program. Can that be?'

'She's one of the headliners at the Flow and Glow Festival this year. I'm going if I have to sell my car.'

Lee ended up on the far side of the room, closer to a wall than she likes to practice, but she had an extra cup of coffee when she got to Santa Monica, and she's a little jangled. The wall might come in handy for balance, all things considered. The woman next to her is doing a series of deep hamstring stretches when she looks over at Lee and smiles.

'Lee,' she says, beaming. 'It's Shelly Mance. I used to come to Edendale when I lived out in Silver Lake. You were my first teacher.'

She scoots over and gives Lee a big hug. It isn't that Lee doesn't remember her; it's just that she doesn't remember her exactly. One of those faces that look familiar, like a tune you know you've heard before but can't place. Like a lot of the women in the room, Shelly is all in white and wearing big silver jewelry. When did people start wearing jewelry to yoga class? Lee opened Edendale Yoga almost six years ago, and even though she remembers most of her students, there's a certain amount of blurring in some cases.

'You might not remember me,' Shelly says. 'I used to be a lot heavier.'

The fog starts to lift. Shelly definitely was a *lot* heavier, but Lee isn't going to touch that topic. 'Didn't you used to have purple streaks in your hair?'

'Don't remind me, please.'

Lee remembers her as a diligent student with a lot of flexibility. Someone who'd obviously done gymnastics before adolescence and probably went through a lot of yo-yo weight shifts. Lee's not in a position to judge in that area. 'Do you still do those amazing splits?' Lee asks.

'God, I can't believe you remember that. You inspired me so much. Actually, I'm a teacher now, too.'

'Good for you,' Lee says. There are so many people who claim to be yoga teachers these days, you always have to be careful about a follow-up question. It's like asking an actor if he's been on TV or a writer if she's been published. 'At this studio?' she says.

'No. I wish. This place is amazing. At YogaHappens. They hire a few big stars and then a ton of recent trainees like me to fill in the schedule. The pay is lousy, but it's good on-the-job training.'

Lee nods. Shelly's words confirm what she's suspected for a long time. YogaHappens, the mega chain that tried to hire her last year, charges students a fortune for classes and mostly offers instructors who are learning as they go along.

'You should come up to Edendale again to practice,' Lee says. 'We're about to open a whole new wing. On top of that, we don't burn incense.'

'I know; it's a little heavy today. It's good I brought my inhaler.' She slips this out of a pocket and takes a puff. 'I'd love to come study with you again. I'd probably appreciate you even more now. Half the time I was in classes back then, I was staring at Alan. He's so gorgeous, and you guys have such a great marriage. Everyone looks up to you. You do know that, right?'

Lee feels the familiar stab in her chest when she hears this, although it's true the pain gets less sharp every month. It's been almost a full year since they split up.

'You don't have to worry about being distracted by Alan anymore.' She smiles at Shelly and decides to leave it at that.

'Oh. Okay. Sorry?'

'Don't be,' Lee says. 'I'm not.'

The awkward silence is broken by David Todd's entrance into the studio, and almost immediately, Lee feels the discussion drift away from her. He's not tall – probably only a few inches taller than Lee. He has the sinewy limbs of a natural athlete and the huge, winning smile of a cartoon character. He's wearing thin-framed eyeglasses, an improbable and endearing touch. His training as a master of some esoteric form of martial arts is clear from his posture and the solid, confident way he strides into the room. But at the same time, he manages to inject a note of self-mockery into his movements, which gives his walk an adorable puppy dog quality that Lee just falls for. A lot of teachers Lee's interviewed for positions at Edendale present themselves with the grim seriousness of a funeral director. It's nice to see a smile. He's wearing an unpretentious T-shirt that makes him look completely unaffected and even more sexy.

Before he's opened his mouth, Lee feels gripped by a sensation that's so unfamiliar, she doesn't recognize it at first. *Oh no*, she thinks. *I'm falling in love.*

He goes to one of the windows and opens it wider. 'Let's get rid of this smog,' he says, batting at the incense smoke.

Lee is actually happy, for the first time in a very long while, that she and her husband are in the process of getting divorced. David Todd is exactly the teacher she needs at the studio to fill out her roster of instructors, and Alan was difficult about hiring male teachers at Edendale. *They're not worth the trouble*, he always said. *They hook up with students, and next thing you know, we'll have a lawsuit on our hands.* Too bad Lee didn't realize sooner he'd been talking about himself. The last thing Alan wanted was competition for attention and students to seduce. If she's felt a little overwhelmed by everything that's been going on at Edendale recently, at least she's able to make her own decisions about hiring. And suddenly, that seems like a very good thing.

Between teaching, running the studio, and taking care of the twins, Lee doesn't make it to more than one class a month, and that's in a good month. She gets to Edendale as early as she can and does her own practice, but that often involves a rehearsal for the classes she'll teach that day, interrupted by making notes on her sequence and alignment. As David settles onto his mat at the front of the room and does some exaggerated and amusing stretches of his neck that make him look like an elastic superhero, Lee remembers how much fun it can be to be in someone else's hands.

'I don't know about you,' David says, 'but I am in a completely ridiculous mood today. I just got back from a visit to my family in Chicago, and I've got jet lag, family lag, and the sugar blues. I know, it's too much information, but I'll try to make it seem relevant in some way by the end of the class. So . . . stick around, folks.'

Sharing personal information is risky, but somehow his ironic tone and enormous grin make it work. He's transformed himself from an intimidatingly fit and attractive teacher into the dorky guy with a complicated family everyone can relate to. And maybe fall in love with. Almost everything he says elicits the fond laughter that comes as much from being adored as it does from being funny.

The real magic kicks in when he starts to teach. He leads the class through one of the most original flows Lee has seen in a long time. He manages to incorporate traditional sun salutations with martial arts kicks and graceful movements that have a touch of Martha Graham in them. At the same time that he's moving around the room and making people laugh together as a group, he's offering such exact and detailed verbal cues for the poses that Lee finds herself slipping into dragonfly (always a tough one for her) and a floating half moon with more grace and ease than she's ever felt. The good humor and the constant smiles he elicits just make everything a little easier and everyone a little less tense.

Lee's often felt that the überserious, reverential tone some teachers adopt makes students feel constricted and, in some way that she hasn't quite figured out yet, competitive. As if they're striving to be the holiest, not aiming to have fun. She tries for a light, irreverent tone, but DT is pulling it off with more charm and less sweat than she's ever managed.

What amazes Lee most is that at the end of class, when he has the group in savasana, their eyes closed and a folded blanket resting heavily on their stomachs, he circles the room offering adjustments and goes back to his opening comments about visiting his family. But this time in a more quiet and somber tone, appropriate to what he's saying.

'Because what I realized this weekend, is that no matter how much I love my family – and despite all of our differences, I really do love them – the people I feel closest to are you. Maybe you're thinking that I don't even know you. And in most cases, it's true. But here, in a room like this, with everyone working together in the same spirit, breathing in unison, wrestling with gravity, and reaching a little bit past their limits, I feel as if we're connected in spirit, if that makes sense.

'And so the truth is, I don't know what else to do but to keep coming back to all of you, here and everywhere else I teach, because even if it sounds dumb, even if it doesn't make a lot of sense, you feel like my real family.'

Lee can hear his footsteps getting closer to her, and then she feels the warmth of his hands pressing lightly against her forehead.

'This is what I believe in and love, and this is what keeps my life on track.'

It's not that this is so unusual or so profound, but he says it with such sincerity that Lee finds herself genuinely moved. It's as if all the losses she's felt over the past year sweep over her along with the wound that Shelly opened at the start of class, and she's forced to acknowledge, finally, that what's kept her going, even more than her twins (though she hates to admit that), is the feeling of connection and love she gets from her students and the studio. She can't imagine what she would have done in the past year without that. Lying on the floor with her eyes closed and tears running down the sides of her face, she knows that she will do whatever it takes to make the expansion of the studio a success. She has to. There just isn't any other option.

And right now, she knows that convincing David Todd to give up his nomadic ways and come teach at her studio is a big part of that. It's meant to be.

'He's amazing, isn't he?' Shelly says to Lee as she's rolling up her mat.

'He is,' Lee says. She feels as if she's been on a long, thrilling ride at an amusement park, but without the dizziness and nausea. She's physically energized and a little spent emotionally. 'Do you come to his classes a lot?'

'As often as I can. If you want, I can introduce you to him. I always have questions.' Shelly rolls her eyes.

Lee looks to the front of the room, where there's a long line of students waiting to talk to DT or, for all she knows, get his autograph. There's no chance that it's a fast-moving line, and she has to get back to Silver Lake to teach. She goes to the cubby wall in back and scribbles a note on one of the business cards Lainey insisted she have made up. Maybe they weren't a complete waste after all.

'If you can hand this to him,' Lee tells Shelly, 'I'd be really grateful.'

'I'll tell him it's from the best teacher in L.A. And that includes him.'

Katherine is in her sewing room, flowing through a few sun salutations, trying to work off her frustration about having killed the entire day waiting for her landlord to show up. She was supposed to go to class in Santa Monica with Lee, but she had to cancel. She knows that having a home yoga practice is, in many ways, the ideal, but she's never been able to stick with it for more than twenty minutes at a stretch. As soon as she gets to a pose she doesn't like, she either skips it or goes for a snack. When she hears people talking about their amazing home practices, she suspects they're talking about ten to fifteen minutes of honest effort that devolves into a nap or masturbation.

As she's trying to motivate herself to do at least one boat pose (her Pose of Dread), she hears a rapping on the window. She pops up and sure enough, there's her landlord standing on the deck out back, peering through her window, hands cupped around his eyes.

Tom (she refuses to call him Tommy, as he keeps suggesting she do) doesn't seem to understand the basic concept of ringing a doorbell. He's always appearing around corners and looking in windows and arriving unannounced. At least today she was expecting him to show up, even if she was expecting him hours earlier. She's known for a long time that he has a crush on her, and since he's married and basically harmless, and the crush has worked in her favor for the entire time she's been renting her perfect little Craftsman cottage, she's never objected too much. There's something creepy about his random appearances at the house and his slumped posture, but he hasn't ever crossed into Major Problem territory, and the fact is, she's dated a lot of guys who were way creepier than Tom.

She points toward the front of the house and meets him at the door.

'The doorbell wasn't working, Tom?' she asks.

'Oh, well, I thought I heard you out back, so . . .'

She leads him into the kitchen and pulls out a chair for him at the little vintage dinette set she got for a song on Craigslist. It would be a lot more comfortable to have him sit in the living room, but the view of the hills and the distant reservoir from the huge wall of windows there is so stunning, she worries that it will remind him of how far below market value her rent has been for the past three years.

'Nice table,' he says. 'Was this my mother's?'

'No,' Katherine tells him. 'I put most of her furniture down in the basement over a year ago. I was worried about the wear and tear.'

'Not that it matters to her anymore, but thanks,' Tom says. 'New tattoo on the shoulder there?'

'Not that I know of. Nothing new in that department in a long time, Tom. No plans, either.' The tattoos stopped right around the time she finally quit drugs, and even though she was tempted to get a tiny fireman's badge with Conor's name on it somewhere on her right arm, the whole process is so closely associated with the most miserable period of her life that she couldn't bring herself to do it. On top of that, she knows her own track record with men too well to believe that inking a guy's name (even an amazingly great guy's name) into her skin would be a good idea. 'You want some mint tea?'

'Yeah, why not?' Tom says. 'So fucking hot out there, I can't breathe.'

His shirt is soaked with sweat. When she first moved into the house, Katherine tried to get Tom to go to a yoga class. It definitely would have helped his lungs and, for better or worse, he probably would have enjoyed the sight of all those leggings and halter tops. But of course he never went, and Katherine decided it wasn't her business to push. She pours him a glass of cold mint tea and sits opposite him at the table.

'Thanks for coming by,' she says. And then she launches into the speech she's been rehearsing all day: 'So a couple of weeks ago when we had that freaky rainstorm, I noticed a little damp spot on the living room ceiling. I had Conor go up on the roof with me, and he thinks a lot of it looks pretty tired. He and I can do some patching, but I think you should have a look. It might be time for a bigger job. And if it is, I'm happy to help with some of the cost.'

Tom peers down into his glass distractedly. 'So that thing with Conor is working out okay, then?'

Harmless enough as a question, even if it is beside the point. 'It's working out fine.'

'It's been almost a year, right? I'm happy for you, Katherine. I always thought you deserved a nice guy. I knew one was going to come along one of these days. He live here now?'

'No, Tom. Just me. I'd tell you otherwise. Conor and I are both pretty independent.'

'No plans to move in together?'

'I've never been a big one for long-term plans.'

'At a certain point, though, you have to think of the future, Katherine. We all do. Like it or not.'

There's a tone in his voice that makes Katherine a little uncomfortable, as if he's crossed into preachy generalizations that are clearly about something other than her relationship with Conor. The fact that he's stopped looking her in the eye is another worrisome sign. She'd always rather hear the bad news first, so she says, 'Something on your mind?'

'Not mine,' he says. 'My sister's.'

Katherine takes a long, deep breath. This, almost certainly, is the bad news she's been dreading ever since she fell in love with this house and moved in at a crazy-low rent with the understanding that once Tom's mother's estate was settled, it might go on the market, and she might be asked to leave at a moment's notice. Strangely, though, she feels calm. She's faced worse things in her life than this and she's learned that freaking out isn't going to change anything. All the deep breathing, all the vinyasas really have helped her cope.

Tom still isn't saying anything, isn't able to glance up from his mint tea – which, after one tentative sip, he hasn't touched. Lack of sweetener, no doubt. Despite Tom's pop visits in hopes (she's sure) that he'll come across her prancing around the house naked (as if she ever does that!), she feels bad for him and decides to help him break the bad news to her.

'You're putting the house on the market,' she says. 'Am I right?'

He nods, still without looking up. Katherine can see so much discomfort in his posture, she feels she ought to defend his actions. She's always been better at defending others than defending herself.

'It's your house,' she says.

'I know, but –'

'No buts. I've been the luckiest tenant in L.A. the whole

time I've been here. Don't think I don't know it. Look at this place. I knew the terms when I moved in.'

'You're an amazing girl, Katherine, you know that?'

'I'm a realist,' she says. 'Let me get you some sugar for that tea.'

'You know, the one thing I got out of my sister is an agreement that you can stay for another three months. And also that we'd sell the place to you without the Realtor. That way you'd save all those fees. Could be a major help.'

Katherine nods. Big help, she's almost sure. 'Just out of curiosity,' she says, 'any idea about the asking price?'

'We don't know exactly yet, but definitely under two.'

It's pretty much what she figured whenever she thought about the house, not that they'll get what they want in this economy. Not, frankly, that she'd be able to afford it even if they cut the price in half and then divided by two.

But she meant what she said about having been lucky all these years. It's that – the positive – she focuses on the whole time Tom is sitting at her kitchen table, sipping the tea, making small talk that starts tiptoeing into awkward territory only as he's about to leave. ('All that yoga must be doing something for you. Look at those legs. Wow.')

When Conor knocks at her door about an hour later, she's in a surprisingly cheerful mood. After Tom left, she went out and spent too much money at the Cheese Store, not that she and Conor really know that much about cheese. Still, if you can't afford a two-million-dollar house, it's nice to know you can at least (almost) afford some really good French Comté to put into the soufflé.

'Something smells good,' he says and wraps his arms around her. 'And I'm not talking about dinner.'

Conor would compliment her if she'd just come in from running a marathon, and he'd mean it. Katherine never knew men could be so genuinely nice until she met him. They've been seeing each other for a year now, and she still hasn't uncovered any flaws. Although in a pinch, perfection sometimes comes close to being a flaw.

'You're in a good mood,' he says. 'Did Tom show up?'

'He did,' she says.

That's when she throws herself into his arms and starts bawling.

Graham, the architect who designed the new studio space for Lee and is serving as the project manager on the renovation, is standing in what will be the new reception area. He's examining the detail work on the river stone wall he more or less insisted Lee put behind the desk.

'I'll have the contractor come back and reset a few of these stones,' he tells Lee. 'Some of the work they did is a little sloppy.' He taps something into his iPad, which is encased in black leather. Everything Graham wears or carries is either black or white.

'Really?' Lee says. 'They look perfect to me. You were right about putting those in. It changes the whole feel of the entrance.'

Lainey gives Lee a nudge that's about as subtle as everything else she does. 'I was wondering about those stones, too,' she says. 'The row at the top. I have them on our list of questions.'

Graham looks at Lee and winks. 'If there's one person I want to be happy, Lainey, it's you.'

Graham is a tall, lean man who shows up at the studio in freshly laundered white shirts and black jeans that look as if they've been ironed. His graying hair is always slicked back tidily – literally, not a hair out of place – and he gives off the faint smell of woody aftershave. When Lee first talked to him about the job, she was reassured by his meticulous appearance; a sloppy architect wouldn't cut it. So far, he's proven to be as careful and detail oriented as his perfect hair and starched shirts suggest, and even if the project is running forty percent over budget and a month behind schedule, she's delighted with the results. When the new space opens, Edendale is going to be a much larger and more beautiful place than the funky little studio she opened when she and Alan first moved to L.A.

'I'd like you to look at the doors to the bathrooms, too,' Lainey says. 'I'm not sure that frosted glass gives enough privacy.'

'But they're beautiful,' Lee says. She was a little worried about the glass, but didn't want to risk sounding prudish by bringing it up.

'They make the hallway back there look bright and twice as big,' Graham says. 'Anyway, Lainey, it's a yoga studio. People are half-naked in class with their butts in the air. The most you'll see is a few distorted shadows. Trust me, no one will care.'

'I'm going to be using the bathrooms, too,' Lainey says. 'And trust me, I *do* care. And I think we should look at the exhaust fans, too. Someone might need to take their medical marijuana before class, and those fans need to suck out the smell *completely.*'

'We'll take another look,' Lee says.

It's important to placate Lainey. In the month and a half since Lee hired her, she's come to rely on her judgment and advice more and more. Lee has started to wonder if her frequent references to the benefits of legalizing marijuana are motivated by more than an impersonal interest in the California economy, but even so, her ideas tend to be solid. 'When do you think we'll be able to open?'

Graham puts on a pair of round black-framed glasses that make him look like an aging Harry Potter. He goes over a few notes and shrugs. 'Right now, I don't see any problems with sticking to our target. Eight weeks from today should be good. We'll still have a few rough edges, but nothing anyone will get hurt on.'

'If we schedule the opening for then,' Lainey says, 'we're going to hold you to that date.'

'I wouldn't cross you, Lainey,' Graham says, taking off his glasses. He winks at Lee again. These conspiratorial winks at Lee have become a habit when Lainey is around. In private, he's more serious and businesslike, although it's true he has managed to slip the fact that's he's divorced into the last couple of conversations they've had. He invited her out for a business lunch one afternoon, but fortunately, Lee got out of it gracefully. The meticulousness that makes him so good at his work and so attractive as an architect makes him less attractive to her in other ways.

Lee is not looking for more complications right now. Although it would be nice if David Todd at least responded to the message she left for him.

As soon as Graham has gone, Lainey gives her a

talking-to about being too eager to please. 'He's working for you,' she says. 'You don't have to be so agreeable and yoga-ish about everything.'

'We make a good team,' Lee says.

'You let me be the bitch, in other words.'

'I wouldn't put it in those words, but . . .'

'Don't apologize. I'm comfortable in that role.'

Once it was clear that Lee wasn't going to be able to run an expanded business the loose way she'd run Eden-dale since the start, she hired Lainey to oversee the books, run the registration desk, and play 'bad cop' with the volunteers and other teachers when a little discipline is called for. Lainey made it clear in her interview that she'd never done an asana in her life and had no interest in starting. Sometimes, Lee suspects Lainey's lack of experience in yoga is one of the reasons she hired her. She'd prefer not to think about the kind of stereotyping on her part this suggests, but truthfully, there are times when there seems to be some correlation between budding yogi and flaki-ness in practical matters.

They head back to Lee's office in the old wing of the studio, and Lainey drops herself into a chair. She gives Lee a penetrating look that almost makes Lee wince. A pronouncement, suggestion, or scolding is coming.

'Whatever it is,' Lee says, 'I'd prefer you tell me right out.'

'I've been working on something for a couple of weeks,' Lainey says. 'Yesterday, I finally got a contract for you. I told them you'd give an answer by the end of the week.' She starts to casually pick at the sleeve of the blouse she's wearing and adds, 'Don't let me down on this one.'

'Okay. Do you tell me what the contract is for, or would you rather I just sign without knowing?'

'The latter, obviously, but I'll fill you in anyway.'

Lee meets her gaze, briefly distracted by trying to see if her eyes are red.

'I've been talking to the organizers of the Flow and Glow Festival. I'm guessing you've heard of it.'

'I have.' Flow and Glow is an annual four-day yoga festival that takes place in the Sierras. Thousands of students attend and scores of teachers are enlisted to instruct. It started out modestly but quickly became the main yoga event of the year, with teachers lobbying madly to get invitations and students saving up for months in advance for the enrollment and lodging fees. Lee has been listening to students and teachers rave about it since it started, four years ago, and even though she's been tempted to go, she's never had the time. Besides, it's the kind of mass gathering that she's always stayed away from. She doesn't much like crowds, and she isn't crazy about classes in the bright sun, and from what she's heard, there's a huge amount of competition among the teachers for top billing, as if it really is a rock festival. It's the kind of thing someone like David Todd would never participate in.

'I have a feeling I'm going to disappoint you on this one.'

'You haven't even heard me out,' Lainey says.

Lainey is a large woman, older than Lee by about five years. Lee feels protected by Lainey's practicality, her efficiency, and even her controlling streak. She was an administrative assistant in the biology department at UCLA before the university started trimming staff. This job is a step down for her in terms of salary, prestige, and benefits, but she appears to be completely committed and even happy. 'Talk to Lainey' has become Lee's favorite phrase. She only wishes she could say it to Michael and Marcus, her twins, when all hell breaks loose at home.

Lee wanted someone to take over more of the business matters, but occasionally she feels as if she's at Lainey's mercy.

Lainey hauls herself up from her chair. She has a habit of wearing corduroy dirndls with peasant blouses, outfits that suit her personality somehow, even if they don't flatter her bulky body. She digs through some papers on Lee's desk and hands her a brochure for Flow and Glow.

'Five thousand people attended this thing last year. This year? Maybe double that. If you perform here, or teach, if you prefer –'

'Teach sounds more up my alley.'

'I figured. You *teach* in front of hundreds of students over the course of the weekend. Your name and your picture are seen by tens of thousands of people who visit the website and the Facebook page. These brochures are sent out to every yoga studio in the country. Being one of their teachers immediately gets you on the road to stardom.'

Stardom. Lee flashes briefly on an uncomfortable moment she had last week as she was teaching, a moment when she felt a swell of pride and ego about the fact that thirty-five people had crowded into the studio to take her class. She felt energized by the crowd and by what she sensed was an eagerness on the part of students to do their best to please her. She used the moment to warn students against the perils of letting ego steer the ship, a reminder to herself.

She opens the brochure and sees that half the middle page is devoted to pictures and a biography of Kyra Monroe, referred to here as 'the international yoga priestess'. She feels her face getting a little warm, and it's not from the heat of the day. The bio lists a series of accolades and honors Kyra has received from assorted publications and yoga alliances, and mentions her bestselling videos, podcasts, and *The Inner Outer*, her 'groundbreaking' book on 'spirituality and the eroticism of the asanas'. If all that isn't enough to make you believe Kyra is going to completely rearrange your DNA, there's the fact that 'Priestess Kyra will be introducing a new line of franchise opportunities for the trademarked Kyra Monroe Harmonic Balance Explorer Yoga System'. Whatever that means.

Lee doesn't remember Kyra as blond, but it has been a long time.

'I'm not saying you're wrong,' Lee says. 'I'm just saying it isn't for me.'

'I've spent weeks negotiating this,' Lainey says. 'You can spend a couple of days thinking about it. They've offered you seven classes, the same number as Baron Baptiste, and only one less than Kyra Monroe.'

Kyra Monroe is getting more exposure than Baron Baptiste?

Lainey turns at the door. 'Let me know by Friday, okay? Until then, I'll assume it's a yes.'

Of all the things Graciela has missed about L.A. in the past six months, the one she's probably missed the most is heading up to Silver Lake for Lee's yoga classes. This isn't what she expected. She lived her whole life in L.A., and before getting the job as a backup dancer on Beyoncé's concert tour, she'd barely left Southern California. She would have guessed she'd miss the crazy sprawl of the city; the hot, dry air; the view of the Pacific from Santa Monica Pier; the sad, sweet yellow sunsets; even the constant hum of the insane traffic. If nothing else, she would have guessed she'd miss Daryl a whole lot more than she has. At least more than she'd miss a funky yoga studio in Silver Lake. And she definitely wouldn't have guessed she'd miss that funky yoga studio at this moment, as she's in the last third of a class with Richard Pale, one of New York's hottest yoga teachers. Mr Intensity.

In the five days she's been in the city, Graciela has heard about this class, Intensity Plus, from half a dozen different people.

Oh, you have to try Richard Pale's class when you're here. It's unbelievable.

I almost died halfway through.

He kicked my ass.

It was so hard, I started crying. I loved it.

I couldn't move the next day.

For a lot of yogis she's met lately, the best classes are the ones that make them cry and send them running to an acupuncturist. She's not really into that, but on the other hand, she couldn't resist the challenge. It's part of what her friend Zana calls 'the insane-ification of yoga', the trend to push endurance, strength, and flexibility to the limit.

And then there's Mr Pale himself — insanely fit, insanely handsome, and oozing an insane amount of sexual energy.

Richard Pale is such a movie star, she's heard.

He's a rock star.

He's gorgeous.

Or, the highest compliment you can pay someone these days: *He's a yoga star!*

Studio number seven in this Midtown yoga palace is filled with a group of the most hard-core yogis Graciela has ever seen. More well-earned New York hyperbole. Women – and a surprising number of men – with serious expressions and equally serious muscles. To warm up, about two-thirds of them were levitating up into handstands and then effortlessly floating their feet through their arms with their legs hovering off their mats or doing complicated scissor arm balances or folding in standing forward bends with their heads between their legs. Everyone is pretty much in his or her own world, but there's still a feeling of competition in the air that's undeniable, even if you're not supposed to acknowledge it. She's noticed a lot of this at the studios she's visited in her travels. So many people seem eager to establish their credentials before class begins, doing their best moves before the teacher arrives – just in case those postures aren't part of the flow – and trying to pass them off as mere warm-ups or preparatory stretches. A year ago, Graciela would have been so intimidated she would have left, but now she knows she can keep up with the best of them if she wants to, and more important, that she doesn't have to try.

Thank you, Lee.

Graciela used to think L.A. was full of hyperbole, but it's nothing compared with New York. Everything here is '*the* best' or 'the *most* delicious' or '*the* most expensive'. The funny thing is, she's bought into all of it. From the minute she got out of the limo in front of the Four Seasons, she was in love with the city. It helps that it's May, and that everything is in bloom and the weather has been a balmy dream, day after day. But there's more to it. There's a mixture of beauty and sophistication that she knows she doesn't fit into, but she loves it even so.

Richard Pale, with his milky skin and jet black hair and eyes, is flipping up into a one-armed hand balance and lowering his feet toward his head, all while instructing the class to follow suit in a voice so calm and steady he could be sitting in a rocker. Insane. But what can she do except try it out? When she did street dancing, she did moves like this, only more quickly and with less graceful balance. She pops up into an approximation of the pose, and Mr. Intensity comes over and adjusts her slightly. 'The more intense the effort, the brighter the enlightenment,' he says. 'I want everyone to come and check out the alignment of this yogi's shoulders.'

He keeps his hands on her hips as the rest of the class gathers around.

'This looks great, right?'

A murmur of approval.

'Beautiful woman in beautiful pose.'

Graciela's shoulder is starting to tremble and she wants down.

'Unfortunately, this is all wrong. This is how people develop major injuries over time.' He helps her down, and she folds over into child's pose, trying to catch her breath. 'Now we're going to rebuild this pose from the ground up. With our beautiful, raven-haired yogi as our model.'

Later, as she's leaving the class, Mr. Intensity pulls her aside and says, 'Thank you for being such a good sport. I only picked on you because you're so strong. You must be a dancer.'

'Thank you,' she says. 'I'm a dancer, but I'll be an unemployed dancer soon.'

'Come back and see me,' he says. 'I'm doing a teacher training next month. You'd be an amazing teacher.'

Ever since rehearsals for the tour started, about eight months ago, Graciela has been getting compliments. She's never had so much attention from so many people, heard so many men and women – musicians and other dancers, complete strangers, even a few genuine celebrities who came to the concerts – tell her how talented she is. And how beautiful. They've been on the road for more than six months now, and at some point, several months ago, back when they were in Brussels, she finally let the praise sink in and allowed herself to accept that maybe some of it was true, and that just maybe she wasn't going to be punished for allowing herself to believe it. She doesn't have to resort to hearing the constant drone of her mother's verbal abuse, telling her she looks like a *puta*, can't dance, ought to have had two kids by now. She can listen to these other voices. Or try to.

'I don't much like being the center of attention,' she says. 'Anyway, I'm headed home to L.A. in a couple of days.'

'Check my website. I'm doing a training out there early next year.'

And then he bows and gives her a friendly little hug. Except when you look like Mr Intensity, it's almost impossible to hug or smile or even bow without it having a flirtatious edge. It must be tough.

In the marble locker room, Graciela tells herself she's happy to be headed home. Even if she hasn't missed Daryl desperately, it will be good to be with him again. He's told her he's changed, that he's learned to control his anger, and she really wants to believe him. They never talk specifically about what happened, probably because it's too painful for both of them. Referring to his 'anger' is as close as they ever get to mentioning what he did to her.

Graciela walks out into the lobby of the yoga studio. It's as spacious and glamorous as a hotel lobby, and at long last, she can say that she knows a thing or two about hotel lobbies. She goes to one of the watercoolers and fills up her bottle. When she turns around, Jacob Lander is standing behind her, grinning.

'I thought that was you,' he says. 'I could tell by the hair.'

And then, he reaches out and touches the tips of her long, wavy dark hair. A little bold, but maybe a little shy, too.

Graciela tries to act nonchalant, but *Jacob Lander* recognizes her by her hair? From the *back*?

'I guess it's getting a little too wild,' she says.

'It's wild. Definitely wild. I don't know if you remember, but we met at the opening night party for your New York concerts. I'm Jacob Lander.'

She bursts out laughing. Like maybe there was a chance she wouldn't know who he is? Or would have forgotten that they had talked for about ten minutes and, when she said it was her first visit to New York, he told her his three favorite places in the city? (The Staten Island ferry, Bethesda Terrace in Central Park, and some hole-in-the-wall steak house she's forgotten the name of. ('Oh, and in case anyone asks you, Yankee Stadium, of course.')

Graciela has never been a huge sports fan, but when Daryl moved in with her two years ago, she ended up watching a lot of basketball and baseball, just because he always had the games on. Then, too, there are certain people, like Jacob Lander, who have crossed over from sports figure to international sex symbol. He shows up in *People* magazine, on *E! News*, and in the tabloids more often than a lot of movie stars. There are rumors that he's had affairs with everyone, including some musical talent she's gotten to know pretty well this year.

And despite the fact that he's a womanizer and an all-around superstar, he still has the reputation for being a *nice guy*. He's not especially young, but he has a round face that's handsome, boyish, and kind; beautiful green, almond-shaped eyes; and smooth olive skin. She knows he plays for the Yankees, and she's pretty sure he's a pitcher. Or maybe shortstop?

'I'm Graciela.'

This time it's Jacob who laughs. 'Did you think I'd forget your name?'

'I didn't think you'd remember it.'

'You're underestimating both of us!'

She's not totally sure what he means by this, but it's obviously supposed to be a compliment. 'I didn't figure you for the yoga type,' she says.

'I come a few times a week when I'm in town. I get way fewer sprains and pulled ligaments since I started. You'd be shocked at how many guys in pro sports do it. Though it's true, mostly in private sessions. Don't want to be seen falling on their asses in public. What class are you taking?'

'I just finished Richard Pale's class,' she says.

'Mr Intensity! Damn, you're serious about this, aren't you? This time of year, I can't risk anything that extreme. Mostly go for the restorative. So you don't get enough exercise dancing nonstop for two hours every night?'

'It's not really nonstop,' she says. 'It just looks that way. Besides, I had an injury over a year ago, and a yoga teacher in L.A. helped me work through it. That's how I got the gig. Every time I take a class, I feel like she's looking over my shoulder.'

'Guardian angel?'

Graciela shrugs. 'More like a really good friend.'

For the most part, the Achilles tendon injury (and the real way the accident happened) seems like ancient history now, but mentioning it this way brings it back to her – all the pain, all the hard work it took to get past it.

She hears a gong in a studio and she nods toward the door. 'I think your class is starting,' she says. 'Good luck.'

'I need some luck,' he says.

'How do you mean?'

'I'm hoping you're gonna agree to give me your phone number.'

Graciela is so genuinely baffled by this comment (he can't possibly be asking for her number), she hesitates for a moment.

'An insider's walk around the city?' he says.

'I don't have a pen,' she tells him.

'I have an amazing memory, girl.'

She can hear the instructor's voice in the yoga room.

She's had opportunities galore over the past six months, and she's resisted them all. But the tour is ending, and for some crazy reason, she trusts Jacob Lander. Maybe more than she trusts herself.

'Just for a walk?' she asks.

'That's what I'm offering.'

'I'm . . . I'm not . . .' She doesn't know how to finish the sentence. How is her having a boyfriend relevant to an offer of an innocent stroll around Manhattan?

'Single?' he says. 'I didn't think someone who looks like you would be alone. He's back in L.A.?'

She nods.

He grins at her, showing off the most adorable pair of dimples she's seen on a grown-up. Then he says, 'Don't forget, Graciela, you're in New York now.'

Lee has decided that coconut water is a little like Lady Gaga: one day completely unheard of, and the next so ubiquitous it's dizzying.

Two years ago, you could buy a little foil pouch of the stuff in a few stores. She tried it once and thought it was . . . okay. Today it's so wildly popular among yogis, the little retail section at Edendale can't keep it in stock. Tina, the young woman who takes care of the sales, orders it by the crate and still they are always running out. Lainey insisted they raise the price to four dollars apiece, not for the sake of profit (she claimed) but so that they would sell less and wouldn't have to keep reordering. Oddly, the price increase only bumped up sales.

'I warned Lainey that would happen,' Tina said. 'A lot

of studios sell it for six or eight dollars, so people were worried ours was bad quality until we raised the price. They thought it was past sale date or even made from concentrate. I'd *never* stock a brand from concentrate.'

Lee has read all the claims about it being a perfect way to hydrate, that it's ideal for athletes, and – inevitably – that it's 'nature's Viagra', the highest compliment you can give something, apparently. No doubt it has its virtues, but she had a cooler of filtered water installed in the studio, and you'd think more people would opt for the free hydration. Probably in a year or less it will be replaced by another liquid trend (remember Vitaminwater?) or found to be the cause of deforestation or impotence.

She's contemplating this on her mat at the back of the studio while observing a teacher who's giving a demonstration class at Edendale with an eye toward getting hired. It's not a good sign that Lee's mind has wandered to coconuts. The teacher, a young woman named Whatley Nettles, is an amazingly adept yogi who moves with great conviction and strength. When she stands in warrior pose, her legs appear as solid as marble. But for almost all of the seventy-five minutes of class, she's been at the front of the studio, practicing on her own mat as she talks. It's an impressive feat, and while it's true she's made some verbal adjustments to a couple of students, Lee has the distinct feeling that she's more interested in her own workout than in teaching.

'Move your hand around your thigh. No, not that one, the other one. Not your calf, your thigh. That's your knee.'

It would be so much easier to simply go over and assist, but that would mean missing out on a posture herself.

After class, Lee thanks her and praises her skills – as a practitioner.

'One thing I'm curious about, though,' Lee says. 'Do you always practice while you're teaching?'

'Not always. But today I'm on the move all day, and this was the only chance I had to do my own practice. You know how it is. If I don't get a chance to practice I get really cranky, and . . . not fair to the boyfriend. Is that a problem?'

'Not necessarily,' Lee says. 'It's just that it makes it hard for you to know what the students are doing and to adjust them when you need to.'

Whatley is rolling up her mat and about to zip it into a leather case. Lee can tell from the frown that she's not happy with the comment. 'It's not all about *me*,' she says. 'At some point, these students are going to have to take responsibility for their own lives and their practices. I'm sure you agree. So I'm getting them ready.'

In fact, there's no point in arguing with her. Lee knows that she isn't going to hire her, precisely because for Whatley it *is* all about her. It's one of the problems she's been having in finding a teacher she really loves. Studios are so eager to fill spots in their teacher-training programs – for a lot of studios, it's their most reliable source of income – they call out the best students and flatter them into enrolling. Which makes some kind of sense, except being an expert practitioner and being a committed teacher are often two different things.

'I'll let you know by tomorrow,' Lee tells her. 'And if you're thirsty, just ask Tina for a coconut water on your way out.'

'Is it from concentrate?'

'No, it isn't.'

'Great. I'll definitely take one.'

Back in her office, Lee listens to her messages: one from Alan about changing plans with the kids again, one from her mother, and one from David Todd. As soon as she hears his voice, she feels herself flush and then tries to get a little more composed. She's only going to ask him if he'd consider teaching at Edendale.

He answers the phone in the cheerful tone she recognizes from his class, and when she mentions her name, he says, 'Right. Thank you for leaving the nice message.'

Since Lee didn't introduce herself to him after class, she isn't sure he knows who she is. 'I was on the left side of the room,' she says. 'Crunched up against the wall?'

'I know. You don't exactly fade into a crowd.'

'It depends on the crowd.'

'You're too modest. I've been hearing about Edendale for years now. You've got a big reputation, but still kind of underground. That's my favorite kind of place.'

'I'm glad you feel that way,' she says. Sensing that she has to tread a little carefully, she adds, 'I'm doing some expanding, and I'm looking for a few teachers I respect. I didn't know how hard it would be to find someone good.'

There's a long pause after she says this, and Lee knows, as the silence goes on, that he's going to turn her down.

'I'm pretty much at my limit now,' he says.

Lee grabs at the 'pretty much' as an indication that there's some room for negotiation, a small window of opportunity.

'I'm not good at doing a hard sell,' she says, 'but I'd love to talk to you. Your teaching wasn't like anything I've seen before.'

'I felt the same way about your practice,' he said. 'It's beautiful.'

It's amazing to her that after all these years, this particular compliment about her yoga still has the power to make her happy. Especially when it comes from someone like David.

There's another long pause, and then he says, 'I'm working with some kids tomorrow, and if you'd like to come watch, that would be great. See the rest of what I do professionally. We can go out afterwards and talk, but I'll take you at your word about not doing a hard sell.'

A few minutes after Lee has hung up, Lainey comes into her office to tell her that the enrollment numbers at the Flow and Glow Festival are now approaching ten thousand.

'Sounds like a real boon,' Lee says, 'for the organizers and sponsors.'

'And the teachers. Just saying.' She scrutinizes Lee and adds, 'You look kind of flushed. Something exciting happen?'

They're at least two-thirds into the shooting of *Above the Las Vegas Sands*, and so far, Stephanie has gone to the set every day. It isn't exactly what she was planning, but Sybille Brent, who bankrolled the bulk of the film's budget, asked her if she would. 'In case the director wants some last-minute changes in the script,' Sybille said, 'or, more to the point, he or the actors start improvising. I know he's the director and it's his movie, but you're the screenwriter and I'm producing, and between us, it's *ours*.'

It means that Stephanie has had no time to work on the new script she started before the shoot began – an original this time – and hasn't made it to a yoga class at Edendale in well over a month. Her body feels stiff and heavy, and she's actually had a couple of dreams in which she's effortlessly doing handstands, tossing her leg behind her head, and receiving praise from a teacher who looks a whole lot like Lee. Then she wakes up and realizes that she's more or less put her personal life on hold for professional reasons. Yet again.

Still, showing up at the set daily has paid off. Sybille was right, as usual. How is it that Sybille, who has never been involved in a film before and doesn't even live in L.A., can get so many things right? And how is it that Stephanie got so lucky in connecting with her?

The director of *Las Vegas Sands* isn't yet thirty. It was a coup to have him sign on to the film, one arranged by the executive producer and helped along by Sybille's generosity. Three years ago, he made a movie called *Bananafish*, about a young woman's obsession with J. D. Salinger. It got stellar reviews and brought in almost twelve million at the box office, huge for a movie that was made (allegedly; Stephanie would love to see the accounting on the *actual* budget) for less than two. The screenwriter got nominated for an Oscar, as did the supporting actress. The former nomination was well earned. In Stephanie's opinion, the latter was one of those mercy nods they give annually to whichever star past the age of eighty decides to do a final role.

Despite her admiration for *Bananafish*, Stephanie smelled trouble the first time she met Rusty Branson. He had about him the distracted air of someone who's let success go to his head, along with (very possibly) other things. The first couple of meetings Stephanie had with him, he barely looked her in the eyes. He nodded in a vague, noncommittal way at everything she said, all the while focusing his gaze on something fascinating on the blank wall behind her head. Stephanie felt tolerated more than respected, and it was clear he didn't consider her anything like an equal. He's a skinny redhead with the studied, unwashed sloppiness that a lot of young directors seem to think makes them look talented.

Sybille asked Stephanie afterward what she thought of him and then added: 'And no bullshit. I'm counting on you.'

'It's obvious from his movie he knows what he's doing,' Stephanie said. 'But I'm guessing he's not as smart as he believes he is. Worst of all, he thinks he's slumming by doing this movie.'

'I agree. So why did he do it?'

'Tough times in Hollywood?' Stephanie said. 'Steven Spielberg didn't call him after *Bananafish* with an offer from a major studio? On top of that – and maybe I'm just flattering myself here – I think he likes the script. Grudgingly.'

'I know he does. And that's why you have to make sure he sticks to it. They're your words. Protect them.'

'Something else,' Stephanie added. 'I get a feeling he resents women in the business. One of those guys who thinks that women can't do movies as well as men. He likes the script, but he still believes we shouldn't have been let into the boys' club. The greasy hair and body odor are like a challenge: "Go ahead and make some girly, superficial comment about shampoo." He's not going to get it from me.'

'I suppose that explains the lack of eye contact. I love when men think women are inferior but are intimidated by us anyway. When you have a lot of money, you can put them in their places.'

Stephanie now wishes she asked Sybille why she herself wasn't planning to be on the set daily, but because she's come to think of her as such a private person, with a mind and will of her own – and the divorce-settlement money to support both – she's always let Sybille take the lead. So Sybille's decision to head back to New York shortly before the movie actually went into production was curious, but something Stephanie accepted without pressing, in the same way she'd accepted Sybille's generosity.

The production has taken over an old schoolhouse in a decrepit neighborhood in East L.A. They spent two weeks in Las Vegas doing exteriors, and now the rest of the movie is being shot here. Today, they're filming in the 'bedroom' of a 'house in Vegas', and it's one of the more important scenes in the movie. In it, Imani's character has to seduce her rival's husband, leading up to the film's climactic wedding scene.

At the moment, there is no seduction going on. The actors are draped in bathrobes, and Rusty Branson (whom Imani privately refers to as Bananabrain) has begun to raise his voice.

'We're not talking full frontal, Imani. I'm saying waist up.'

'Yeah, I heard you. And I'm saying no. The script says nothing about nudity, and I'm not doing it. End of story.'

'She's trying to seduce him, for Christ's sake. Who the fuck wears a bathrobe to seduce someone?'

'Dietrich seduced Gary Cooper in a tuxedo,' Imani says.

'She's comparing herself to Dietrich,' Rusty loudly announces. 'Maybe we need to call another diva alert.'

Stephanie can see Imani starting to fume. Rusty likes to toss around the term 'diva' when he's talking about Imani. Sometimes fondly, when things are going well, and sometimes – as now – not. As Imani has explained it to Stephanie, it's the term every African American actress gets slapped on her if she happens to have her own ideas and carries some clout. Even though Imani's career has been limited to TV up until now, she's the biggest name they have on the picture, and it's no secret that it will help distribution and with foreign markets where *X.C.I.A.* is just starting to air.

Stephanie knows this is once again her moment to intervene and point out that the scene as written includes no nudity, even though she sees Rusty's point.

'Where's Daniel?' Imani asks.

'With Renay,' someone says.

'Yeah, but *where*?'

Imani's niece is a beautiful, strangely quiet girl with a gloomy demeanor that Stephanie finds a little unnerving. Probably she's just intimidated being around movie people – she grew up in suburban Texas – but even so, it's hard to get more than a few mumbled words out of her at a time. At least she's a dedicated babysitter. It wouldn't completely shock Stephanie if she turned a corner one day

40

and saw Renay nursing Daniel herself. Still, she has a habit of wandering off with the baby and ending up on some upper floor of the school where they're shooting. Imani has never opened up to Stephanie about any of her concerns about Renay or why she's on the scene at all, so Stephanie has stashed it into the Not My Business category and tried her best to ignore it.

She gestures to Rusty, and the two of them retreat to the hallway. Since the hallway is still lined with battered lockers, it always makes Stephanie feel as if she's back in high school in Jacksonville, Florida, a period of her life she's not eager to revisit. On top of that, unlike the rooms where they're filming, there's no air-conditioning blowing out here, so it's stifling.

'Let me guess,' Rusty says. 'You're going to side with Imani again and call Lady Bountiful back in New York and bitch to her if I don't agree with you.'

'To be honest, I was going to make an observation,' Stephanie says. Her ability to stay cool through all these potential disasters relates directly to the work she's done with Lee over the past year. She really has to figure out a way to start going to classes again, since the private sessions Imani has been paying for are just a little too intimate to be really effective. Both Stephanie and Imani end up being embarrassed by them.

Rusty is looking off over her shoulder in his distracted way. 'Go ahead,' he says, bored. 'Let's hear the latest set of excuses.'

'Imani had a baby a few months ago,' she says. 'She's still nursing.'

'Your point?'

'It's not the right moment to ask her to do a nude scene. Or half-nude, for that matter.'

'So it's my fault she didn't bother to get in shape for the movie? You told me you and she were great yoga buddies. I'm not seeing any Madonna abs here.'

'It's four months, Rusty.'

'Do you have any idea how much slack I've cut her because of that damned baby?'

'Don't think she doesn't appreciate it.' Positive feedback. She's read somewhere that it works wonders.

'If the kid's such a problem, why bother accepting the role? Or for that matter, why have the fucking baby to begin with?'

'Think of it this way,' Stephanie says. 'The baby has gotten your movie a ton of publicity already. Big comeback for Imani's life and her career. It's a great hook. I know it's a pain, but it'll help us all out in the long run. It's the perfect angle to take for articles when the movie comes out. *Oprah Magazine*, *Vanity Fair*. The publicists are crazy for it. And it's going to appeal to exactly the audience for this movie.' It's possible that some of this is true.

Rusty shakes his head with something like disgust, but the fact that he doesn't raise any further objections makes Stephanie feel certain that she's scored her point, without damaging his ego, and that he's going to back off.

'Rusty,' she says, 'do you know the baby's name?'

'What's this, a trap?'

'His name is Daniel. And you might get Imani to agree with you more often if you could refer to him by name every once in a while instead of saying "the baby" and "it".'

Now he actually peels his gaze off the wall and looks

Stephanie in the eyes. 'I'll be happy to be done with this movie,' he says. 'It'll be good, no doubt, because *I'm* good. The word of mouth on this is already off the charts. So when you get nominated, you'll have *me* to thank.'

That said, he heads off to the boys' room.

Stephanie sticks her head into the converted classroom, catches Imani's eye, and gives her a thumbs-up. She steps out the side entrance of the school. It's hot outside, the sun that unrelenting blaze of white that she hates, although there's at least some air moving. She finds a patch of shade under a fire escape and takes out her phone.

'I know you have good news,' Sybille says. 'I could tell by the ring.'

'One more crisis averted,' Stephanie says. 'Something about babies and boobs. You don't need to know. I'm not even sure why I'm calling you.'

'You're getting burnt out,' Sybille suggests.

There's soft music and a hum of conversation in the background. Sybille is probably lunching in a quiet restaurant somewhere in Manhattan. Her life seems to revolve around elegant lunches and vaguely defined meetings with lawyers and financial consultants. It should sound vapid and dilettante-ish, but because Sybille is always so honest about herself, it never comes off that way. It's amazing how much you can get away with in life as long as you own up to it.

'Not exactly burnt out,' Stephanie says. 'Just a little tired. Headed toward exhausted.'

She hears Sybille speaking in a soft voice to someone, clearly one of her attendants – a waiter or perhaps the person cutting her hair for five hundred dollars. Stephanie, on the other hand, has been letting Roberta cut her hair.

'How about this?' Sybille says. 'How about you come to New York sometime soon? Just for a few days. I'll put you up at a wonderful place and pamper you shamelessly. You've earned it.'

'It's tempting, but a little far to travel.'

'You'll be very comfortable. There's something I've been meaning to talk about with you anyway, and it's probably easiest in person. We'll call it a business meeting, if that would make you feel better.'

Stephanie hesitates, and Sybille says, 'Bring Roberta. We'll have fun. I promise to leave you alone ninety-eight percent of the time.'

Stephanie took Roberta to a dinner Sybille had arranged in L. A. before she went back to New York, but she hasn't gotten into any specifics with Sybille – or anyone else – about their relationship. It seems a little too soon. She's not used to hearing people mention Roberta in this casual way, almost as if Sybille assumes they'll be traveling together, and she's uneasy about it.

'She lives in San Francisco.'

'I realize. They have flights from there, too, dear. We could book her through LAX so you can have someone to talk to on the plane.'

'I'll ask her and let you know.'

'Perfect. And Stephanie, you do know how good this movie is, don't you?'

'It's all in the editing.'

'It's in the writing. Doors are going to start opening for you.'

*

44

Katherine's massage client is a tall, slim woman who does yoga at Edendale at least six days a week. Every time she comes to see Katherine, she tells her how important the practice is to her and how it's changed her life for the better. At the same time, she complains endlessly about how *difficult* it is and how hard she's *working* at it and how much she's *giving up* to fit so many classes into her schedule. She's one of those my-*namaste*-is-bigger-than your-*namaste* people that drive Katherine a little crazy. *Couldn't you maybe try to have fun?* she feels like asking.

On the other hand, Natasha works at it *so* hard, she's turned into a good client. She's always overstretching a muscle or straining her lower back, and as soon as she feels a twinge, she makes an appointment with Katherine, demanding she 'fix' it right away so she won't miss a day of classes. If there isn't a twelve-step program devoted to asana addiction, there should be, especially since for some it's turned into a competitive sport. Katherine knows a thing or two about addiction, and when someone like Natasha misses a day of classes, the anxiety and physical jumpiness that set in look very much like other withdrawal symptoms.

Today Natasha came in with a neck problem that Katherine suspects is due to straining her scalene muscles, probably during some kind of extreme twist. The difficulty of treating her is that she has trouble remaining silent long enough for Katherine to do her work. Last week, Natasha signed up for the Flow and Glow Festival in the Sierras. Ostensibly a nice vacation, but she's so nervous about not getting into the classes she wants, she's been having trouble sleeping.

'But you'll get into something, won't you?'

'Yeah, but last year I got shut out of Shiva Rhea's class and Rodney Yee's. There's no way I'm letting that happen again. It was a nightmare. Every major yoga star in the country was there. I found out when the online scheduling for this year's classes opened and I stayed up until midnight and was one of the first people registering. It was an emotionally stressful experience, trying to make all those choices.'

'Maybe don't focus on it right this minute,' Katherine says.

'I'm trying to put it behind me,' Natasha says. She quiets down, but starts up a few seconds later. 'You're not going to believe what happened to me.'

Katherine's doing a myofascial release on Natasha's neck, and so Natasha's words come out a little garbled. 'Maybe wait until I finish with this stretch,' Katherine says.

'My boyfriend proposed.'

Katherine has a moment of confusion because Natasha makes the ostensibly happy announcement in a tone of joyless anxiety.

'It helps if you can relax everything for another minute or so.'

'You're probably going to think I'm crazy, but you know how important my yoga practice is to me, right?'

Ultimately, it's the client's time, and sometimes it seems to Katherine her clients get more from talking than from the work she does on their bodies. Sometimes, she just has to give in to the therapy session. She could use a little therapy herself these days. Ever since she got the news from Tom about the house, she's been feeling off kilter.

It's just a house, she keeps reminding herself. A *thing*. But it's been a living presence in her life, almost like a relationship. She's never lived anywhere she's loved so much or felt so at home in, not even where she grew up. Well, especially not there.

'You mean your boyfriend doesn't do yoga?'

'He does; it's just that he only does kundalini. I know it's supposed to be great and everything, but I'm sorry, it's just not what I think of as yoga. The turbans and the gongs and everything? And half the time, they're just sitting there breathing.'

'Have you taken any classes?'

'Please. I don't have the patience for that. I mean, I once dated a hard-core ashtangi, and that was bad enough. One of those ropy guys that have been doing the same practice for twenty years? Totally rigid? Men who do ashtanga religiously are super intense. Fortunately, they're such control freaks, they tend to have incredible staying power in bed, so at least there's *some* upside to it.'

It's amazing what people consider problems, but Katherine has heard of issues with this sort of mixed marriage before. As far as she can tell, it has nothing to do with the yoga itself and everything to do with the personality trait that draws certain people to certain styles of yoga – the detail-oriented precision of Iyengar, the strict sequencing of ashtanga, the overheated bullying of Bikram.

'Maybe if you went to some of his classes, he'd come here and you could meet in the middle.'

'I'm not very good with compromise,' Natasha says. 'I was hoping you'd tell me it wasn't going to work and I shouldn't accept the proposal.'

'That's not the kind of advice I give.' *I'm having enough trouble*, she feels like telling her, *getting you to stop talking for two minutes.*

After Natasha has left, Katherine goes into Lee's office. Lee's sitting at her computer with her ubiquitous cup of coffee in front of her. She looks up and smiles at Katherine, a little strain showing in the corners of her mouth.

'I just gave one of the toughest classes I've ever given,' she says. 'It was exactly the flow I had planned, but I had one of those mornings, and somehow, it leaked out.'

'Phone call from your mother?' Katherine asks.

'Alan.'

'Even better!' Katherine was never a fan of Alan, even when he and Lee had an ostensibly happy marriage. He was always preening and condescending, and Katherine knew more about his infidelities than she cared to know. 'I wish I'd been in class. I could have used some tough love.'

'Bad morning?'

'Not exactly.' She hasn't discussed this with anyone yet, but sooner or later she's going to have to, and Lee is the most logical person, even if she knows in advance what Lee will say. 'Conor and I had a talk last night. He thinks the two of us should look for a place together.'

Lee has blond hair and a flawless complexion, and when she smiles, her face literally does light up, a glow that comes from someplace inside. 'And?'

'It would help with the rent.'

'It's been a year, Kat. You practically live together as it is. Think how much more convenient it would be.'

'I know. But for some reason, I keep thinking about all the inconveniences. I'm used to having my own bathroom. I can go to bed whenever I want. He and I don't like the same kind of music.'

'What did you tell him?'

'I told him I'd think it over.'

On top of all the other things she hates about her hesitation, Katherine can now add that it makes her sound a little like Natasha. Except Conor is willing to go along with any kind of yoga Katherine wants him to do.

'Whatever it is we decide, I have to start looking soon.'

'Sometimes, you just have to take a chance,' Lee says. 'Speaking of which, I heard from someone who teaches a Brazilian blend of yoga. He calls it Yoga de Janeiro. Are you interested in taking a class and reporting back? I was going to do it myself, but Alan keeps changing times with the kids.'

Yoga de Janeiro does not sound like Katherine's style, but it's the least she can do for Lee. And who knows? It might help her reach a decision. 'I don't have to wear a thong, do I?'

'That's voluntary,' Lee says. 'Thank you for doing it.'

The next morning, Lee stops at Café Crème before going to the studio.

She's not sure how there could be a connection, but the truth is, since she and Alan broke up, she has been getting more and more into coffee. Maybe it's that in the weeks after he finally moved out for good, she needed the extra caffeine jolt just to get herself out of the house. Whatever it is, she knows she's going to have to cut back. She's up to six cups a day, although two of them are espresso, which, as everyone knows, has less caffeine. She's pretty sure.

She orders a large latte and then, thinking better of it, downsizes to a medium.

'With an extra shot of espresso,' she decides last minute.

While she's nervously waiting for it – in the past couple of weeks she's noticed that she gets edgy while she's waiting to be served, another bad sign – she calls Alan. He has the boys, and she wants to make sure he's still planning to bring them to the studio after school. She hasn't been spending as much time with the twins as she'd like, mostly because she's been so busy with the studio. She keeps telling herself it's a good thing that they're getting more and more connected to their father, but part of her feels left out. She'll have to plan an excursion with the boys.

He answers the phone in his typically aggrieved tone.

'In case you're checking on me to see if I'm up,' he says, 'the answer is yes. We're all having breakfast, and we'll be at school early.'

A simple hello would have been nice, but it's probably asking for too much. Twice this month, Alan has brought the kids to school almost twenty minutes late. It's funny how, after all that happened between them, Alan's tone always suggests Lee is punishing him. *Victimhood*, she feels like telling him, *is really unattractive*.

'I didn't doubt it,' she says. 'I was just making sure you're still planning to bring them to the studio after school.'

'Don't you think I would have told you if I'd changed my plans, Lee? Give me a little more credit than that.' He does one of his big sighs and then says, 'But since you're making such a *big deal* about it, I'm supposed to sub for a kirtan teacher at Maha in Brentwood, and I was going to ask you to pick them up if it isn't too *inconvenient*.'

Why the sarcastic tone? Lee is paying about eighty per-cent of the bills for the boys and, despite the advice of friends and lawyers, is still covering Alan's health insurance.

The barista hands her her cup; she gulps it gratefully and then takes a deep breath to try and calm down. She's learned that it's easiest to deal with Alan as he is instead of wasting time trying to turn him into an adult.

'I'll figure it out,' she says. 'And look, I know it's a little far off, but I wanted to give you a heads-up about the end of next month. I got offered a position at the Flow and Glow Festival, and Lainey thinks I should accept it, so I'm hoping you can take the boys for the last week of the month. I'll e-mail you the exact dates.'

There's a silence on the other end of the phone long enough for Lee to walk out to the sidewalk and polish off half her cup.

'Alan? Are you there?'

'You got offered a teaching spot at Flow and Glow? How did *that* happen?'

'I'm a yoga teacher, remember? It doesn't seem like it's totally out of left field.'

'Okay, Lee, I can really do without the sarcasm. You do know how tough it is to get positions, don't you? It's like some nobody getting to play on a Dave Matthews tour.'

The more he objects to her going, the more convinced she is that she's going to accept. 'So do you think you can handle the kids?'

'Jesus, Lee. Did it ever occur to you that *I* might want to go to the festival this year? I mean, did it cross your mind that you're not the only person with a life and a career?'

'You got offered a gig there? That's great.' Not for her, but any paying gig is a big deal for Alan and ultimately good for everyone.

'I didn't say that, did I? I said I might want to go. And yeah, I'm working on a few things, too, so stay posted.'

It would be terrible if, at this stage of life, Lee started getting passive-aggressive, but the truth is, she takes a certain amount of pleasure in having been so supportive of Alan that he can't legitimately blame her for any of the problems he's having in his music career. If it weren't for her, he wouldn't have gotten into playing live music for yoga studios around town and begun to have some of the success he never had on the folk music scene. As far as she knows, he's given up his singer-songwriter dreams and has started to bill himself as a spiritual guide and 'Yogic musical therapist'.

'Let me know how it goes,' she says. 'My mother would love to spend time with the kids. She could come out here and stay in the house. She hasn't seen them in a while.'

'I'm not sure I'm comfortable with that. She's never liked me, and I don't want her poisoning the kids' minds against me. Anyway, I can't stay talking anymore. As it is, you've kept me on so long with your great news, it's going to make the kids late for school. And Marcus might want to stay here another night, so if he does, you'll have to bring him back.'

There's no right or easy answer to this. She and Alan

have an organized schedule of who has the boys when, and for the most part, they've tried to keep them together, just to minimize the feeling of the family being broken in two. But everyone agrees that if the boys want to stay in one place for an extra day or two, they can make the request. This is the third time Marcus has asked to spend an extra night with Alan. Marcus was always the more easygoing of the twins, the one who seemed most sensitive to her feelings. She can't deny that there's something painful in this sudden about-face. Sipping her coffee and crossing the street to the studio, she feels like getting Marcus on the phone and asking him why he doesn't like her anymore. Instead, she says, 'Tell him it's all right with me, as long as we can work out the logistics.'

'I'll leave that up to you,' Alan says. 'You've always been good with managing other people's schedules.'

Great start to the morning, Lee thinks. *Get ready, yogis; class today is going to be fierce.*

Later in the afternoon, Lee double-parks in front of the kids' school and sits on the hood of the Volvo, waiting for the boys. The air is hot and dry, but she finds it comforting, and the sunlight on her arms is soothing. She's definitely been spending too much time inside these days.

A bell sounds and the school doors open, and an exuberant flock of kids spills out, like birds released from a cage. She's struck, as she always is, by the rowdy, friendly diversity of the school and she feels a jolt of happiness that she and Alan, after much debate, opted to keep the boys in public school, even when some of their friends found it too chaotic and went in a different direction. One good decision they made together. She spots Michael, stumbling out of the school and jostling for a backpack with a boy she's never seen before. He used to be a more aggressive kid, but since she got him doing yoga at the Good Doggie kids' classes (no longer taught by Barrett, who had the good sense to leave the studio after her affair with Alan came out), he has started to calm down. This is just friendly tussling and nothing more. A few seconds later, Marcus saunters out alone, backpack dropping off his shoulders, his head bent over something. A cell phone? Except the boys don't have cell phones.

Ever since they were babies, she's dressed them in the same clothes and kept their hair the same length. Before having twins, she always found it a little ridiculous and maybe disturbing when she thought about parents making mirror images of their kids. What she realized when she had her own twins is that it's a way to treat them exactly the same, not favoring one with certain styles or colors of clothes. It's an unconscious way of saying they are loved equally. So it bothers her that Marcus has decided to let his hair grow into a shaggy mop while Michael is still asking for the crew cut they always liked. Marcus insists that it's just because he hates getting it cut, but it's obvious it has something to do with Alan's shoulder-length hair.

Michael runs out to meet her, and she gives him a big hug. 'How was school, mister?' she asks.

He shrugs. 'It was okay. Boring. I think one of these teeth is coming loose.'

She bends down to inspect a loose canine tooth and

says, 'I give it another few days. Maybe a week. No apples for you.'

'Do you think this is going to bleed a lot when it comes out?'

'Probably not a lot. But you're so grown-up, it won't bother you anyway.'

Michael, who was born six minutes before his identical twin, has always been out in front when it comes to height and teeth, as if that six minutes counts for several months.

When Marcus comes over, he's put whatever it was he had in his hands away. She wraps her arms around him and drinks in his smell, trying not to notice that he stiffens a little at her touch. 'Have a good day, young man?' she asks.

'I got an A on a math test,' he tells her. He shimmies out of his backpack and hands her a rumpled piece of paper.

Math has never been his strong suit, but in one of the many transformations he's undergone recently, he has suddenly started to take it seriously and enjoys doing his homework. 'I'm going to put this up on the wall in my office at work,' she says.

'Sorry, Mom, I wanted to show it to Dad, too.'

Don't take it personally – her mantra for child rearing. 'I'll make a copy,' she says.

She gets them into the backseat and makes her big announcement as they're pulling away from school. 'So here's what I thought, guys. I thought we'd go on an outing today.'

'You have class,' Marcus says.

'Not today. We're going up to Griffith Park. Someplace you really love.'

'Soccer field?' Michael asks with excitement.

'You go there all the time. This is special.'

When they hit a traffic snarl, Lee turns on the radio, but all she can find is grating pop music and talk shows about environmental disaster.

By the time they make their way through the traffic and get to the park, it feels as if the best of the afternoon has already passed. Michael is asleep in the backseat, and Marcus is fiddling with a stopwatch she's never seen before. The air is a sulfurous yellow and unnervingly still, and even before Lee pulls up in front of the station for the miniature-train rides, she realizes that she's miscalculated. This used to be the boys' favorite outing in the city, but she can't remember the last time they were here. Were they six? Maybe younger? It's almost as if her whole plan is a crazy attempt to bring everyone back into a happier and more settled time. Parents are walking into the quaint little train station, holding the hands of kids who look a good five years younger than the twins.

Michael wakes up in time to look out the window and weigh in with an unenthusiastic, 'Oh. This.'

She's not going to show her disappointment at the reaction. 'Come on, guys,' she says. 'It's Travel Town. You love this.'

She tries to be cheerful and energetic as she steps out of the car, but the afternoon heat slams into her, and she feels her enthusiasm for this outing draining from her body. The problem is that since she's already started, she has to follow through.

She opens up the back door and the boys stagger out. That's when Marcus, in a sweet and loving tone, delivers a line that strikes her like a blow to her stomach: 'What if someone *sees* us, Mom?'

'What do you mean by that?' she asks. 'You mean sees you with *me*?'

'I mean here. It's, like, a thing for little kids.'

'Well, I hate to break the news,' she says, 'but compared with a lot of people on the planet, you *are* little kids. Now let's go. Don't be so negative.'

She heads up to the counter to buy tickets, and the forced cheerfulness of the man in the ridiculous uniform is only insult onto injury. Maybe it wouldn't be quite so bad if the heat weren't so intense, adding another layer of discomfort and pointlessness to the outing. 'That much?' she asks when she's told the price.

'Everything goes up, lady,' the man croaks. 'The state's broke, last I heard.'

She hands the kids their tickets and says, 'There'll be a nice breeze once we get moving.'

The boys have that stunned, stoic look they get when they're trying to please and simultaneously block out their surroundings. It's the look they get when she takes them to the dentist or for their flu shots. The miniature trains look even smaller than she remembers, and if the youngest children look happy and excited, the adults certainly do look foolish, sticking up out of their seats on the tiny railroad cars like oversize dolls. At least there's a canopy so they won't be in the blazing sun.

They file onto one of the trains and the boys insist on having seats of their own, one behind the other, probably so they can slump down and attempt to be invisible. This leaves her in her own seat with nothing to do but listen to the other adults trying to coax excitement out of their four-year-olds: 'Wow! Look at that! That train's backing up! See how that one pulls the other one? Isn't that great?'

Being here brings back, vividly and in painful detail, the memory of the last time they came. It was more than four years ago, shortly before Christmas. The railroad was decorated for the holidays, and they were a happy little family, and as far as she knew, everything was absolutely perfect. The boys were in silent awe at the magical lights, and she and Alan held hands the whole time, her head against his shoulder with the boys on their laps. It wasn't the New England Christmas scene she'd grown up with, but it summoned up her own childhood, or the happiest parts of it, anyway. *Merry Christmas*, Alan whispered to her, and she believed everything was going to be exactly that happy, magical, and beautiful forever.

Now the landscape in front of them looks yellow and uninviting. The boys look overheated and miserable. Seeing them here, where she hasn't seen them for years, she realizes how surprisingly tall and grown-up they've become, even just in the past year, while she's been so occupied with other things.

Before the train moves, her phone starts ringing in her bag. It's Graham, the architect. 'I'm at the studio,' he says. 'We need to make a decision about paint color for the ceiling. Any chance you'll be here this afternoon?'

'I'm with my kids,' she says. 'How about in a couple of hours?'

'I can't stay that late. I'll call tomorrow and we can book something else.'

She looks over at the disgruntled boys and realizes that this is a way to get out of the situation with a little dignity. A perfect escape.

'I'll be there in thirty-five minutes,' she says.

She stows the phone and steps off the train, feeling more energetic than she's felt all afternoon. 'Sorry,' she tells them. 'That was Graham. We have to go back to the studio. We'll come back another time.'

The boys leap off the train and start to shove each other playfully. They dash over to a kiosk with information about upcoming events, and for the first time since she picked them up at school, they look like they're having fun and are happy to be with her. Amazingly, they look very much like five-year-olds again.

Katherine and Conor are going to West Hollywood to attend the Brazilian yoga class Lee asked her to check out.

Katherine is behind the wheel of Conor's truck, and she can tell he's nervous but trying not to show it. 'A little easier on the brakes, babe,' he says.

'I keep confusing the pedals,' Katherine says. 'Don't make it worse.'

'You're doing great. Don't worry about it.'

Shortly after Conor moved to L.A. from Boston last year, he bought a small Ford pickup truck from a guy on Craigslist. When Katherine asked him why he needed a truck, he shrugged and said, 'To haul stuff around', as if it was obvious. Katherine couldn't understand what it was he was planning to haul, but almost every weekend Conor helps a friend or colleague from the fire department move furniture or load wood or transport a giant pile of mulch or soil from one place to another. He's happiest when he's in the middle of a project that involves sweat equity, Home Depot, and, usually, a fair amount of beer.

Katherine has been trying her best to get everywhere on her bike, but Conor insists she needs to learn how to drive the truck and get comfortable with the standard transmission and the clutch when they go out together, because 'you never know when you might have to'.

She's teased him again and again about being the ultimate Boy Scout, but secretly, she loves that he thinks of these things in advance and has helped her become so much more adept in practical matters. If Tom, the landlord, really did want them to repair the roof of the house, Conor knows a handful of people who would have come over and organized a roofing party, complete with music and drinks.

'What's this class called again?' Conor asks.

'Yoga de Janeiro,' Katherine says. 'The website calls it a traditional Brazilian practice that was developed five years ago.'

He laughs. 'Am I going to end up feeling like a complete ass?'

'It's possible. But I will, too. And anyway, what a cute ass.'

Yoga de Janeiro and Wagner Emerson, its creator, burst onto the L.A. scene about six months ago and the class quickly became the one everyone was talking about and trying to get into. These days, the new classes everyone talks about with that crazy excitement that borders on the sexual are hybrids. 'Yoga plus or minus' is how Lee describes them. Yoga merged with ballet or acrobatics or kickboxing. Yoga and salsa. Yoga and gymnastics. Yoga and swimming. Disco yoga. Piloga. Yoquatics. Katherine suspects Yoga on Ice will be next, but for all she knows, it already exists.

She's all for fun, but she's a little wary of the hybrids, so many of which turn out to be either a standard vinyasa class done to reggae or an awkward blend of two disciplines that somehow manages to bypass the best aspects of each. Why is it, she wonders, that as soon as something gets popular, people have to attempt to change it or 'improve' on it in ways that rarely turn out to be an improvement?

Whenever Katherine attends a yoga class with Conor, she's reminded all over again of what she loves about him. He plunges into every class with an open heart and an enthusiastic spirit that she admires and envies. He'll lurch and stumble, land on his face or on his butt, but keep going with an endearing grin on his face. He was that way right from the first time Katherine convinced him to attend one of Lee's classes, without having a clue what he was getting himself into.

Sure, I'll try it, Conor said, a phrase that seems to be his motto for life. It's probably the attitude that made it possible for the two of them to get together, despite her doubts and fears. *Just try me*, he said to her when she told him she was bad at commitment and afraid she was going to end up hurting him. She's been 'just trying' him for a year now. She's had her share of regrets and moments of wondering if this is right, but nothing unmanageable. But suddenly, between the sale of her house and what, if she's right, would be another major factor, the stakes have risen by a lot.

'Slow down for this right, babe,' Conor says. 'Inch over into that lane. Don't worry about the honking. Fuck 'em if they can't let you in.'

The room looks like a large dance studio. There are mirrors on the walls, and some effort has been made with the lighting to give it a nightclub atmosphere for this particular class. There are maybe a hundred people on their mats, and a surprising number of the women look as if they might actually be Brazilian. Less surprising somehow is the fact that many are wearing outfits that might be considered modest on the promenade in Rio, but that look like bikinis here. As for the men, Katherine would guess that the bulk of them are more interested in each other's Speedos than in anything the women are wearing.

'I feel *way* overdressed,' Conor says quietly.

He's wearing the baggy blue basketball shorts and paint-splattered LAFD T-shirt he always wears when he exercises. Overdressed or not, he's drawing a lot of attention from both sexes, as he always does in yoga classes. It's his height and his red hair and the fact that he looks so insanely and irresistibly out of place.

'Me, too,' she says. 'I should have worn my thong after all.'

Conor bends down and kisses her on the neck and whispers, 'When are we having our talk, Brodski?'

'We're in Brazil, Mr. Ross,' she whispers back. 'Let's not discuss business while we're on vacation.'

He slaps her butt affectionately, and Katherine suddenly wishes they really were in Brazil, or anywhere they had some privacy. Conor has proven to be the ideal lover for her in more ways than she could have hoped. He is, no question about it, the most gentle man she's ever been involved with, but he has an aggressive side that comes out during sex that puts her over the edge. She's always been sexually drawn to men who are rough around the edges, but she's never given herself over to them completely because she's never trusted them. With Conor, she doesn't hold anything back. She trusts him to take care of her and to never let things get out of hand. What amazes her most is that things seem to be getting more passionate and intense the longer they're together, a totally new experience for her.

So far, she's managed to avoid answering his suggestion that they buy a place together. Why mess with a relationship that's actually working well for the first time in her life? Why try to improve it, like the teachers combining yoga and luge or whatever the next big thing is?

And besides, if her suspicions turn out to be correct, their 'talk' might be a bigger discussion than Conor thinks.

The lights in the studio dim more, and everyone gets to their mats and quiets down. Then music starts pounding from the speakers – rumba remixed with an edgy hip-hop beat – and a roar of excitement fills the room. By the time the instructor appears, the studio feels like a crazy dance party. Wagner Emerson is a short, muscular man who's probably on the wrong side of thirty and might be past forty. He's definitely working it. He's shirtless, and his tanned torso is so smooth and hairless, it looks as if he's been polished. Between that and the cap of platinum hair, he's ready for a *Men's Health* photo shoot or maybe a porn movie.

There's no way Lee is going to go for this, Katherine thinks.

Even so, the music is infectious, and Wagner's patter, delivered in a drawling accent with ample Portuguese thrown in (which, magically, Katherine suddenly seems to understand), is hard to resist. The warm-up movements – a lot of pelvic thrusting – lead into a sort of strip-club variation on sun salutations. *Poor Conor*, she thinks, afraid to look in his direction.

Once she drops her resistance, her judgment, she does start to feel great. There's something genuinely sweet and affable about Wagner Emerson that is charming. Despite the lascivious grin, the laser-smooth pectorals, and the boy-from-Ipanema accent, which she suspects Wagner practices so every word ('rrrotate you hips, so you making a big, beautiful circle with you big, bea-*u*-tiful asssssss') sounds like a comically exaggerated come-on, his flow does have an exhilarating beat and rhythm. Not quite yoga, but not entirely unrelated, either. He somehow manages to work pranayama into the movements – not an easy task considering the speed of it all. The subtext makes it feel like this is a build-a-better-orgasm workshop, but it's not as if you can claim that breathing and muscle control doesn't have its pleasurable applications off the mat. She once read an article online in which Bikram addressed it head-on and claimed that once you'd done his yoga, you 'couldn't get it down' for days. (As if!)

So fun, so fun, so fun keeps pulsing through her head to a sultry samba beat.

There's a sudden roar of laughter and applause, and when she dares to turn around to see how Conor is managing, Wagner is standing behind him giving him an adjustment to loosen up his pelvis that involves grinding his hips into Conor's big, muscular butt. It's one of the most lewd things she's ever seen in a yoga studio. And Conor? He's just laughing, blushing, and winking at Katherine with a very sexy look in his eyes.

He's giving it a try, Katherine thinks. And watching him in this ridiculous posture, feeling a little light-headed and ridiculous herself, she thinks that if he's willing to try *this*, to just go with it, shouldn't she be willing to try living with him?

She gives Conor a big, exaggerated thumbs-up. What she means by this is: *Let's do it. Let's call the real estate agent tomorrow morning. Let's give it a try.* She'll translate later, in case he's too confused to get it now.

At David Todd's invitation, Lee is driving to a martial arts school on West Pico, not far from Santa Monica.

When she was leaving the house this morning, she found herself changing outfits three times, a bit of craziness that made her angry with herself. She's meeting with him to discuss a job, one he's more or less already turned down, and in fact, she knows absolutely nothing about his personal life. He could be married, for all she knows. Or gay. Or any other combination of factors that would make her outfit completely irrelevant. She's found a few stray rumors on the yoga blogs about DT being seen around town with various teachers, but she doesn't lend any of them credibility.

There's something deeply humiliating to her about her own eagerness to meet him, but then again, she's never been totally comfortable with her feelings about men. She was always a serious student in high school and college, so focused on grades and making sure that she would get into a good medical school, she never thought all that much about sex. Or never thought it had anything to do with her. It was for girls who had different interests and goals. Norm, the boyfriend she had from eleventh grade all the way to college graduation, was a smart, dorky guy who was mostly, she now realizes, a placeholder so she wouldn't have to think about relationships and could turn down the offers that came her way. She and Norm had cozy, routine sex that always left her longing for something else without knowing what, exactly, it was she wanted. She remembers one Sunday afternoon when she was a junior in college and had flown out to Chicago to spend a weekend in his dorm. It was February, and they were under the covers together, and they'd just done what she thought of as 'making love', and she burst into tears because she felt so empty and unaccountably alone with longings and disappointments she didn't understand. *What's wrong?* he asked her. And because she didn't know what was wrong and didn't want to offend him, she said, *Nothing's wrong. I'm just happy.*

She'd always known that she was attractive, but it wasn't until she discovered yoga that she felt connected to her physical self. It was as if it had unlocked the athletic

66

potential she'd kept bottled up while she was studying organic chemistry and anatomy. She'd memorized every muscle and bone and organ in the body, but somehow missed the obvious point – that she herself has a body. When she started practicing, she discovered it, and learned, too, that she could be confident about it. She hates when people make lewd references to yoga and double entendres about 'positions' (Kyra Monroe, are you listening?), but it was true for her that being in touch with her physical self in a new way made her feel connected to her sexuality for the first time in her life. When she met Alan, she threw all caution overboard. The very first time he touched her, she realized exactly what it was she'd been crying about with dear, ineffectual Norm. Ultimately, it was a bad marriage with Alan, but it was always great sex, enhanced, for both of them, by the work they did on their bodies in the studio.

For the past year, it's been easiest to focus on other things, just as she did when she was a student. It's exciting and disappointing that meeting David Todd has put a wrinkle in all that carefully maintained repression.

There are more martial arts schools in L.A. than yoga studios, and the one she's looking for turns out to be in an unassuming strip mall, wedged between a dollar store and a chain drugstore. She gives herself one last glance in the mirror on the visor. *I'm getting older*, she tells herself, and then snaps shut the visor. It's just a business call.

The first thing that hits her when she walks in is the smell of ground-in sweat that's reminiscent of the gymnasium in her junior high. If she could get away with having a place as funky as this, she wouldn't have any worries about keeping up with the bills. Nor would she ever want to walk in the door.

There's no one at the desk in front, so she follows the sounds of stark electronic music to a long narrow studio in the back. There, a group of about a dozen teenagers – boys and girls, every race – is standing in a circle, watching David going through a series of dance-like kicks and lunges in the middle of the room. He seems only partly aware of his surroundings, as if he's transported himself to a different place, and as the kicks get higher and the circles he's spinning in get faster, he looks as if he's taking flight. He's wearing a pair of cotton drawstring pants and nothing else, but even so, Lee finds herself focused on the faces of the kids in the circle, who can't seem to look away from the performance. When he comes back to earth and finishes with a bow, there's a reverential silence, and Lee notices one girl on the opposite side of the room, a wild-looking kid mottled with tattoos and a crazy mop of hair, brushing away a few tears of awe.

'It's mostly Japanese budokon,' David tells her, 'but I blend in a lot of traditional asanas, too. You couldn't get these kids to come to yoga. So I emphasize the martial arts and sneak in the rest.'

'Someone refers them to you?'

'Schoolteachers, mostly. They're kids with big problems. Drugs, violence, family stories you can't believe. I work with a few groups. They can keep coming if they stay in school. The truth is, I make a difference with only about ten percent of them, but sometimes, it's a huge difference.'

'Do the schools pay you?'

'Lee, are you kidding? This is California. Unless they decide to legalize pot and get some new revenue, it's volunteer work.'

'You should talk to my assistant,' Lee says. 'She's big on the legalization issue.'

Sitting across the table from her at a café on Montana, David looks a little older and more tired than he does in front of a class. He has a handsome, angular face with light hair that keeps falling under his glasses and into his eyes. He has a scruffy little goatee, too, and there are a few gray hairs scattered in it. All of this makes him even more attractive to Lee, as if he's earned the lines in his face and is comfortable with himself. He put on a loose green T-shirt that's stretched out at the neck and completely hides the lean torso Lee saw in class. It's an appealing mixture of confidence and lack of vanity – more or less the opposite of the two men she has been on 'dates' with in the past six months. Those were fix-ups arranged by her friend Lorraine, an artist in Silver Lake. The dates turned out to be endurance tests with men who were simultaneously so insecure about themselves and so narcissistic that neither one asked her a single question, and then they seemed hurt and surprised when she shook their hands good-bye.

David digs his fork into a chocolate peanut butter tart that's either the most disgusting or the most delicious thing Lee has ever seen. 'You really should try this,' he says. 'Then I'll feel less guilty about having ordered it. I'm working on my sugar addiction, but . . . slowly.'

'From what I've seen, you don't need to worry about it

too much,' Lee says. Open-ended kind of comment, but still too flirty?

'I've got a lot of demons in my past,' David says. 'They take different forms all the time, but for the most part, it's best to stay in balance. Or try to.'

Lee takes a bite of the tart, and her taste buds go on high alert. 'I can see how you could get hooked on this.'

'You can get hooked on anything in life.'

'Coffee's my vice of the moment,' she says. 'I keep telling myself it's better than cigarettes.'

David starts to tap the back of his hand with his fork, as if he's trying to decide whether to tell her something. Finally, he says, 'I looked you up online.'

'Oh? Anything interesting?'

'Some old footage from an interview you and Kyra Monroe did on TV a while ago.'

Lee can feel herself cringing. 'I didn't realize that had resurfaced. I hope you didn't watch it.'

'I stopped as soon as I saw where it was going.'

'Even if that isn't true, I appreciate you saying it. I hate even thinking about it.'

David cocks his head. 'It is true,' he says, as if it would never occur to him to lie. 'A lot of people think you're pretty amazing. Have you read some of the things your students have written about you on Yelp?'

In fact, Lainey has made sure that Lee keeps following the reviews the studio gets online, and while she tries not to get too invested in the praise, she takes a certain amount of pride in what all these anonymous reviewers are writing. 'I think you should come up to Silver Lake and see for yourself,' Lee says. 'I'm probably overrated, but I'm open to constructive criticism.'

'The word "compassion" comes up in almost every comment.'

'I'm a good actress.'

'Some things you can't fake. And I love that you're keeping it so low key, not buying into the big commercial monster that's trying to gobble us all up. You have to fight against them every chance you get.'

'What I'd love,' Lee says, 'it to make Edendale more of a community. Silver Lake has its share of kids in trouble, too. Not to be too hard-sell about it, but I think you should come and check us out.'

'I get a lot of offers, and right now, it's easiest to stick with what I've got. If I came, it would just be to take a class. I need a little more compassion in my life.'

Lee is relieved that he hasn't turned her down completely. If nothing else, she'll have a chance to see him again. She'll work on him.

He picks up a napkin and says, 'Do you mind if I . . . ?' and then reaches out and dabs at her chin. 'Sorry, but I feel responsible since I insisted you taste this.'

'It didn't take much coaxing.' She checks her watch and gets up from the table. 'I have to go. I have to pick my kids up at school.'

'How old?'

'Nine and nine. Do the math.'

He gets up with her, and they walk out into the bright afternoon heat. The traffic is starting to pick up on Montana, and Lee wonders if she should call Chloe to get the kids. If she did, she could go shopping down at the farmers' market. Maybe David would want to come along. He stops on the sidewalk and touches her arm. 'I read about you and your husband.'

'*That's* online?'

'Everything is if you know where to look. Anyway, I'm sorry. It can't have been easy.'

'Actually,' Lee says, 'it turns out to be a lot easier than living together was at the end.'

'Even so.' He brushes the hair out of his eyes and changes out his glasses for a pair of small, round shades. Definitely a hippie, a type Lee has always been drawn to. 'I just went through an ugly breakup a few months ago myself. I decided to focus on work for the next year to try and get clear. No dating, nothing.'

'I guess I'm in the same phase,' she says.

He reaches out and gives her a big hug, and Lee can feel the hard muscles of his chest and stomach pressed against her for long enough to be confusing. She isn't sure if he's just told her he's available or totally off-limits. She lets it go and focuses on the fact that he's coming to Edendale for a class. She's going to see him again. At the moment, that seems like enough.

Graciela moved out of the Four Seasons as soon as the tour left New York, two days ago. Obviously, she couldn't pay for it on her own, and, equally obvious, she wasn't about to accept Jacob Lander's offer of staying with him for a few days. Not that she wasn't tempted. Jacob lives on the fifty-seventh floor of a brand-new building on Columbus Circle. It is, without a doubt, the most glamorous apartment Graciela has ever seen. Basically, it's like an aquarium floating in the sky, with views all around – of the Hudson River and Central Park and down to lower Manhattan. She saw it briefly when he asked her to come up with him while he dropped off a present for his housekeeper's kid. It's minimally furnished, and there's something about the way there's no clutter at all, *anywhere*, that makes it feel a little sterile and un-lived-in, like a spectacular hotel suite waiting to be occupied.

But that goes along with Jacob's personality. He's a huge neat-freak. He has someone in every day to clean the bathrooms and the floors and polish everything else, and, by his own admission, takes several showers a day. At this point, that's just one of the many things about him that she finds almost unbearably adorable. He has a host of funny vain qualities that somehow read less like vanity and more like his attempt to keep his complicated life in control, to organize all that fame and money so he is master of it instead of being ruled by it.

Being with him has made her realize that Daryl's idea of trying to control his own life is mostly about manipulating and controlling *her*.

She checked herself into this place on the Upper West Side, a short walk from Jacob's building and within sprinting distance of about eight different yoga studios. The Belleclaire is a big step down from the Four Seasons, but it's clean and quiet and there's something cozy about its homey charm.

Her room is on the ninth floor of the hotel and faces an air shaft in back, although thanks to the arrangement of the buildings behind, an air shaft with a sliver of a view.

Not like looking at Central Park, but it's quiet and makes her feel safely insulated from the world. No one can see in. And considering what she's facing back in L.A. (and more to the point, the complications she's creating for herself right now), she appreciates that.

She walks down the curving staircase to the small, oval-shaped lobby. The elevator is slow and creaky, and she's been feeling especially energetic since she met Jacob anyway. The desk clerk waves and smiles at her. He's young, obviously gay, a little chubby, and a crazy fan of Beyoncé. He came to the concert twice, and he recognized her as soon as she checked in. It's the only time that's happened beyond the stage door, and it immediately made her feel close to him somehow, partly out of gratitude. She waves back at him, but then realizes that he's waving her over to the desk.

'How's it going, Lyle?' she asks.

'I mean,' he says, 'how could I be anything but happy on a day like today?'

'I get the feeling you're always happy,' she says.

'I'm paid to look that way.'

She hasn't told anyone about Jacob. He's made it clear that he tries to keep his personal life as quiet as possible, and she can understand why. There have been moments when she's been tempted to tell Lyle, of all people, but then, she isn't sure what she'd tell him. She's been 'seeing' Jacob? So far it's just been one tour of the city, a lunch at an out-of-the-way place in lower Manhattan, and a yoga class they took together. The most physical contact she's had with him is feeling his hand on her back when he holds a door open for her, but even that is enough to send a current of excitement through her whole body. She can tell he's attracted to her, and she isn't sure if she's grateful or disappointed he hasn't made more of a move. An hour ago, he called to change their lunch plans and asked her to come to his place instead, with no explanation other than saying he was in the mood to make burgers.

'I should hurry,' she says. 'I'm supposed to meet a friend.'

'Before you go,' Lyle says, 'you had a call here this morning while you were out running.'

'Really? There was no message.'

'It wasn't that kind of call. Just a guy asking if you were checked in here.'

'He didn't leave a name?'

'Nope.' Lyle pauses in a way that's clearly meant to make a point. 'He didn't.'

There's no doubt in her mind the caller was Daryl. Checking up on her. She told him that she had postponed her return to L.A. because she wanted to explore New York with one of the other dancers. Then she called him as soon as she moved into the Belleclaire, described her room, making it sound a little less appealing than it actually is. It's obvious he still didn't believe her.

'What did you tell him?'

'We don't give out that kind of information. Not if it's asked that way. Especially for a celebrity.'

'Real celebrities don't stay at this hotel.'

'You'd be surprised. Anyway, if he'd just asked to be connected to your room, we would have done it. Or said we don't have anyone listed under that name, if you weren't here. So keep that in mind next time you're stalking someone.'

'Will do,' she tells Lyle.

She should tell him it's probably her boyfriend, but right now, she doesn't want to refer to Daryl that way. Why is it, she wonders, that since meeting Jacob, she's been getting angry at Daryl for what he did, for the first time?

Out on the sidewalk, she starts to feel a familiar stab of pity for Daryl, despite what he did to her, despite the way he gets jealous and angry about her success, despite everything she's done to try and help him all these years. *If he'd just asked to be connected to your room*, Lyle said. But how would Daryl know that? How many hotels has he ever stayed at? He grew up in East L.A. in an apartment so small he had to share a bed with his two brothers until one of them was killed in gang violence in the neighborhood. It isn't as if she grew up with a lot of opportunities, but compared with Daryl's childhood, hers was idyllic. He's always told her that meeting her is the best thing that's ever happened to him, and she knows this is true. A year ago, she would have asked the wrong questions at a hotel, too. She's been places she never believed she'd see, while Daryl has been stuck in L.A., doing the same low-level deejay jobs, not getting where he wants to go.

She walks down Broadway, suddenly feeling as if the streets are dirtier than she realized and noticing that the wind is blowing around a lot of dust and trash. She takes out her phone and calls Jacob's number.

'Hey, Gracie,' he says. 'Running late?'

'No. It's not that.'

'Okay. You sound a little funny. Where are you?'

'I'm on Broadway. But . . . I don't think I should come

up for lunch. I'm thinking I might change my flight and try to go back to L.A. tonight. I'm sorry.'

He's silent for a long time, and then he says, 'You can't do that. For one thing, the flight would cost a fortune, and then for another, you'd always wonder if maybe you missed out on the best burger of your life.'

She laughs at that, even though she doesn't find it funny, and then she feels so sad and confused, she starts to cry. 'I'm sorry,' she says. 'I just can't.'

'Tell me where you are,' he says. 'I'm coming to get you.'

Lainey is so happy when Lee tells her she is going to take her advice and accept the offer to teach at the Flow and Glow Festival, she actually leaps up out of her chair and gives Lee a hug.

'I think this is a great decision,' she says. 'It's going to bump you to the next level where you belong. You're a star, Lee. You just don't realize it yet.'

Lee's first thought on hearing this is that David Todd would disapprove. But how much can that matter? She met him in Santa Monica three days ago, and he still hasn't shown up at Edendale for a class as he said he would. Maybe he was just trying to placate her by saying he'd come. Or maybe she's getting way too impatient.

'Let's not get ahead of ourselves,' she tells Lainey.

'I'm just relieved,' Lainey says. 'I accepted the offer over a week ago, so it would have been messy if you decided against it.'

'At some point,' Lee says, 'we should have a talk about that.'

'I agree,' Lainey tells her. 'But let's wait until after you see how amazing you look in the photos I sent them. You went up on their website yesterday.'

Back in her office, Lee decides that she might as well call her mother. She's going to have to do it sooner or later, and it's usually best to get the least appealing chores out of the way first.

'Lee!' her mother shrieks. 'I'm so happy you called me, honey. I've been thinking about you all day. Is something wrong?'

Lee checks her watch. It's not even one o'clock back in Connecticut, but from the sound of things, her mother has had her first glass of wine already. In the past year or so, the cocktail hour seems to have been pushed closer and closer to noon, but Lee can't decide if it's her place to bring it up or not. The past twelve months have been rough for Elaine and hopefully the drinking is just temporary and will settle down once all her legal problems get resolved.

'Nothing's wrong, Mom.'

'I'm so happy to hear that, honey. I just get worried because I never hear from you, and when I do it's usually with a problem or a favor.'

Lee feels as if she's been caught. She *is* calling with a favor. 'Everything's going well here,' she says.

'I wish I could say the same, but, well, let's not get into it. I know you don't want to hear about *my* problems.'

In fact, Lee really doesn't want to hear about her mother's problems. She knows too much already, and there's nothing she can do to help.

A little more than a year ago, Elaine fell under the spell

of Lawrence, a yoga teacher she met at the YMCA, and decided to go along with his plan to turn her house into a yoga retreat, with classes held in the barn and people sleeping in the moldy converted basement. Elaine has always been competitive with Lee and her sister, and Lee can't help but believe that if she didn't own a yoga studio, her mother wouldn't have gone along with Lawrence's half-baked plans.

'Has the lawyer sorted things out?' she asks.

'He's working on it, but I don't know if he's going to be able to get all the charges dropped. The neighborhood association is being disgusting. It's all homophobia. That's what Lawrence said, and of course he's right.'

Inexplicably, Lawrence is always right in her mother's eyes, even though he's caused her nothing but trouble, and based on the evidence, is always wrong. 'I thought you got along well with the association, Mom.'

'Now you're blaming Lawrence. Don't go there, Lee. I feel so bad for him, honey. I know you think he's a big phony and that he's using me as if I was just some old lady who has a crush on him, but you haven't met him. He's such a decent, sweet, *handsome* young man. And he's been so upset about all the trouble he's caused, he had to get away for two weeks, just to relax.'

'I'm sorry to hear that.'

'I can tell from your tone you think it's all his fault, but it really isn't. And don't worry, he didn't *ask* me for the money for the trip; I *offered*. Saint Barts has always been a healing place for him and Corey.'

The last Lee heard, Lawrence had convinced Elaine and Bob, Lee's stepfather, to invest in renovations for the barn and the house and then, without Elaine's knowledge, began holding late-night yoga classes in the barn. These became so popular, the neighbors started to complain about the noise and traffic. That's when Elaine learned that Lawrence hadn't applied for any of the permits he claimed to have gotten, and that the classes were hot nude male yoga he advertised on some questionable social networking sites. The lawsuits regarding code violations began shortly thereafter.

'To be honest, Mom, I was calling with a question.'

'You mean a favor, honey?'

'I suppose. It's about the boys.'

'You know I'd do anything in the world for them. I love them so much, and Bob and I never get to see them, almost as if you're ashamed of us or something, and are trying to keep us away from them. I don't blame you about Bob. I don't like being seen with him in public either, but he *is* their grandfather, honey.'

'I'm going to be teaching at a yoga festival in June for a few days, and I was wondering if you might want to come out here and spend some time with the boys.'

There's a long silence on the other end of the line, and in the background, Lee can hear her mother opening and closing cabinets and rattling bottles. 'Alan too busy?' she finally asks.

'He might be playing music at the same festival.'

'He better be careful. He might make enough money this year to qualify for income taxes.'

'If the timing's bad, Mom, I can always get one of my teachers to babysit,' Lee says. 'I just thought it could be a good break for you. Get away from all the problems there.'

'Oh, Lee. Don't make it sound like I wouldn't *crawl* out

there to see them, because you know I would.' Lee can hear the squeak of cork against glass, undoubtedly as her mother works open one of her big wine jugs. 'I'm going to start putting money aside right now. Unless you'd like to chip in something.'

'I'd be happy to, Mom. I was coming to that.'

'Oh goodie. When little Marcus called the other day, I was so happy to hear from him, I almost burst into tears. He was trying out his new cell phone.'

'Oh, really?'

'You sound surprised. You didn't know he has a phone?'

'I suspected. It's just that Alan and I had an agreement to wait a little longer to get them phones, so –'

'Oh, Alan didn't buy them, honey. It was his new girl-friend.'

This comes as such a surprise to Lee, she says nothing. It's not that she didn't imagine Alan was seeing someone; it's just that she didn't suspect that person would be buying phones for her kids.

'Are you there, Lee? Now don't tell me you didn't know he has a girlfriend. Me and my big mouth.' There's more squeaking of cork.

'Don't worry about it. It's fine.'

'She's a yoga teacher, too. You must be a dime a dozen out there.'

'I have another call coming in, Mom. We'll talk later and make plans.'

Graciela is standing on the corner of Broadway and Seventy-third Street waiting either for Jacob Lander to show up or to get enough courage to turn around and go back to her hotel. There doesn't seem to be a right choice or even a better one, and she feels rooted to the spot. The city is too hot and humid, and the traffic on Broadway feels threatening, whizzing past in its relentless way. She suddenly misses L.A. more than she has in months, the dry heat and ocean and even poor Daryl. She looks down at her phone, wondering if she can call him, and then, without thinking about it, she calls the one person she trusts most.

'Graciela!' Lee says, sounding genuinely happy to hear from her. 'Are you back? We've missed you.'

'I'm still in New York,' Graciela says. 'I decided to stay a few days longer.'

'I don't blame you. It's an amazing city, isn't it?'

'I guess,' Graciela says.

'Is everything all right?'

More than anything, Graciela wants to ask Lee for advice. What should she do? Or more to the point, what would *she* do? It isn't just that Lee got her past her injury and helped her get ready for the audition. There's something about her personality and the way she teaches her classes that makes Graciela believe that she's a truly decent person. Maybe she doesn't always make the right decisions (her choice of husband probably counts as a mistake), but it's hard to imagine her making selfish or hurtful choices. Lee has changed Graciela's life more than anyone she can think of. She started on the outside, with the physical, and somehow, the changes worked their way inward.

'Everything's okay,' she says. 'I'm just standing on a

street corner, and I'm a little worried I'm about to do something foolish.'

'Do you want to tell me more?'

'I guess I just wanted to hear your voice.'

'Do you know when you're coming back?'

'Sometime in the next week. I have an open ticket. I'm staying at a little hotel in the West Seventies that I like a lot. It's quiet.'

Lee seems to be thinking this over. The funny part is that even though Graciela is feeling too awkward and afraid to give any details, she has a strong impression Lee knows anyway. She's like that. Graciela often wondered if Lee didn't know exactly how she got her injury all those months ago. Not that she said anything, and not, most likely, that she would. After a little while, Lee says, 'You're a good person, Graciela. I hope you know that. Just ask yourself what you really want, and go from there. Don't second-guess it. And start coming to class again when you get back to L.A. I promise it will help, whatever you decide to do today.'

Graciela is still trying to figure out what it is she wants when she spots Jacob jogging up Broadway. He's sweating when he reaches her, and he takes her by the arm, right above her elbow.

'I wasn't sure you'd wait for me,' he says.

'I almost didn't.'

'That's what I was afraid of.'

Looking at him, so confident and handsome, it's hard to imagine he would be afraid of anything. Someone walking along the sidewalk stops and does a blatant double-take. It wouldn't surprise Graciela if he hauled out his phone to take pictures. Jacob puts his arm around her waist and leads her down Seventy-third Street, toward the river. He's walking quickly, and Graciela has to race to keep up with him. It's shady here and suddenly quiet, as if all the clatter of Broadway has evaporated. It isn't until they're on the corner of Riverside Drive that Jacob stops and turns to her, his face glistening with sweat and his cheeks flushed.

'Why would you do that?' he asks.

'Do?'

'Call me and tell me you're running off. I spent the whole morning shopping for you. Do you know how much I was looking forward to making this lunch for you?' He takes a tendril of her long hair and brushes it off her face, and then says more tenderly, 'Do you?'

'I'm sorry. I didn't want to disappoint you. I wanted to come, too. I was looking forward to seeing you all day.'

'What happened?'

'I told you, when we met . . .'

'You have a boyfriend. I know that. Have I pressured you to do anything?' He moves his hand from her hair to the back of her neck and massages it gently. 'I don't want to make things complicated for you, baby. I know we're on borrowed time. I just like being with you. I like it a lot.' He puts his arms around her and pulls her into his chest, and she can feel the heat of his body through his shirt and smell the clean, chemical smell of starch.

'I like being with you,' she murmurs into his chest. And then she reaches her arms around his back. She can hear his breath slowing down, as if he's getting more calm. Why would she mean this much to him? 'I'm not used to this,' she says. 'I'm not used to feeling this way. It's confusing.'

He reaches down and holds her chin in his hand. 'I know it is,' he says. 'Life's confusing and complicated, but sometimes you just have to follow your best guess.'

Across the street, someone is getting out of a cab, and without either of them saying anything, Jacob signals the driver. The taxi pulls over to the curb, and Jacob opens the door for her. When they're both inside, he gives his address to the driver and pulls her against him in the backseat. He leans down and kisses her forehead. 'It's only lunch,' he says.

'I'm not hungry,' she whispers.

'Neither am I.'

As the taxi pulls up in front of his building she hears Lee's voice. *Just ask yourself what you really want.* She doesn't know if this is the best choice or the right one. She guesses things are going to be complicated. But she does know that it's exactly what she wants. More than anything.

As soon as it became obvious that Imani wasn't going to have a free minute to get back to yoga classes at Edendale and start getting herself into shape, she called Becky Antrim and asked her to recommend a teacher who'd come to her house twice a week and give her private sessions. Becky seems to know everyone connected to yoga in L.A. She's been doing it religiously for years and has the body to prove it. She started back when she was on *Roommates*, the iconic sitcom that made her a superstar. She subscribes to a dozen or more blogs and Twitter accounts that point out the best class in town on any given day, and when she's not on a movie set, she goes to at least one.

'Brilliant idea!' Becky said. 'I was wondering when you were going to start up again. I have a friend whose job is matching people with private yoga teachers. Like a shrink who just does referrals. Let me ask her.'

Becky presented Imani with six different teachers, each one connected to a celebrity. Did she want Steve Martin's yoga teacher (Steve Martin does yoga?) or Natalie Portman's or the guy who supposedly tours with Lady Gaga or . . . ?

'They all do yoga?' Imani asked.

'Honey, come on. *Everyone* does yoga.'

In the end, Imani went with Tara Foster, mostly because she's known for being somewhat gentle, and she isn't linked to any celebrities with Madonna- or Demi Moore-like intensity. She stayed with her because during their first session, Imani discovered that if she asked Tara a few questions about her private work, she could tell stories for a good thirty minutes while more or less giving Imani a massage.

Imani invited Stephanie to join her today, and now, in the late afternoon, Tara is finishing up her hour with them. Today's class was about hip openers, but mostly, it has focused on a two-week vacation that Tara took to Hawaii with a country singer and her family. She got first-class accommodations, all meals, an astonishingly high weekly salary, and ten tickets to the singer's sold-out concert at the Hollywood Bowl next week.

'And how many sessions did you have to do with her?' Imani asks. She's asked this question at least once before, but she knows that if she doesn't keep Tara talking, she's going to suggest she and Stephanie come out of their supine twists, and Imani's not looking forward to that. Basically, she's running out the clock.

'Supposedly two to three a day,' Tara says, 'but she got a little resentful at the idea of doing *anything* since it was her one big vacation, and she just wanted to lie around. We had one session the first day and maybe two in the last week.'

'We're in the wrong business, Stephanie,' Imani says. 'In my next life, I want to come back as Tara. Flat abs and all.'

'Let's do an inversion before we finish up,' Tara says. 'And really, it wasn't the best two weeks of my life. I had nothing to do, and the family treated me pretty much like staff.'

'I love that we can talk during these sessions,' Stephanie says. 'I've never talked while doing yoga before.'

'One of my clients takes business calls during class,' Tara says. 'Plus there's a whole issue in studios now because so many students try to sneak in texting while they're in child's pose. They hide their phones under the edge of their mats. I know one teacher who builds in a water and Twitter break after sun salutations.'

Imani sees this as an opening for further discussion, hopefully enough to avoid the inversion altogether and get them right into savasana. 'How does the businessman hold the phone? Or is he on speaker? And do people know you're doing yoga or does he pretend he's at his desk?'

Ten minutes later, Tara is packing up her mat and props, and Imani is handing her the envelope with the check tucked inside. Tara always looks Imani right in the eyes as she's taking the envelope, making it seem, to the greatest extent possible, that this part of the transaction isn't really happening. She explains to Imani that she's going to a yoga festival at the end of next month and won't be available, and then says, 'I've been hearing about your movie.'

'Oh? Who from?' Imani asks.

'I work with Cheryl Hines, and I guess she's heard about it from a few different people who think it's going to be a big hit. Cheryl says hi, by the way.'

'See if you can find out who's spreading the word,' Stephanie says. 'I'd love to know.'

Tara grimaces and says, 'I'm not sure I can do that. I really have to be discreet, for professional reasons.'

'I understand completely,' Imani says.

What she really understands is that for the past sixty minutes, Tara has spilled the beans on pretty much everyone she works with. Not in a malicious way, but because, like everyone else in the world, she loves talking about what she does.

Sometimes Imani thinks of these yoga teachers who drive from client to client as information systems that crisscross the city. On the plus side, it's a good way to learn what's going on. On the negative side, if one client has the flu, that's bound to spread quickly as well.

After Tara has left, Stephanie says, 'I saw what you were doing. You can't manipulate a teacher in a regular class that easily.'

'Why do you think I'm paying the big bucks for privates? Once the movie's done, I'm going to start going to classes again. I need a kick start, though.'

'I love hearing that people are talking about the movie

already,' Stephanie says. 'I'm beginning to get a good feeling about it.'

They're sitting beside Imani's pool, staring off into the approaching twilight. It would be the perfect moment for a cocktail, but since Imani's nursing, she can't. She knows that Stephanie can't either, but she has her own, very different reasons for that. Glenn keeps telling Imani she can have a glass of wine with dinner if she wants. He's a pediatric surgeon, so she ought to take him at his word, but the last thing she needs is one more item to add to the ever-growing list of reasons to wonder if she's being a good enough mother to her little prince.

'I hate getting my hopes up, but I've got a good feeling, too. Rusty's a dick, but he's a talented dick.'

'I know how tough it's been with the baby,' Stephanie says. 'We're lucky you agreed to the start date.'

Problem number one, Imani thinks, but says nothing. In retrospect, she shouldn't have accepted the role in *Las Vegas Sands* at all. She should have waited. But once she got past the first trimester of her pregnancy and started to believe (in no small part thanks to Lee's guidance and instruction) that she really was going to be able to carry this baby to term, she developed a Superwoman complex and thought she could do anything. Bring it on, whatever 'it' happened to be. And on top of that, she couldn't wait any longer to get back into the game. She'd left *X.C.I.A* almost two years earlier, and she was rapidly approaching irrelevancy. She thought – was hoping, really – that once she had Daniel, she'd stop caring so much about her career, about being a 'celebrity', whatever that means. It hasn't worked out that way.

'Daniel sleeping?' Stephanie asks.

'Renay took him out in the stroller. They should be back soon.'

'So it's working out with Renay?'

Problem number two. There's enough skepticism in Stephanie's tone to make it clear she's guessed that something is up in the Renay department.

'Renay's trying,' Imani says. 'The main thing is, she really does seem to love Daniel.'

Renay is the fifteen-year-old daughter of Imani's older sister, Gloria. When Imani told Gloria she was looking for a live-in nanny, Gloria suggested Renay. She was having unspecified academic problems, and Gloria saw this as a good opportunity to give her a break from school, do something interesting, and 'grow up a little bit.' In typical fashion, Gloria didn't stop to ask if it was a good opportunity for Imani.

Imani agreed to the idea mostly to please her sister. For years, Gloria has been tossing barbs at Imani about her career, as if it's horribly unfair that her life is so much easier and better than Gloria's. As if her success in acting has nothing to do with talent or hard work and is all the result of the fact that she was 'given all the looks' in the family. That's a double whammy because there's always a tone in Gloria's voice that suggests she's somehow or other been defeated by having a pretty younger sister. So Gloria's weight problems are Imani's fault, too? And Imani's marriage to Glenn is one more unfair stroke of luck while Gloria's multitude of bad choices around men is entirely out of her own control?

But then, Imani herself has never quite gotten over the

feeling that she's always been disproportionately lucky. What would happen if she ever got *really* famous? Becky Antrim, who is *really* famous, told her you never get over the guilt entirely, although reading about your husband's infidelities with the most beautiful actress in the world in the tabloids helps bring your ego back to earth.

Imani flew Renay up from Texas a couple of weeks before the start of the shoot. She hadn't spent a lot of time with her niece since Renay was a kid, and the last she remembered, she was an awkward eleven-year-old with skinny arms. She was surprised to see a tall, lanky teenager emerge from the gate area, looking more attractive than Imani would have guessed, a rolling suitcase in one hand, a fat novel by Dickens in the other. *Academic problems?* Imani wondered.

But as soon as she got into the car, it became clear that Renay, for all her good looks and intelligence, was depressed. She rarely looked at Imani directly, and when she was asked a question, she answered in as few words as possible.

Imani was so baffled about how to deal with Renay, she seriously considered sending her back home. But she has this adorable habit of talking to Daniel in a Donald Duck voice that's so cute and sweet, Imani decided to let her stay. She hoped she'd help her come out of her shell more, but that doesn't seem to be happening. It's almost as if she's traumatized.

Since it's beginning to get late and Glenn should be home from the hospital soon, she asks Stephanie if she'd like to stay for dinner. Glenn is the most agreeable man on earth, so no matter how exhausted he is and how *not* in the mood for company, he's always the perfect host.

'I'd love to, but I can't,' Stephanie says. 'I have a ton of organizing and packing to do for the New York trip. I'm afraid it means I won't be on the set for a few days.'

'I'll make it through,' Imani says. 'I'll turn into "diva from hell" just to piss Rusty off. When are you coming back?'

'We're coming back early next week.'

'Sybille's coming back with you?'

'Not that I know of. My friend Roberta's coming with me.'

Imani nods. It doesn't take a brain surgeon to figure out that Roberta is gay, and based on the way Stephanie lit up the time Roberta appeared on the set unannounced, it's obvious that their friendship is close, if not closer. But the disappointing, boring truth is Imani can't say anything about it until Stephanie decides she's ready to discuss it. She knows there's at least one live-in boyfriend in Stephanie's recent past, but Imani has learned that people are always full of surprises when it comes to love and sex.

'Lee called me a little while ago,' Stephanie says. 'Graciela's in New York. She thinks I should check in on her when I'm there. She decided to stay in the city longer.'

'Is something wrong?'

'Lee's too discreet to say, but I got the feeling Graciela might be in trouble.'

Imani gives her a look. 'Oh! *That* kind of trouble!'

'I'm guessing.'

They look at each other and start to laugh. Everything

about Stephanie, from her manner to her face, has softened in the past year. 'You know,' Imani says, 'that might be the first time I've seen you cut loose and laugh. You should do that once a day, at least.'

'You think?'

'I hear it's great for the immune system. If Tara is right about the movie, your life is going to change. You're going to have to be prepared for it.'

It isn't until after Imani has walked Stephanie through the house and ushered her out the front door that she realizes how late it is. Renay has been gone for over an hour now. On top of that, it's nearly dark. She calls Renay's cell phone, but there's no answer. Trying not to let panic creep up on her, Imani puts on a pair of running shoes and goes out to the sidewalk. She starts walking west, then thinks better of it and turns east. She reminds herself how good Renay is with Daniel, how unlikely it is that she'd be stupid enough to walk outside of the neighborhood and into high-traffic territory she doesn't know with a baby in a stroller. Which begs the question: *Where the fuck is she?*

Graham is showing Lee the improvements he made to the wall behind the reception desk.

'Well, not me personally,' he says. 'The contractor. But he wouldn't have done it unless we pushed.'

'It looks perfect,' Lee says. She thought it looked perfect before, too, but there's probably no need to let Graham know that, since he seems so proud of all the fine-tuning he's done. 'I hate to sound ungrateful for the wall,' she says, 'but I'm getting a little worried that we still don't have a floor.'

'Minor detail, Lee. Floors are quick and easy. We can have that done in a day. I'm hoping you're going to change your mind about the hardwood.'

Putting in a hardwood floor to match the old studio has been a bone of contention since they started the project. Graham, who's worked on several other studios, wants to use a composite that resists heat and humidity, is a bit sticky, and is the trendy flooring, he assured her, in studios all over L.A. Lee prefers the way the wood looks, the way the sunlight makes it glow, the slight give it has when you jump.

'I'm pretty set on the wood,' she says yet again. 'I'm trying to be a trendsetter, in my own retro way.'

'But let's say you want to offer hot yoga classes. The PEM flooring is much better for a hot room.'

Over the years, Lee has done her share of heated yoga. She knows how good it can feel, and she knows about the benefits. But she can't get past feeling that there's an element of sham involved in the craze surrounding it. Students leave a hot yoga class exhausted and drained, feeling purified and cleansed, but the truth is, there are scores of poses and arm balances you'd never teach in an overheated room. People sweat so much they're slipping all over, and a really difficult posture becomes dangerous, especially when students are on the edge of heat prostration. She'd rather her students leave feeling cleansed and limber because of the poses they do. Otherwise, they could go to a sauna for the same feeling.

'Not a big hot yoga person,' she says.

He smiles at her and folds his arms around his clipboard. How he keeps his shirts so spotlessly white is a mystery to Lee. Maybe he has a supply of them in the backseat of his Mini Cooper.

'Speaking of trends,' he says, 'I saw you on the Flow and Glow website. Beautiful photos.'

'I didn't know you practiced, Graham.'

'I don't. I just like to keep up on my clients. I'm doing more yoga studios at the moment than restaurants, if you can believe it. So when I talk about the floor, I know my stuff. Let me show you some of the work I've done. I'll take you out for dinner and we can go through photos and floor samples.'

He says this in such a casual way, Lee isn't sure whether he means it as a date or not. On the other hand, he could easily bring his laptop to the studio and show her the photos here.

'Everything's a little crazy right now,' she says. 'I haven't had time for a meal out in weeks.'

'All the more reason,' he says. 'Bring the kids. I'd love to get to know them better.'

He's leaning against the desk, and there's no mistaking his stance now, open and a little provocative. He is a handsome man, intelligent and kind, and he's been incredibly nice to her all along. But that just adds to the argument for turning down the invitation rather than misleading him.

'I'll get back to you on that,' she says. 'And let's set a date for the floor. I've started to announce the grand opening, and it would help to have a floor down.'

'All right. It's up to you, but I think you're making a mistake.'

She can't tell for sure if he's talking about the dinner or the PEM flooring.

Lee goes into her office at the back of the studio and pulls up the website for the Flow and Glow Festival. She might as well face it now.

The website is a combination of commune-with-nature spirituality and hang-out-with-the-superstars glitz. The photos of the locale are pretty spectacular – yoga classes on a mountaintop, beside a river, in view of a waterfall – but the photos of the teachers and the students seem to emphasize, in a subtle way, their skimpy, sexy outfits and their suntans. Most of the embedded videos from last year's festival are of the after-hours parties, which include a lot of fire eating and free-form dancing.

She thinks back to her own training with her teacher in New York, the long, grueling hours she put in, learning every posture, step by step, a long tradition handed down, given to her as a kind of gift. In those days, this event, with so many thousands of participants, would have seemed like science fiction. At some point, she's going to have to explain to David Todd that she's doing this and why. Assuming he ever shows up.

Along with the fire eating are a few videos of the ubiquitous Kyra Monroe. Lee takes a deep breath and clicks on one of the tabs. There's Kyra, lean and pretty, hair blowing in the wind as she instructs a class of what appears to be hundreds, giving instructions in her most kittenish, seductive voice, prowling in between mats, playing the star.

Shortly after Lee moved to California and opened Edendale, *Los Angeles* magazine did a story on five 'hidden gems' on the L.A. yoga scene. Somehow, despite the fact that she'd just opened the studio and was teaching classes with five and six students, they chose her as one of the teachers profiled. It was when yoga was beginning to explode in popularity, and thanks to the article and some beautiful – if slightly inaccurate – photos, Lee got a lot of media attention. There were more profiles in a couple of neighborhood papers, a hugely favorable review on the Accidental Yogist blog, and, finally, the opportunity to appear on *Good Morning, L.A.* With Kyra, one of the other hidden gems. This was the interview that DT found online.

Lee had had a premonition that the TV appearance might not be a great idea, but Alan had told her she'd be a fool to turn it down. *I'd do it in a minute,* he'd said, as if there had been any doubt about that. *If you don't want to go, tell them your husband can do it.* She hadn't been able to bring herself to remind him that her husband hadn't been asked.

The TV appearance started off as a fairly straightforward interview with informed and interesting questions about running a studio, and if Kyra's yoga top seemed a little weirdly low cut, Lee didn't think much of it at first. After a couple of minutes of interviewing, the questions started to get more suggestive ('I'll bet your boyfriend likes that one, eh?' 'Speaking of positions, any bedroom tips?') and Lee did her best to smile through it and maintain her dignity.

When the demonstration portion of the interview started, it became obvious the host was going to play the whole thing like a party game, suggesting one more ridiculous contortion after the next, until she and Kyra were locked together in a lurid twist, her nose buried in Kyra's conveniently exposed cleavage. The host was hooting.

'I think we invented a new one here – porno pose.'

As she and Kyra were leaving the studio, Lee said, '*That* was embarrassing.'

Kyra looked at her with a surprised grin. 'You're kidding. We thought you'd think it was fun.'

'We?'

'I made a few suggestions to the producer during the preinterview. You have to make sure it's lively and a little outrageous, or they don't invite you back. Trust me, we're going to get *lots* more offers after that little performance.'

'Trust me,' Lee said, 'I'm going to turn them down.'

'Gee, I didn't know you'd be so uptight, Lee. Sorry about that. Really.'

Funny, Kyra didn't sound sorry, never mind *really* sorry. And if she was going to choreograph the whole thing with the producers, she could have had the decency to cast herself as the one with her face buried in someone's boobs.

Lee stayed in Silver Lake and happily worked the way she wanted to work. She met Kyra and her then-husband at a couple of conferences, but it was always awkward. Kyra used the *L.A.* magazine profile and TV 'performance' to build on her fame, and Lee watched as she turned up in more and more magazines and videos, saw advertisements for her workshops, heard rumors that she and her ex were pitching a reality series about their lives called *Twist and Shout*.

Well, to each her own, but Lee hated the way the couple always treated her with a condescending tone, as if there was something tragic about the path she'd chosen.

She's still looking at the website when the door to her office bangs open and the twins rush in. Individually, they can be fairly calm and sweet, but when the two of them are together, they're like their own weather system, changing the temperature in the room and creating little squalls. Lately, she's been so happy to have the two of them together, she's welcomed the storms.

'I was getting worried about you,' Lee says. 'Did soccer run over?'

'Dad was late picking us up,' Michael says.

'He was stuck in traffic,' Marcus says. 'It wasn't his fault.' He's taken on the role of defending his father every chance he gets, so Lee has made a special effort never to criticize Alan in front of them, even about the most minor things.

'One of my students was complaining about the traffic, too,' she says. 'What matters is, you're here now. Next time, just give me a call to let me know, okay guys?'

Lee has been waiting for the kids to bring up the subject of their new cell phones, just so she doesn't have to be the one to open the topic, but so far they haven't said anything, a big disappointment. As for Alan's new girlfriend, really, she couldn't care less. Good luck to Alan – and more to the point, good luck to the girlfriend.

'Marcus,' she says, 'did you get a cut on your face?'

He reaches up and touches his cheek. 'Just a scratch,' he says. 'It's not a big deal.'

'I know, but come here so I can have a look.'

Grudgingly, he drops his backpack onto the floor and comes behind her desk. He's getting more touchy about her kissing him, but she can't help but reach out and grab him in her arms and wrestle him onto her lap. 'My big grown-up boys,' she says and kisses the side of his face. 'I think we should wash that out and put a little something on it.'

He squirms out of her arms and leans on her desk, peering at her screensaver, stick figures doing poses.

'It didn't bleed or anything. So it can't get infected.' He touches the mouse; her screensaver dissolves and the Flow and Glow website flares to life. 'How come you're looking at a video of Kyra, Mom?'

She doesn't think anything of it at first, and then Michael comes behind the desk and gives his brother a punch in the arm. 'Shut up, Marcus,' he says.

Lee looks at the two of them, red faced and about to start a fight with each other, and she pieces it all together. And then the irony of it hits her and she starts to laugh. *What a wonderful, perfect little couple*, she thinks.

'I think we need to have a talk,' she says. 'About the cell phones your dad's girlfriend gave you.'

'You mean Kyra?' Marcus asks.

I breathe in, I breathe out. I show up on my mat and do the best I can. 'Yes,' she says calmly. 'I mean Kyra.'

Imani realizes that she's started to circle the same streets over and over, calling out Renay's name in an increasingly desperate tone of voice. Her breathing is getting ragged, and she feels as if she's working herself into an all-out panic attack. She wants to talk to Glenn, but some part of her feels responsible for this. After all, she shouldn't have let Renay take Daniel out so late in the afternoon, and if she hadn't been talking with Stephanie about her damned career, she would have noticed how late it was getting, and why the hell did she decide to invite Renay to L.A. in the first place when she knew pleasing Gloria was impossible no matter what?

She sits down on the edge of a lawn, pulls her knees up to her chest, and starts to rock back and forth. It feels as if she dashed out of the house an hour ago, but probably it's just been a few minutes. She checks her watch and decides that if Renay hasn't shown up in five minutes, she'll call Glenn. She has a plan, and that always makes her feel better.

She gets up off the lawn and starts toward home. That's when her phone rings.

'Aunt Harriet?' The voice is tentative.

'Renay,' Imani says, trying her best to keep her voice level. 'Care to tell me where you are?'

'I'm sorry, Aunt Harriet.' Gloria has forbidden Renay to call Imani by her professional name, and even at a moment like this, Imani finds herself annoyed. 'I think I'm a little lost.'

'All right, I figured you might be. But you and Daniel are okay?'

'I was trying to get to the park, and I think I went the wrong way. I'm not sure where I made the wrong turn. I had my map with me, but . . . I'm kind of tired.'

The real shock to Imani is that Renay has just uttered three complete sentences to her. Progress.

'I want you to stop walking, wherever you are, and tell me what you're looking at.'

In the background, Imani can hear cars passing by and

the sound of Daniel crying, the latter an oddly and unexpectedly comforting sound. It's his 'I'm hungry' cry, and hearing it, Imani feels a pang of longing to be nursing him and pride that she can distinguish one cry from another.

Renay describes a street scene with such a surprising eye for detail that it begins to sound familiar to Imani. The café with the little green tables, the bench with the names painted on it in pink, the gas station with the inflatable man waving in front. Is it possible that she's in Silver Lake?

'Stop someone and ask them if you're in Silver Lake, honey.' When it's confirmed that she is, Imani, against her better judgment, shouts, 'Renay! How the hell did you get all the way out there?'

'I just kept walking. I didn't realize it was so far.'

Focus on your intention, Lee is always telling them in class. Her intention right now is to get Renay and Daniel home so she can feed her son and *ship Renay on the next flight back to Texas*.

'It's all right, sweetie,' she says, trying to soften her tone. 'As long as you're both okay. I'll bet you're hungry, too. Just stay where you are and don't move. You're about ten blocks from my yoga studio. One of the teachers can probably come pick you up in about two minutes. I'll meet you at the studio in half an hour.'

As she's jogging back to the house to get her car, she decides to call Katherine. It's not like they're great pals, but it's close enough to an emergency, and suddenly, the little group of women she met at Edendale feels like family.

*

Katherine and Conor are looking at an apartment on the less fashionable border of Silver Lake and Echo Park. Chloe's mother, alleged to be one of the best real estate agents in the area, has agreed to show them places, mostly as a favor to Chloe. Carolyn is much more at ease showing houses worth a couple million, and Katherine has a sneaking suspicion that she's hoping this bit of charity will put her in line to list Katherine's house. Or Tom's house, as Katherine keeps reminding herself.

Carolyn is probably fiftyish, but she has that weirdly uniform appearance that Katherine has noted on an awful lot of real estate agents she's met in L.A. As if going to the same doctor for the same Botox treatments and lip injections and brow lifts is part of the licensing procedure. For some reason, people want their real estate agents, like their movie stars – and increasingly, their yoga teachers – to give off an air of ageless glamour. Carolyn is an attractive woman, but at the same time, there's something about the cut of her clothes, the soft, highlighted hair extensions, and the adjustments she's made to her face that give her the look of a reality-TV housewife, an entirely different species than a real housewife.

She's waiting for them in front of the building, an uninspiring four-story concrete block with parking beneath. 'I guess we get our own space,' Conor says to Katherine. 'That's a plus, Brodski.'

This is the third apartment they've looked at, and so far Conor, in his optimistic way, has managed to find only good things to say about each place. The price is right or the light is good or he really prefers a shower to a bathtub anyway or gee, the Thai restaurant next door whose kitchen exhaust vent is right outside the bedroom window is reported to have excellent food and think how much shopping and cooking time it will save them.

Katherine, on the other hand, has experienced a mild depression bordering on despair each time she's pulled up in front of these faceless buildings. She keeps reminding herself that she's been spoiled by her/Tom's house, and that a few years ago, before she moved into the bungalow, she would have found any of these places perfectly acceptable, and that really, you can adjust to anything in life if you put your mind to it. 'I love that dress, Katherine,' Carolyn says. 'Please tell me you didn't make that yourself.'

Katherine just smiles and Conor puts his arm around her waist. She and Conor have discussed Carolyn's penchant for complimenting Katherine's reconstructed vintage dresses. Maybe she's sincere, but since Carolyn herself has never appeared in anything less than designer outfits she accessorizes with eight-hundred-dollar shoes and voluminous handbags that, like show dogs, have titles and pedigrees, Katherine can't help but hear a note of condescension in her praise.

'As you can see,' Carolyn says, waving vaguely, 'there's off-street parking. I know it isn't what you're used to up in the hills, but this neighborhood is getting super fashionable.'

In the couple of days they've been at this, Katherine has learned how to translate real estate language. 'Getting fashionable' means 'You'll definitely want to live here – in ten years.' So maybe 'getting super fashionable' means five years.

Carolyn leads them up a set of stairs clinging to the outside of the building, her heels clip-clopping and pretty much everything about her looking preposterously out of place here. As she's wrestling with her big set of keys, she says, 'I talked to the owner, and he assured me that once they leave the windows open for a few days, the smell will be gone. Also, don't worry about the carpet. He promised me they're going to have it replaced. Unless the cleaner can do something.'

The front door leads directly into a weirdly shaped kitchen with a loud refrigerator and a greasy hood over the stove. It's one of those crazy rooms that are vast, but because of the angles and doors, are almost impossible to imagine furnishing.

'I'll bet you love these Formica countertops, Kat,' Carolyn says. 'Period detail. I think I read somewhere that you can use bleach to get these burn marks out.'

She looks as if she's about to touch the counter, but then thinks better of it.

'I'll show you the bathroom, but again, they haven't had the cleaners in yet. They promised me they'd resurface the tub if the stains don't come up. And by the way, there's a note on the sheet that says those are rust stains, not blood.'

Katherine sticks her head into the bathroom, but can't bring herself to walk all the way in. 'It's . . .'

'Small, I know. But the landlord says not to worry about the smell of mildew. Apparently it's coming from upstairs, not this unit.'

'No window in here?' Katherine asks.

'From the outside, it looks like there might be one covered up by the vinyl wall behind the tub. A small fix.'

'I guess we save money on window shades,' Conor says.

'I'm going to remember that line,' Carolyn replies.

The bedroom is painted an institutional shade of blue – nursing home? psychiatric ward? – but the carpet is an indeterminate color. 'I've never seen windows that high,' Katherine says.

'I guess it gives us more wall space to put the bed,' Conor says.

Carolyn is looking at her listing sheet. 'So there you have it. Not palatial, I'll grant you, but it has potential.'

'So there's no living room?'

Carolyn starts to shuffle her papers. 'Interesting question.' She puts on a pair of jeweled eyeglasses. 'Oh, I see. They call the kitchen a "great room". Living, dining, kitchen combination. Open floor plans are really popular, as you know.'

Katherine looks at Conor and makes a little pout, then the two of them burst out laughing. He takes her in his arms, turns her around, presses his chest against her back, and rests his chin on the top of her head. 'I told Conor I could live with him anywhere,' she says, 'but maybe I was wrong.'

Carolyn shrugs. 'It needs some work. You said you love projects, Conor. This would keep you busy for a while.'

He lets go of Katherine and takes a spin around the place on his own, while she and Carolyn make awkward time-filling conversation about Chloe and how much she loves teaching at Edendale. When Conor comes back, he says, 'Do you think the landlord would let me do a little carpentry?'

'I don't think it would take much convincing.'

When Conor slips a little notebook out of his back pocket and starts sketching and jotting down some estimates of dimensions, Katherine has a feeling she might be looking at her new home.

Outside, Carolyn shakes their hands and says, 'Believe it or not, this is going to go quickly once it actually hits the market. If you're at all interested, you should probably let me know as soon as possible. It's not the worst place I've been to recently, and you're both busy. It's roomier than it looks, unless you're thinking about kids.'

Katherine feels as if she's just been stung. About six months after they began dating, Conor started dropping hints about how much he loves kids and how he really looks forward to being a dad someday. He had more sense than to come out and make a suggestion about the two of them, but it's always hanging in the air somewhere between them, especially now that they're planning to move in together. He's never pressed Katherine about details of her past, and he's never shown any signs of being judgmental, but he's basically a pretty conventional guy. He would make a great parent. And Katherine knows that she would not.

'We'll talk it over,' Katherine says.

In the truck on the way back to the studio, Conor says, 'I don't think that was rust in the bathtub.'

'You looked? You're braver than me, Mr. Ross.'

'Of course I am. I'm letting you drive, aren't I?'

'You're insisting.'

'I know, but I can tell you're starting to like it. You just don't want to show it. You're not as open-minded as you pretend.'

'I don't like thinking someone knows me better than I know myself.'

'It would be nice to find a bigger place,' Conor says. 'And don't get nervous; I'm not talking about a family. Just a little room to hide from each other. And I wouldn't mind a dog.'

If they do take this place, sign a lease for a year, there really wouldn't be any question about kids, about a family. She has had more than her share of family in her life.

'You do know,' Katherine says, 'that I'm never going to be the type who's going to want a house in the suburbs and three kids and an SUV, don't you?'

'I'm not so sure,' Conor says. 'Once you get used to driving this truck, all bets are off on the SUV.'

'No, Mr Ross. I'm serious. I never want to mislead you.'

'And why is that, Brodski?'

'Because I love you too much to do that. And I want to remind you of my million and one faults.'

'I knew about the million, but what's the one?'

'Please, Conor,' she says. She can hear a note of desperation in her voice, one she doesn't like, but it's important to her, before they move in, before they get that much more deeply involved, to know he understands her and accepts her as is.

He reaches for her hand and says, 'Hasn't it crossed your mind that I love you because of all the things you think are faults? You just have to keep being yourself.'

Katherine feels her phone ringing in the pocket of her sundress and hands it to Conor. 'If this is one of my old boyfriends, tell him I moved to Glendale and started raising labradoodles.'

Conor looks down at the phone. 'It's Imani,' he says. 'You haven't heard from her in a while.'

'Are you mad at us, Mom?' Michael asks.

As a matter of fact, she is, but she knows that a good portion of her anger is displaced rage at someone else. She's tempted to tell the boys she's 'not mad but disappointed', but since that was her own mother's favorite passive-aggressive way of expressing anger and simultaneously inducing guilt, she heads in a different direction.

'I thought we had an agreement about secrets,' she says. 'Specifically that they weren't good for anyone, so we wouldn't keep them from each other.'

'Yeah,' Marcus says. 'But Dad said it wasn't really a secret, just something we weren't telling you yet.'

Not telling her yet is apparently Alan's specialty and his favorite way of making an outright lie sound insignificant. When she confronted him about his affair, he acted as if he didn't know why she was so upset, since he was 'going to tell you about it when the time was right'.

'I don't know, honey. That sounds a lot like keeping a secret to me. Doesn't it to you?'

'Dad told us you didn't want us to have phones,' Michael says. 'And Kyra said that since it was a safety thing, it was more important we have the phones and not tell anyone for a little while.'

'And by "anyone" she meant me, specifically?'

The boys look at each other and shrug. 'I guess,' Michael says.

'And by "a little while" she meant how long?'

'I guess until you said it was okay for us to have phones.'

The logic of this is so pricelessly Alan, she almost starts to laugh. Alan clearly has found his perfect match in Kyra.

There are about a dozen other questions Lee wants to ask the boys, but she really doesn't want to pull them into the middle of any more parental drama than they're already in. But there's one more question she can't resist asking.

'I guess you also weren't supposed to mention to me yet that your dad and Kyra have been seeing each other?'

Michael is groping in the bottom of the pockets in his baggy pants. 'Can I show you the phone anyway, Mom?' he asks.

'You might as well.'

Marcus begins to dig out his phone, too, and suddenly Lee feels relieved that they're so excited to show her something, to share it with her. It's a consolation prize, but better than nothing. No wonder they've been so eager to spend time with Alan these days. Two people to dote on them, one of them willing to hand out expensive and irresistible gadgets. If she started dating, would they be happier to spend time with her? Although she can't imagine DT lavishing them with electronic gadgets. Budokon lessons? Surely they'd love those.

'Dad said you don't like Kyra, so we shouldn't talk about her to you,' Marcus says. He pulls a new iPhone encased in a green holographic cover out of his pocket and starts playing a game.

'You guys know that your father and I aren't together anymore, so he can see whoever he wants. It doesn't matter if I like her or not.'

'Oh, okay,' Michael says. 'So you mean you don't like her?'

'I didn't say that, honey. I never knew her very well, and I haven't seen her in a long time.'

'Yeah, but you didn't like her when you *did* know her?'

'The important thing is that *you* like her, since you seem to spend time with her,' Lee says.

Quite a while ago, she finally got it into her head that you should never write anything in an e-mail that you don't want potentially broadcast to everyone on the planet. More recently, she came to realize that talking to the twins is the conversational equivalent of e-mail and that she can't say anything in front of them she doesn't want repeated to Alan and now, apparently, Kyra Monroe. The more she thinks about this pairing, the more perfect it seems. Kyra and Alan are clearly soul mates and deserve each other. If they make each other happy, it can only be a good thing for her in the end. Which doesn't excuse the fact that Kyra is buying the kids things she knows Lee doesn't approve of and then encouraging them to lie about it to her. A big talk is definitely overdue.

In the meantime, she might as well accept something she's obviously not going to be able to change. She takes out her own phone.

'Okay,' she says, 'give me your numbers so I can get them in my contacts list. Marcus, you go first.'

'So the kid just wandered off with the baby in a stroller?' Conor says. He has his arm slung across the back of Katherine's seat, which somehow or other makes driving a lot less intimidating, almost as if she's not really doing it alone. 'It's right up at the light and then your second left.'

'I've never met Renay,' Katherine says. 'Lee did once or twice and said she seemed a little spacey. Maybe she just lost track of where she was.'

'So why would Imani let her babysit in the first place? She must be able to afford pretty much anyone.'

'You're asking the wrong person,' Katherine says.

When it comes to parenthood, there's a lot that's mysterious to her, so she usually keeps her mouth shut. When she hears people talking about their parents, their families, and their childhoods in warm and nostalgic tones, she feels as if she's living in a parallel universe. The best thing she can say about her childhood and her own mother is that she survived both. Barely, but the past is the past. When, during one of several attempts to reconnect with her mother, Katherine asked her what had made her think it was a good idea to lace her babies' formula with tranquilizers and sleeping pills (admittedly a loaded question), her mother turned self-righteous: *Those pills were expensive and they weren't easy to get. And don't think I didn't want to take them myself. But I didn't. I gave them to my kids.* She puffed up with obvious pride at the mere thought. *So you can accuse me of being selfish all you want, Kathy, but it isn't going to stick. You try telling me there's something wrong with a mother making sure her kids get a good night's sleep.*

How do you argue with that? And yes, in a crazy way, her mother really *had* thought she was being a good parent by hitting the streets of Detroit to score pills for her infants instead of herself. That's the model she has for motherhood. Not promising, and not a cycle that anyone in her right mind would want to keep going.

They pull over to the address Imani gave her and sure enough, there's a teenage girl sitting on a bench gently rocking a stroller, with her nose buried in a thick book. Katherine was somehow expecting a younger version of Imani, but even from a distance, she can see that Renay is tall and thin, and with the way she's bent over the book, at least a little humiliated and repentant. *Don't worry*, Katherine feels like telling her. *I'm in no position to judge you.*

Katherine does a fairly decent job of parking, and she and Conor walk down the street. He takes her hand, something he does so often that Katherine has almost forgotten how sweet it is. 'Renay,' she calls out. 'I'm Katherine, your aunt Imani's friend. She told you we were coming, right?'

Renay finishes reading a page, sticks a marker into her book, and puts it on a rack under the stroller.

Conor squats down and peers at Daniel. 'How's the little guy doing?'

'He's hungry,' Renay says. 'But he's okay.'

Katherine watches as Conor lifts the baby out of the stroller with practiced ease. He has three sisters, all of whom have babies, although Katherine has lost track of the exact number of nieces and nephews. Daniel's an adorable little thing with a big head and a comically disgruntled expression, like an old man with a gripe against the world. He looks up at Conor and blinks, and Katherine is amused at his expression, which seems to be saying: 'Get me the fuck out of here!'. He's making some garbled attempt at communication, a futile pursuit at this stage, which just makes it that much more poignant. How can people bear the vulnerability of their babies? Katherine would be constantly on the verge of tears.

'I told Imani we'd take you and Daniel up to Lee's yoga studio and wait for her there. You've been there, remember?'

Renay gets up off the bench without answering and starts to collapse the stroller. 'You don't have a baby seat,' she says.

'We got Imani's okay,' Conor says. 'It's only a few blocks. Let me help you with that.'

He passes Daniel to Katherine. He's heavier than Katherine would have guessed from looking at him, and a good deal less scary to hold than she feared. There's something heartbreaking in the way he just trusts that Katherine, a complete stranger, is going to take care of him. She rests his head against her shoulder and starts patting his back. When he turns his face a little and nuzzles against her neck, Katherine feels something inside her melt.

'Don't get any ideas about me driving,' she tells Conor. 'I'm not taking that on.'

'You get a pass this time,' he says. 'But thank Daniel, not me.'

As they're heading up to Edendale, Renay says, to no one in particular, 'Do you think my aunt Harriet is going to send me back home?'

Katherine looks at Conor. There's a tone in Renay's voice that's hard to read, a cross between anger and anxiety. But she's so mopey and furtive, it's a relief to hear her say *something*.

'Why would you think that?' Katherine asks.

She turns to look at Renay and catches her rolling her eyes. 'Because I walked out of the house and got lost with her baby?'

Katherine leans against Conor and the two of them burst out laughing. 'You've got a good point, Renay,' he says. 'Very good point.'

'I bet she'll understand,' Katherine says. 'Once she cools down.'

'I don't think she likes me much to begin with. She and my mom don't get along.' She adjusts Daniel so that he's tighter against her chest and then, without looking at Katherine, she says, 'I like your dress.'

'Miss Brodski makes her own clothes,' Conor says proudly. 'Pretty talented lady.'

'Don't believe him,' Katherine says. 'I mostly take old clothes and fix them up a little.'

Renay has on jeans and a little gray blouse that doesn't fit her right and isn't the best color for her skin tone. It screams H&M, but with a few adjustments it could be a lot more flattering. She'd love to trim up the sleeves so they show off more of Renay's slim arms. If she lopped off the collar altogether, it might be a cute look. Renay has one of those long, lean bodies that can wear pretty much anything, and it seems a shame she's going with this. She's got nice cheekbones and a really long neck, but her hair is straightened in a dry, stringy way. With a super short haircut and the right neckline, she could be a knockout.

'What are you reading?' Katherine asks.

'*Great Expectations*. My English teacher gave it to me before I left for L.A. I don't want to get too far behind.'

'That's Dickens, right?' Conor asks. 'The one with the old lady with the wedding dress?'

'Right. Miss Havisham. Did you read it?'

'I'm sure I was supposed to. I probably read the outline or the illustrated comic book version.'

Since high school was all a bit of a blur and she's never been much of a reader, Katherine keeps her mouth shut. Part of her wishes she had been the type of high school student who'd read Dickens on her own, who'd been a little more interested in what she could learn about life from books and a little less interested in what she could learn on the streets. She's come to the conclusion that firsthand experience is vastly overrated. Usually, it's an excuse for a lot of regrettable behavior.

'Do you sew?' Katherine asks.

Renay shrugs. 'I guess. A little.'

'You should come visit me sometime. I can teach you a few simple tricks that would make that blouse even prettier than it is.'

'My mother tried to teach me, but we ended up fighting.'

Katherine is willing to bet that this sums up Renay's relationship with her mother very neatly.

'Katherine's a patient teacher,' Conor says. 'She puts up with me, after all.'

Katherine watches as Renay checks out her dress again and then scans the tattoos on her upper arms. 'I know I don't look like the sewing type,' she says. 'But it's really fun to learn, especially if your mother isn't teaching you.'

*

116

After Imani has nursed Daniel and changed him at the changing station in the studio bathroom, she starts to feel a little calmer. He's fine, safe in her arms, and that's what matters. She looks at herself in the bathroom mirror. Okay, so she's had better days. She's had better months, too. Her eyes are puffy from crying and her skin looks dull. Even if she gets a good night's sleep (doubtful), the makeup girl on the set is going to have her work cut out for her tomorrow. She takes a weird kind of pleasure in thinking about how miserable Rusty-fucking-Branson is going to be when he sees her. Maybe she should grab some ice cream on the way home, get nice and bloated, and really piss him off.

Or . . . maybe not.

She goes back out into the studio and joins the others in the lounge. So far, she hasn't been able to look at Renay, but being here, she feels more generous and inspired, as she always did when she entered the studio during her pregnancy, as if there's something in the atmosphere of easy friendship here that brings out the best in her. Lee is having a cup of coffee, nervously pacing back and forth. No doubt she hasn't had the best year of her life, and she always does her best to keep it under wraps, which might be the better part of getting past it. There was some drama going on with the kids when she arrived, but Chloe took them out for dinner so Lee could get ready to teach her 7:30 class.

'Feeling better?' Lee asks.

Imani puts Daniel down on the soft cushion of the sofa and he sighs, looks up at her with that scrunched-up face of his, reaches out his hands, and starts laughing.

You're just the loveliest person I know, she thinks. *I hope you stay this nice for a long while.* She can't resist picking him up again and squeezing him. She has moments with him when all the people around her fade into the background and it's just the two of them. It sometimes happens with Glenn, although she tries hard to never let it show.

'He's blissed out,' Imani says, watching him. 'It's so easy to make him happy. A meal and a clean diaper.'

'And how's his mother?' Lee asks.

'Not the best afternoon.'

She could tell, as soon as she showed up, that everyone was feeling protective of Renay, as if Imani was going to come in and bite her head off. She would have felt the same way if she was in their position, but she still can't shake this spark of anger every time she glances in Renay's direction, or, well, the desire to bite her head off. It's lucky they're all together, because now she can get out what she has to tell Renay on neutral territory.

'I called Glenn as I was driving over,' she says. For the first time, she looks Renay in the eyes. 'We agreed that we're going to make things easier for everyone and get a nanny who worked for one of his patients.'

Renay nods. 'It was a mistake. I'm really sorry.'

'I know, honey. And I know it wasn't a great afternoon for you, either.'

Renay shrugs and says, 'Did you tell my mother?'

'I haven't called her yet.' It hadn't occurred to her to call Gloria; the last thing Imani needed was more hysteria. She doesn't want to give Gloria another reason to start picking at Renay, so she'll have to give some explanation for shipping her daughter back ahead of schedule. 'We can figure out what we're going to tell her later on. You can stay for a while longer, if you want. You'll have more free time.'

'To do what?' Renay asks.

Imani hadn't thought of that. It's not as if Renay is the type to hang out at the pool, and she certainly hasn't had much opportunity to make friends. In the time she's been in Los Angeles, she's been so quiet and Imani has been so distracted, she hasn't gained much insight into her niece's interests.

Katherine, who's been sitting in one of the puffy chairs beside Renay, reaches out and takes hold of Renay's arm. 'You've got those sewing lessons we talked about, don't forget.'

From the look on Renay's face, she's as baffled as Imani. It's the first time she's felt as if she and Renay are on the same page.

'Renay's going to come to my place a few afternoons a week for sewing lessons. Isn't that what we agreed to?'

'I did?'

'More or less,' Katherine says. 'I'm going to get some thrift-shop specials, and we're going to spruce them up a little.'

Imani thinks this over and rubs Daniel's stomach. He kicks his legs up. 'He's doing happy baby,' she says.

When she originally agreed to have Renay come to take care of Daniel, Imani had it in her head that she might like to play a role in Renay's life somewhere between mentor and madcap Auntie Mame, and even if that clearly isn't going to happen, she hates the idea of sending her back without having made any impact on her, without having shown her something different from what she could have learned in Texas. It would be nice to think that suddenly, after this afternoon, all of that is going to turn around, but what's the use of pretending? Katherine, with her wild past and her unlikely boyfriend, is a more logical candidate to play the role of inspiringly wacky aunt. Imani saw the dress Katherine made for Lee last year, some gorgeous silver thing she copied from a magazine.

She turns to Katherine and says, 'If you tell me what to get, I'll go online and order a sewing machine for her. Something we can ship back to Texas with her when she goes.'

A few minutes later, Lee starts to pull herself together and downs her coffee in a single gulp. 'Class in twenty minutes,' she says. 'I should go get ready.'

From Imani's perch on the sofa, Lee looks thin and a little exhausted. It's the first time Imani has ever seen her look this wired and stressed out, and she suddenly feels as if she's a self-absorbed oaf for having dragged her own problems into the studio once again. Yoga teachers – maybe all teachers – get stuck in the role of caretaker too often. Lee needs a little care of her own. 'You're always ready,' Imani says, because who doesn't feel better after a compliment or two? 'One of the many amazing things about you, Lee.'

'I'm not always ready,' Lee says. 'I'm especially not ready today.' Her voice is cracking in a way Imani has never heard before, almost as if she's angry at Imani for having praised her. 'I had a rough afternoon.'

Katherine's up off her chair in a flash and puts her arms around Lee. 'I thought something was up. What happened?'

'It's nothing,' Lee says. 'I'm just tired. Really, it's nothing.'

But as soon as she says it, she starts crying, hanging on to Katherine a little tighter. 'I'm tired and I've had too much coffee and the kids have been lying to me and you just can't believe who Alan is dating. Not that it matters at all.'

'Get someone to sub for you,' Katherine says. 'If you call someone right now –'

'It's too late. Anyway, I'll be fine. I mean, I look horrible, but I'll be fine. I just hope I don't slip up and start ranting about divorce in the middle of class.'

Imani looks over as the door of the studio opens and a wiry guy with light hair and little round glasses walks in. He checks out the scene in the lounge skeptically, obviously sensing that he's entered what is at the moment a women's kingdom.

'Am I . . . too early for class?'

At the sound of his voice, Lee spins around. 'David,' she says. She reaches for a box of Kleenex on the table in front of the sofa. 'No, not at all. *Perfect* timing. Let me introduce you to my friends.'

Lee is definitely full of surprises today.

PART TWO

About two hours after Stephanie and Roberta take off from LAX, their flight runs into turbulence. Nothing drastic, but bumpy enough to necessitate an announcement from the pilot about seat belts and tray tables and getting permission to find a more comfortable altitude. Roberta, who flew down from San Francisco to meet up with Stephanie's flight to New York, sighs deeply and laces her fingers through Stephanie's.

'What a drag if we crashed the one time I actually got to fly first class,' she says.

Stephanie tightens her grasp on Roberta's hand and says, 'I hate to disappoint you, but I don't think we're going out in style. Not today, anyway.'

'You promise?'

'It's clear-air turbulence, number one. Number two, these planes are built to take about five hundred times this amount of jostling.'

'I'm glad your father was a pilot.'

'Think of it as driving over a dirt road,' Stephanie says. 'A little bumpy, that's all.'

'I hate driving on dirt roads.' Roberta leans her head against Stephanie's shoulder. 'I'd try to sleep, but what a waste of all this luxury.'

'If I know Sybille, there's plenty more coming in New

York. She sent me an e-mail last night and said she knew we'd like our rooms.'

One of the things Stephanie loves about Roberta is that she's a bundle of contradictions. She's incredibly strong, capable, and in control – a plumber, for god's sake, and expert enough with electronics to have rewired Stephanie's living room when she noticed the age of some of the outlets. She has an out-of-my-way-I'll-handle-this reaction to most situations that somehow or other doesn't come off as bullying. And yet, she's prey to these irrational fears and is not afraid to talk about them. She hates to fly, she's terrified of driving on the 101, and the one time they watched the Discovery Channel together, she turned into a squeamish little girl at the sight of a snake. Each time she leaves Stephanie's apartment, she refuses to open the door for herself because of a superstition that it means she won't return.

All of this has made Stephanie feel completely at ease revealing her own fears, in ways she has never done before. In her relationships with men, she tried hard to never appear vulnerable, for fear she'd be perceived as weak and easy to intimidate. Looking back, she has to acknowledge, it was pretty exhausting.

In her relationship with Roberta, she doesn't feel any of that competition, just an openness that's entirely new to her. And yes, after six months of seeing each other, there's no denying that this actually *is* a relationship.

'What did you mean,' Roberta says a few minutes later, her voice a little groggy, 'when you said "our rooms"? Don't tell me Sybille booked us a suite.'

'No, I doubt it.' Stephanie figures she might as well get

this over with now so Roberta will have a few hours to cool down. 'She said she was going to book two rooms, and I thought, well, why not? You know what I mean?'

'Yeah, babe, I do. You didn't want to tell her we wouldn't need two rooms, or two beds, for that matter. You just didn't want to *go there*.'

Roberta untangles her fingers from Stephanie's, pushes back her wide leather seat, and turns her face toward the window.

Stephanie and Roberta have had a few arguments about Stephanie being 'closeted' about their relationship. From Stephanie's point of view, she's not lying about it to anyone, or hiding it. She just isn't discussing it. It's no one's business what she's doing or whom she's seeing. She's always been private about her personal life. If there's one thing she's learned in the movie business, it's that putting your personal life out there – whatever your personal life is – makes you vulnerable in surprising ways. The more people know about you, the more information they have to use against you. Your sexuality, your medical history, whom you're dating, your kid's learning disabilities, your background with alcohol or pills. If you're important, it matters less. At her level, anything can and will be used against you so that some hungry person can make a grab for your crumbs.

Besides which, it's all a little new and confusing to her. It never crossed her mind that she might find herself in a relationship with a woman. *Never once?* Roberta asked when she explained this. Well, maybe it had crossed her mind, but always in the form of hazy feelings and blurry images she didn't process or try to bring into focus. She was too busy concentrating on work. *Or drunk*, she didn't need to add, although that bit of regret always hung in the air. Come to think of it, maybe that's why she was drunk – to help keep all those feelings out of focus.

Roberta turns back to her and props herself up on her elbow. 'There are about ten thousand things I'd like to change about myself, but the way I feel about you isn't one of them. And let's face it, one look at me, and most people hear a medley of Melissa Etheridge's greatest hits playing in their heads. So if you want a little help figuring out how to tell Sybille that I'm not your personal assistant or cousin from up north, just ask me. Happy to be of service.'

A few minutes later, she can see Roberta's rib cage rising and falling, a sign that she's sound asleep. Probably just as well, since the turbulence has suddenly gotten heavier. As an air force brat, Stephanie grew up traveling. Her dad brought her up to think of flying as the most natural and safe means of transportation there is. On commercial flights, he'd put her in his lap and point out the strange, silent beauty of the clouds and the landscape down below and the cold, endless blue above. Whenever she's on a plane, she feels lighter and happier as soon as the wheels lift off the runway, although it's true that she always misses her father when she's flying. Not that she doesn't miss him all the time. She looks past Roberta, out to the slanting sun and the distant clouds. It's hard to know what her father would have thought of Roberta, or more to the point, what he would have thought of Stephanie's involvement with her. Even if he disapproved, it's certain he would have encouraged her to go for whatever made her happy.

She signals to the flight attendant as he's walking past.

'Do you think you could get a pillow and a blanket for . . . my girlfriend?'

He glances down at Roberta and winks at Stephanie. 'Of course.'

Since she's about ninety percent certain the flight attendant is gay, it isn't exactly a big deal saying it, but it feels a little daring.

As he's reaching into the overhead compartment, Roberta turns back toward her. 'I heard that,' she says.

'I thought you were asleep.'

'I was just pissed off and faking it. I liked the way that sounded. I could get used to hearing it. We just need to figure out if you could get used to saying it.'

A few minutes later, when they've flown through the turbulence and Roberta really has gone to sleep, Stephanie gets out of her seat and strolls down the aisle of the plane. Coach passengers can't come up front, but no one says anything when she walks toward the rear of the plane. After only a few hours in first class, the back of the plane looks, sounds, and even smells like a cattle car to her. She feels sorry for the poor slobs in steerage, but not sorry enough to give up her wide seat. Better not get used to this – or any – kind of luxury, because Sybille isn't going to be footing the bill for much longer. Still, she can't believe she never noticed before how packed in everyone is, how cluttered with newspapers and – since coach doesn't serve food anymore – the wrappers from takeout sandwiches and chips. And then there are the babies.

Two rows from the rear bathrooms, she spots a man in the middle seat of a row with a pair of headphones on

and his arms wrapped tightly around his chest. He's rocking back and forth, probably to the sound of the music. It
makes him look a little crazy. Not the type of person you
love seeing on your flight. She'll bet they did a 'random'
extra search of his luggage and shoes.

Stephanie studies his face for a minute and realizes he
looks familiar. He has his eyes closed, but even so, she's
pretty sure it's Graciela's boyfriend, a nervous, insecure
guy she met once briefly at a party Lee gave for Graciela
after she got the spot on Beyoncé's tour. She got cornered
with him and tried to make conversation, but that didn't
go anywhere. A deejay, as she recalls. Kind of sweet but
with a lot of anger about his career and other unspecified
things boiling underneath. Graciela must have sent him
the cash for the flight east. Clearly, she and Imani were
wrong about Graciela's reasons for staying in New York.
She's tempted to introduce herself – these unexpected
encounters are the best way to kill a few minutes on a
flight – but something in his body language and the rocking makes her rethink it. She has her own problems to
focus on, and really, she'd rather not spend more time
back in this end of the plane. Roberta's up front, not to
mention the lunch the flight attendants are getting ready
to serve in first class.

As soon as they enter the yoga studio and Jacob spots the
loops of silken red material hanging from the ceiling, he
grabs Graciela's arm and says, 'What the hell was I thinking of, letting you talk me into this?'

'You like new experiences,' she says.

'I'm OCD about routine. I hate new experiences,' he replies. 'I like you; that's why I wasn't thinking when I agreed.'

'Maybe you'll like the class, too.'

'Just stay close by,' he says.

Does he really think she's going to wander off?

Graciela feels the warmth of Jacob's body against hers and leans back into him. Since he rescued her from that street corner on Broadway (because in retrospect, it does feel like a rescue) they haven't spent more than a few hours apart. He's had training and one game, but otherwise, a spell of rain and atypical scheduling has made it possible for them to be together. If he hadn't agreed to come along to this class, she probably would have canceled her own plans to attend, despite her eagerness to take it. Before she started doing yoga last year, she couldn't have imagined that she'd get excited when she heard about a new class with something original and unusual about it. But now, she starts to feel an itchy eagerness to sample all the new varieties of yoga, the way some people crave dinner at a hot new restaurant.

There's the class itself, and then this side attraction of doing something with Jacob Lander in public. She's not sure why that's such a wonderful thrill, unless it's because he's so careful about going out in public for fear of the paparazzi – both for his own sake, and maybe because of some urge to protect her from ending up with her face under snarky headlines on TMZ or one of the other million and one gossip websites.

'How do we do this?' he asks softly into her ear. 'Do we climb into the material or lie on the floor?'

'I'm no expert,' she says.

The workshop they're taking is Aerial Swing, taught by a teacher visiting from Montreal. Graciela has never heard of her before, but apparently Nicole LaPierre was part of Cirque du Soleil for several years, before an injury got her into yoga. Dana, one of the teachers and a studio manager here, told Graciela that she never feels so free as she does in this kind of class. *It's like leaving all of your worries on the ground while you float in space.* Maybe that was hyperbole, but Dana, a gorgeous strawberry blonde, has one of those mind-boggling practices that combine elastic flexibility and crazy strength. Graciela had to take her word. The idea of rising above all of her worries was so appealing, she talked Jacob into coming with her. Those worries have started to increase daily, rising pretty much in sync with how much she's loving being with Jacob.

There are big loops of what looks like blood-red silk hanging from clamps in the ceiling, giving the studio an exotic atmosphere. A little erotic, a little scary. Like Cirque du Soleil, come to think of it. One woman, who's obviously done this before, is hanging upside down in the sling with her knees splayed out, frog-like, spinning in very slow, lazy circles. She does look free. Uncomfortable, but free.

'I think we should start out on the floor,' Graciela says.

They grab two mats and set them next to each other, much closer than they probably should be. But Graciela can't stand the thought of having Jacob in the same room without being able to reach out and touch him. Maybe he can't stand it, either, because as soon as they're stretched out on their mats, he drapes a leg over her thigh.

'So tell me,' he says, 'do you and your boyfriend do yoga together?'

The question makes something inside her freeze.

Graciela has done her best to avoid any mention of Daryl, and Jacob certainly hasn't brought him up. She's not interested in discussing Daryl, and she's even less interested in asking Jacob if he has a girlfriend somewhere. It doesn't seem possible that he wouldn't, but she hasn't been aware of any phone calls or messages from a likely lover.

With a hot mixture of guilt and anxiety, Graciela says, 'No, we don't,' in what she hopes is a neutral tone of voice.

Jacob is still looking at her, not saying anything, his foot against her leg making very subtle movements that are starting to make her whole body flush. They never did have that lunch he'd been so enthusiastic about preparing for her. They barely made it into Jacob's apartment before they were undressing each other, not because they wanted to see each other's bodies, but because they needed to be skin-to-skin close. Maybe because he's so strong, and is such a competitor by profession, she was expecting a fast, aggressive lover. In fact, he's incredibly sensual and tender, and the way he touches her, pressing all of his weight against her one minute and teasing her with just the warmth of his body the next, makes her feel as if he knows her body at least as well as she does. 'I could do this forever,' he says when they're having sex. And really, it feels as if they have been doing it forever, as if they've always known each other.

Daryl is a different kind of lover, a greedy possessor

of her body who seems to be trying to consume her so he can make sure no one else gets her. Sometimes she feels as if she's being devoured, as if he's making sure that she's exhausted and spent so she can't even *think* about another man. She always loved feeling that wanted by someone, despite the desperation underneath. It made her feel powerful. But that was before Daryl's jealousy and anger and violent outbursts started flaring up so frequently.

'He doesn't do yoga,' she goes on, careful not to mention Daryl's name, not even to refer to him as 'my boyfriend.' 'He plays a lot of basketball with his friends.'

'So you live together?'

'He moved into my place a while back.'

For some reason, it's important to her that he knows it's *her* place. She doesn't want him thinking that the two of them went out apartment hunting together, although why that should matter isn't really clear to her.

Tomorrow (*tomorrow!*) Jacob is flying off to Saint Louis for a game, and she's heading back to L.A. the day after that. In other words, it's almost over. Why not talk about Daryl? This is *just a fling*, she reminds herself. As if she's ever been good at having a fling. As if, really, she even knows what a fling is.

'Your boyfriend's a lucky guy,' Jacob says.

'I'm not so sure about that,' she replies.

'I am so sure,' he says. He runs his hand through her hair. 'You have no idea how beautiful you are.'

She actually blushes, glancing over at a lithe woman on a nearby mat, not sure if she's worried she might be overhearing this or hoping she does. She wants to crawl on top of Jacob, not in a lustful way, exactly, but because she wants to feel their bodies pressed together.

'You're probably more confident after touring for a while, but deep inside, you're still listening to some old doubts you had drilled into your head by a sibling or a jealous friend in junior high or your mother.'

'You're wasting your time in baseball,' she says. 'You should go into mind reading.'

'There's more money in pro sports.'

The teacher and her assistant come into the studio and settle down on mats at the front of class. Nicole LaPierre is a lithe woman with long legs and no chin to speak of, one of those women who aren't exactly pretty but somehow manage to be incredibly sexy with a combination of feline seductiveness and bold self-confidence. She scans the room, and Graciela sees her register Jacob's presence. She pauses for half a second in her introductory comments, and her eyes widen in surprise – clearly, she's impressed. This little flirting makes Graciela feel proud to be with him, and at the same time, so insecure about her own position that she wants to flee the studio.

The magic of doing yoga (or whatever this is) soon takes over, as it always seems to. The teacher talks a little about her performing life (how could Graciela not have noticed before how sexy a Quebecois accent is?) and then starts slithering her long, sinewy body around the silky red material with effortless grace. She has a way of describing these strange movements so clearly that even going upside down and getting tangled up in the stretchy material seems possible and natural. Being upside down and suspended in the air allows Graciela to go into such incredibly deep backbends, she feels as if she's in a different body.

'If you start to twirl and feel like tro-ing up, just focus your drishdi on a spot on your body that's not moving,' Nicole says.

She looks over at Jacob to see how he's faring and watches him hoist himself up the red material, his amazing biceps bulging. He looks so handsome doing this – part gymnast, part weight lifter, and part muscular animal – she can't help but wonder if he isn't simply trying to make himself even more attractive to the teacher and the other women in the class who can't take their eyes off him. It doesn't look even close to what the teacher is describing.

'When you let go of gravity,' Nicole says, 'you'll be amazed at how many new and extraordinary things your body can do. Things you never believed possible. So just trust the slings will hold you and let go. *Let go!* Feel how wonderful it is to fly. And once you see what you can do here when you let go, you start to see the possibility everywhere in your life.'

This is a pretty good description of her whole journey with yoga. Taking small steps and expanding her reach and her flexibility, little by little, has made many things seem possible.

What would happen if she did *let go* of her life in L.A.? Of Daryl? What kinds of new possibilities might open up for her? Maybe she doesn't have to project into the future too far, to all the pain and the problems letting go would create. Maybe all she has to do is imagine taking the first step: asking Daryl to leave. Or telling him she wants to live alone. Maybe she only has to visualize that much of the change.

At the very end of the class, Nicole has them lie full length in the red material. It has so much give, they're practically wrapped in it, head to toe, as if they're in scarlet cocoons. This must be the moment gorgeous Dana described, because Graciela suddenly feels so free of whatever it is she usually worries about down on the ground below, she's caught in a confusing desire to either laugh or cry. She opens her eyes just enough to see out the narrow opening at her feet. Jacob's big, heavy body is swaying in its cocoon close enough so that she can almost feel the warmth radiating off him, but far enough so that they can't bump into each other.

In the locker room after class, a woman changing beside her says, 'Jacob Lander, huh? How'd that happen?' But she says it with a hostile tone, as if she's asking Graciela how someone like *her* got the eye of someone like *him*.

Graciela shrugs. 'He likes my hair.'

As she's walking down Broadway with Jacob, she dares to rest her head on his shoulder. 'Thank you for coming,' she says. 'I loved that.'

'It had its moments,' he says.

He's walking her back to the hotel and then disappearing to get some things together before he leaves. They'll meet later for dinner.

She promises she'll call in an hour, and on the sidewalk outside her hotel, she reaches up and takes his head in her hands and kisses him on the mouth. It's the most aggressive she's ever been with him in public, and a part of her hopes Lyle, her desk clerk friend, sees it.

The clerk behind the desk isn't Lyle but the glum young woman with the faint mustache who always looks at her as if she's planning to steal towels. 'Someone's waiting for you,' she says to Graciela, pointing to the alcove near the elevators. 'And he's been here for a while.'

Tina knocks on Lee's office door and pokes her head in.

'Do you have a second to talk?' she says. 'A couple of people are here with some products, and I'd like your opinion.'

Lee has been sitting at her desk for the past ten minutes trying to work up the nerve to call David Todd. She hasn't heard from him since he arrived at the studio at the worst possible moment and then slipped out the back exit as soon as the class was over. She's punched in his number twice but hasn't put the call through. Did he hate her class? Probably she wasn't at her best, although having him there certainly lifted her spirits. A distraction in the form of vendors might be just what she needs.

'Why not?' she says. 'Do you want to bring them in?'

Tina shrugs. She's been running the retail counter in the studio for more than a year now, but she still isn't completely confident making her own decisions, mostly because she's afraid every product is going to offend someone. Once the new space opens up, she's going to have more responsibilities, and Lee's hoping she'll rise to the occasion. So far, Lee hasn't been able to give her more confidence or cure her self-effacing slouch.

'Might be better to come out,' Tina says. 'They've got some stuff unpacked.'

Lee leaves her phone on her desk and goes out front. As soon as she sees the couple standing in front of Tina's counter, she has a pretty good idea of what's coming. A young man and woman, both the same height, both thin, and both with long dirty-blond hair in dreadlocks. They have on tie-dyed T-shirts and baggy, unstructured pants clearly made of a blend of organic hemp and cotton. They look at Lee and smile broadly, beaming at her with bright eyes that are so intense, they look vaguely alien.

Raw foodists, Lee thinks.

There are so many diet crazes in the yoga world, she can't even keep track of them. Every month or so a new seed or fermented tea or exotic algae emerges as the cure-all *du jour*. She gets endless e-mails and catalogs and sales calls for these substances, each of which seems to have roots in an ancient and now-lost culture that, conveniently, isn't around to defend itself.

Raw foods are high on everyone's list at the moment. It's a subject that confuses Lee. The majority of what she eats – salads and fruit and juices and smoothies – is raw. She spends more time cleaning out the vegetable juicer than she does turning on the oven. But every time she goes to a raw restaurant and reads the menu – raw 'scones'? raw 'pasta'? – she's reminded of those Seventh-Day Adventist vegetarian restaurants in which everything that's supposedly healthy is disguised to look like something that's unhealthy: meat loaf, shepherd's pie, American chop suey. On the whole, she's a little suspicious of restaurants in which every item on the menu is in quotes. And of extremism in general.

A couple of times a month, someone comes into the

studio with a raw food product – cookies or chocolate or a nut mix – that they believe is perfect for the studio's clientele. Many of the salespeople are couples who have a relationship that's so close, they dress and talk alike. Although she's noticed a tendency among a lot of the men to do most of the talking.

Llandra and Lucas started their company two years ago.

'Great,' Lee says. 'What's it called?'

Lucas looks at her with a penetrating stare. 'Raw or Die,' he says.

'That makes the point,' Lee replies.

'It's a choice,' Lucas says. 'Why pretend it isn't?'

Their product line is a collection of raw crackers and breads made out of sprouted seeds and different combinations of dehydrated vegetables and fruit. All have names that hit the mortuary theme hard: Raw Bread or Dead; Coconut Yummies or Cancer; Flax Delights or Irritable Bowel Syndrome. The names are so off-putting, Lee is hesitant to try them, but Lucas holds out the bags in a challenging way, as if he's daring her to turn down the offer.

Although she can't really tell the difference between the Sesame Date Drops or Diabetes and the Coconut Cancer things, they're both surprisingly good.

'They're great,' she says. And then, to try and get a word out of Llandra, she asks her directly if they come up with the recipes themselves.

'We do,' Lucas says. 'Together.'

The more Lee chews, the more she notices a bitter aftertaste, as if something isn't quite right. 'How much are they?'

'Fifteen ninety-five per bag,' Lucas says. 'Except the Kale Chips or Chlamydia. Those are fifteen fifty.'

Lee looks at Tina. Did she really need to get Lee in on this decision? 'To be honest,' Lee says, 'the price might be a little steep for our yogis. Most of them are on a tight budget.'

Lucas snatches the bag out of her hand. 'It all depends on how much they value their lives. They can come up with the money for a yoga class, right? And they could do that at home.'

'Why don't you leave a card with Tina, and we'll talk it over and get in touch?'

'I don't think so,' Lucas says. 'If you have to talk over the choice between life and death, I can't help you out. I guess your yogis like eating dead food so they can save a few pennies. But the thing is, we're not into proselytizing. If you want to encourage your students to commit suicide, that's your choice.'

Once Lucas is outside the studio, Llandra turns in the doorway and says, 'I saw you're teaching at the Flow and Glow Festival. I'm trying to save up the money to go.'

'With Lucas?' Lee asks.

'No, he's not interested.'

Lee reaches into the cash register and hands Llandra a twenty dollar bill. 'I hope you get the money. If I find out anything about sliding registration fees, I'll e-mail you. Do you have a website?'

'Yeah, but Lucas reads the e-mail. I also waitress at the Denny's on South Figueroa. You can reach me there.'

Once the door has shut, Tina says, 'Sorry. I was afraid to try the sample, so I thought I'd ask you. I didn't know if it meant you get cured from cancer or if it gives you cancer.'

'The thing is, Tina, once we open the new studio space, you're going to have a lot more people coming in with products. You really can use your own judgment on most of it. Or ask Lainey. I hate to think what she'd have to say about Raw or Dead.'

'Raw or Die,' Tina corrects. 'Anyway, I think Lainey is more into smoking than cooking, if you know what I mean.'

'But not in the studio, right?'

'Oh, no. She blows the smoke out the back door.'

'I'll talk to her,' Lee says.

Back in her office, she picks up her phone and looks at the blank screen. 'David Todd or die,' she says, and makes the call.

After all that buildup, she gets his voice mail. 'David,' she says, making sure she sounds as cheerful as possible. 'You snuck out after class the other day. I wanted to apologize. I'd had a tough afternoon with my kids and wasn't at my peak. Now you know why we need you here.' *You're going on too long*, she scolds herself. *Wrap it up*. 'Give me a call when you can so I can ramble on some more. It was great seeing you. You'll have to show me that transition you do into titibasana from handstand. I've never seen it done that way. I usually . . .' *Not now. Wrap it up!* 'Bye.'

Stupid, she thinks. *I sounded like an idiot*. What's more pointless or unattractive than all that apologizing? And all that babbling. But she really wants to talk about this particular transition with him. Among other things. She has much to learn from him. So much she wants to discuss.

She jumps when, a few seconds later, her phone rings. That was quick. Except it isn't David Todd.

'Lee,' Graham says, 'we have to make that decision about the flooring this week.'

'But I made the decision, Graham. You just refuse to accept it.'

'It's true,' he says. 'I don't accept defeat easily. Give me one more chance. I'll take you out to dinner and show you the samples. If it's still no, we'll go with the hardwood. No more coaxing. Deal? Do you have the kids tonight?'

'Alan has them.'

'Perfect. I'll pick you up at eight at the studio. Any special requests for restaurants?'

'Anything cooked would be appreciated,' Lee says.

When Sybille Brent's husband of thirty-five years divorced her for a twenty-six-year-old replacement, she ended up with thirty-two million dollars, the 'cottage' in East Hampton, and the apartment on Beekman Place. Stephanie never dared ask Sybille about any of this, and Sybille offered only bits and pieces of her story, without, naturally, mentioning numbers. The specifics came from tabloid stories and one lengthy *New York* magazine article Stephanie read on the subject of the divorce. Among the perils of having been married to a famous real estate developer is, apparently, a ton of unwanted publicity. Among the benefits . . . well, it's hard to think of the money and the real estate as a drawback, no matter how public her husband's infidelities became.

Stephanie told Roberta she thought it would be best if

she went to Sybille's place alone. Sybille had made it clear that she had something she wanted to tell Stephanie, and although she gave no inkling of what it was, it seemed clear to Stephanie that it was serious in nature. Why else fly her to New York? She doesn't know exactly how much of her own money Sybille has put into the film, but she assumes that she wants to tell her she's scaling back on her investment. Maybe she expects some serious belt tightening all around.

Stephanie decides to walk to Beekman Place from their hotel. As for the hotel itself, it's a bit of a disappointment. Apparently, the Regency is known as the site of power breakfasts and deal-making martinis, but the rooms are surprisingly ordinary. Make that the room. As they were checking in, and Roberta was leaning on the front desk, looking at her in a challenging way, Stephanie nervously said to the clerk, 'We'll only need one room. As it turns out.'

'You're doing better,' Roberta said as she kissed her in the elevator. And then, when they opened the door to their room: 'Huh. Maybe we spoke too soon. The other room might have been better.'

It's a warm, windy day, and Stephanie crosses east and in no time at all finds herself in the sheltered enclave of Beekman Place. Everyone's lived here, apparently, from movie stars to politicians. It's quiet and shady, and feels oddly cut off from the rest of the city, despite being a block or two from the mayhem of First Avenue and the UN.

The elevator opens onto Sybille's twelfth-floor apartment, and Stephanie's met by a smartly dressed young woman who introduces herself only as Marie. Sybille is always surrounded by people who are undoubtedly staff but who dress and act casual and informal, as if they're merely helpful friends. 'Sybille's just finishing up on a call,' she says. 'Lovely day, isn't it?'

'It's beautiful. I wasn't expecting it to be this warm.'

'It was an early spring. Let's go this way.'

She leads Stephanie down a hallway and into a dark, paneled library lined with books and filled with heavy leather furniture. Stephanie has only seen Sybille in rented houses or chic, modern hotels in L.A., so it's a surprise to see this traditional and stuffy decor. It's clear that every piece of furniture, probably down to the books themselves, was chosen and placed by someone hired to do so. But maybe it isn't surprising at all. It's not as if she imagined Sybille doing her own shopping and furniture arranging. Beautiful as it is, it seems generic, as if any wealthy New Yorker might live here. It makes Stephanie inexplicably sad, the thought of Sybille in this over-decorated apartment, surrounded only by paid staff.

'I think we could use a little light,' Marie says. She pushes back a set of heavy drapes – no easy task – and then opens an enormously long set of wooden venetian blinds. The room is suddenly filled with sunlight. Stephanie recoils a bit from the view, an almost shockingly beautiful vista of the East River, the water glistening and a barge making its way north.

'I know,' Marie says. 'You wouldn't guess this from the street, would you? The living room is even more amazing. Can I get you something to drink?'

Stephanie tries to make herself comfortable and picks

up a magazine. But within a few seconds, she feels anxious and restless. Maybe Sybille has been disappointed in the scenes of the movie she's been shown. She wishes Roberta – solid, pragmatic Roberta – were here. She takes out her phone and sends a text message to her: *Reaction so far: Holy shit! And all I've seen is the library.*

She's chuckling over Roberta's response (*Steal something for me.*) when she hears the doors slide open. She turns and there's Sybille standing in the doorway, smiling.

'Welcome to New York,' she says.

She's wearing a pair of dove gray woolen pants and a cream-colored silk blouse, both unmistakably Sybille. But in the months since Stephanie has seen her, her friend and mentor seems to have lost a tremendous amount of weight. Her face is gaunt, and her usually bright eyes look as if they've sunken into her skull. Stephanie leaps off the sofa and goes to her. She feels like throwing her arms around her, but they've never had that kind of relationship, and melodrama is clearly not what's called for. She follows Sybille's lead and does a series of cheek kisses.

'I'm so happy to see you,' Stephanie says. Despite Sybille's appearance, this is true. It's hard to feel close to someone as buffered by wealth as Sybille, but Stephanie has missed her terribly.

'We'll get to "seeing me" soon enough,' she says. 'How's the hotel?'

'I love it. We're very comfortable.'

'Marie tried to get you into the Plaza Athénée, but there was nothing available. I hope you weren't disappointed. I've never cared much for that hotel myself.'

'The rooms are great. The room. We only need one, so I canceled the other.'

'I assumed that, but you never want to assume anything aloud in life.' She goes to one of the leather chairs and lowers herself into it slowly, but with the graceful elegance that defines all of her movements. 'Are you happy?' she asks. 'With Roberta, I mean.'

'It's not what I would have predicted for myself,' Stephanie says.

'That wasn't my question, dear.'

This, Stephanie realizes, is what she's missed most about Sybille, her way of being blunt without sounding judgmental.

'She's funny and smart in totally unexpected ways. She seems to understand things.'

'She understands *you*, you mean.'

'Yes, I guess that's it.'

It's hard not to mention Sybille's appearance, but Stephanie knows she has to wait until Sybille's ready to tell her. It has to do with their age difference, but more than that, with the money.

Sybille asks her about the movie, and Stephanie fills her in on a few details of the shoot she's pretty sure she hasn't already told her. They have another three weeks to go, and then they'll go into postproduction. She starts recounting an anecdote in the long history of Rusty and Imani, but halfway in, she has the feeling she's already told her this. She stumbles over her words, confused by what she's saying and talking more and more quickly. She glances away from Sybille and out the window and wonders if she's making any sense. She looks back at the woman who's

147

become such an unlikely friend, and before she has any inkling that she's going to cry, she feels the tears running down her cheeks.

Sybille gets up silently, with the same impaired grace as before, and sits beside Stephanie on the sofa. She takes her hand in both of hers. 'It's all right,' she says. 'Go right ahead and cry.'

Stephanie buries her face against Sybille's shoulder. 'You're sick,' she says.

'Yes, dear. I'm sorry to say, I am.'

'What?'

'I had cancer two years ago, right before my husband filed for divorce. Not an uncommon confluence of events, by the way. The sickness was the one thing I did manage to keep out of the papers. Unfortunately, it's come back. Only this time it's spread.'

Stephanie starts to sob, and then feels Sybille's thin arms wrap around her tightly. She wants to ask her what, where, but then feels as if it isn't her business, and on top of that, how much difference does it make? Sybille is sick.

'I started chemo last week. It's not going to be pretty, but I'm in a position to buy myself as much comfort as possible. I wanted to see you before I got into the thick of it. I wanted to thank you.'

'Me? For what?'

'For the movie. For your friendship.'

'It's you. You've done everything. There wouldn't be any movie without you.'

'I've written a few checks. You wrote the script. You have no idea how much fun this past year has been for me.

It seemed like a crazy idea to try and get into the business; at least that's what everyone told me. But when I met you, I knew something would work out. And it has. Because of you.'

'But you're going to be all right,' Stephanie says. She sits up and looks at Sybille. 'You *are* going to be all right?'

Sybille starts to laugh, a slightly weakened version of the throaty sound she usually makes. 'To be honest, I seriously doubt it. I'll do my best, and put up a "fight" and all of that, but in the end, you learn that there's a certain amount of dignity in submitting to the inevitable. I'm big on dignity.'

'Thank you for telling me in person.'

'That's only part of what I wanted to tell you,' Sybille says. She gets up and goes back to her chair, and Stephanie feels as if they're back to discussing business. 'As you know, I got into this as a lark. A little fun, a little revenge, a desire to prove that I was doing more with my life after being left than running off to a plastic surgeon, which seems to be the usual course among my friends. Not that I didn't do that, too. I hoped the movie would lead to something, something I could do into my next couple of decades. Except now there won't be a next couple of decades.'

Stephanie wants to stop her, to scold her for not being more positive, but surely with what Sybille is going through, it's her right to talk about it in any way she wants.

'And so the lovely, impressive screen credit that is mine in the contract really isn't going to do anything for me. Which is too bad, because the movie is going to be good. Better even than we hoped. What I'm hearing is wild praise about the script. We have distributors interested in the movie already, which, I gather, is pretty much unheard of at this stage of the game.'

If this had come from anyone else – Rusty Branson, for example – Stephanie would have doubted much of it. But Sybille is not one to dabble in overstatement. She feels a rush of excitement, mixed with guilt that she, blessed (as far as she knows) with good health, has the luxury of thinking of the long term.

'So you will be getting my producer credit.'

'You can't do that,' Stephanie says. 'I won't let you.'

Sybille laughs at this and brushes back her hair, and for the first time this morning, she seems like her old self. 'I'm flattered, but you know very well you can't stop me. The papers have all been signed. I will still have a prominent screen credit, but you'll have the one that will be useful to you. I just hope you're prepared for what's coming your way. Don't let it mow you down.'

It's much warmer outside when Stephanie leaves the apartment. Too warm. She starts walking west, but it feels as if it's taking forever, and the hotel seems miles away. She reaches out her arm for a cab, but none stops, and after a few minutes, she starts walking again. On Third Avenue, her feet feel so heavy, it's like being in the middle of a nightmare. She walks north a couple of blocks, and then she starts to run. Sybille is going to die. Like her father died, painfully and too young, and then her mother. Sybille's going to die and Stephanie is never going to see her again. She doesn't care about the movie. What difference does it make? What good are the screen credit and the praise? She's losing this strange and wonderful woman who was responsible for changing her life so completely.

She picks up her pace on Park Avenue and starts running north, looking crazy and a little desperate.

There are men in suits in the lobby of the hotel; they look at her with smug grins and then turn away as if they're embarrassed for her. She jogs sweatily to the elevator. She feels her throat closing as she runs down the hallway and starts knocking on the door to their room, and by the time Roberta opens it, she is crying again. Roberta reaches out and pulls her into her arms.

'The movie,' Stephanie says. 'The movie is going to be really, really good.'

'Why are you so distracted?' Daryl asks.

'I'm not,' Graciela says. 'There's just so much to see on every corner.'

'Oh, so you mean you *are* distracted.'

She decides to let it go.

They're walking along Seventy-seventh Street toward the park. It's a hot, windy day, and the sun is uncomfortably bright. Graciela reaches into a bag she has slung over her shoulder and puts on a pair of sunglasses.

'Where'd you get those?' Daryl asks.

'I don't know. A drugstore, I guess.' She bought the glasses in Paris and they cost something ridiculous, like two hundred euros. She's certainly not going to tell that to Daryl and make him feel threatened and left out. She's already checked herself and made sure she hasn't mentioned any of the places she's been or the people she's met. Things are bad enough as it is.

'Must have been a damn nice drugstore.'

She stops in the middle of the block and stares at him. 'Can we please not do this?'

'Do *what*?'

'I feel like you're grilling me every second. Can't we just enjoy the day and go for a walk in the park?'

'I don't know. You tell me.'

It's been like this since she turned the corner in the hotel lobby and spotted Daryl slumped over on the little bench by the elevator. Every time she thinks of that moment, she shudders. The idea of him buying a ticket and getting on a plane seemed so far outside the realm of possibility, she couldn't believe he was really there. What would have happened if Jacob had walked in with her and taken her to the elevators? But there's no point in even thinking about it; Jacob didn't do that.

The funny thing is, there was a part of her that was actually happy to see Daryl. He's lost weight while she's been on the road, and there's something a little feral about his face and eyes now, but he looked sweet on the bench, tired from the flight, like a little boy waiting to be let into the house. How did he even figure out how to get the shuttle from JFK and then get to the hotel? Seeing him there on the bench, she felt the same mixture of affection and pity she always feels for him, and mixed with it, a little bit of relief. This meant it really was over with Jacob. No more questions about it. She was going back to L.A., back to Daryl; the adventure was over. How could she have fantasized about being with Jacob? Did she really think that Jacob Lander would be interested in her as anything more than a girl he had a little romantic fling with for a few days?

She rushed over to Daryl and threw her arms around him. 'What are you doing here?' she asked. 'I can't believe you're in New York!'

But Daryl's response was a harsh 'So where the fuck have you been?'

'Yoga class,' she said, happy to be able to tell him the truth. Or part of the truth.

'Yeah, but I mean for the past *week*, Graciela. You were supposed to be back already.'

'I told you I was staying on a few days,' she said. She pointed to his backpack. 'Is that all you have for luggage?'

'We're not staying here long,' he said. 'Anyway, I don't have any fancy fucking suitcase.'

Upstairs, he circled around her like he was examining her for signs of betrayal. She found herself touching her face, her neck, wondering if Jacob was visible on her body somewhere. Had his lips left a mark? The scratch of his stubble? Was it possible that something she felt so intensely inside wasn't visible on the surface somewhere?

'What's wrong?' she asked him.

'I'm not sure yet.'

She went into the bathroom and examined herself in the mirror, inch by inch. When she walked back into the bedroom, Daryl was on the bed. He reached out and grabbed her hand and pulled her down on top of him, and then he rolled over and pinned her wrists to the mattress. 'Happy to see me?' he asked.

Except it wasn't a question; it was a threat. And when they had sex, it felt like an attack that gave no pleasure to either one of them. Lying underneath him, looking out the grimy window to the air shaft, all she could think about was Jacob. Was she going to be able to get a message to him? Somehow tell him what had happened? He was at home, waiting for her to show up, thinking everything was fine, and *this* was happening to her. An hour earlier, she'd been suspended above the floor, above all of her worries, in the yoga class. Everything had seemed possible. So why couldn't she call back some of that courage?

When it was over, Daryl said, 'You're different.'

'A lot has happened this past year; you know that.'

'I know more than you think.'

She resents his jealousy, his hostility, his implied accusations, but this time, unlike all those accusations in the past, he's right. He does have reason to be jealous. She is the one in the wrong this time, and she deserves whatever he does to her.

She didn't have a chance to call Jacob, because Daryl didn't leave her alone, not even for a second. Fearing her phone was going to ring and Daryl was going to grab it, she'd turned it off and put it into the bottom of her bag. All of which has made her feel isolated and confined with Daryl – in the little hotel room, in the small Indian restaurant they ate at, even outside on the street, surrounded by thousands of people.

Now, as she's walking to the park with Daryl, Jacob is in Saint Louis. And tomorrow, she and Daryl will be on a plane back to L.A. End of story.

When they reach Columbus Avenue, Graciela spots a greengrocer and tells Daryl she wants to get some water. 'Can I get you something?' she asks.

'No,' he says. 'I'll wait out here.'

She goes inside, relieved to have even this much privacy,

although Daryl is still watching her from the sidewalk. She grabs a bottle and gets in line at the cash register. The man behind the counter is arguing with a customer about the price of a piece of fruit, and the woman in front of her turns around and says, 'This happens every time I'm in here.'

It's Nicole LaPierre. She does a double take and flips her curls. 'You were in my class yesterday!' she says. 'You have an amazing practice. You must be a dancer.'

Graciela smiles weakly at this. The tour ended only a matter of days ago, but she already feels like her claim to that title is fading. 'I am,' she says. 'When I can get the work. I loved your class. It was so much fun.'

'It's good to mix things up a little. I'd rather teach straight Iyengar, but there's more money in the niche market. At least at the moment. There's such a glut of teachers out there, you have to invent something. So why not the circus?'

The fruit controversy at the counter is over, and the cashier rings up Nicole's salad. She smiles at Graciela and waves at her from the door. Graciela feels as if she's dodged a bullet. She saw the way Nicole was looking at Jacob yesterday, but thankfully she was too discreet to say anything. You never know what Daryl might overhear. Graciela stops in the doorway before stepping outside, unscrewing the top on her bottle of water, waiting until Nicole is safely out of sight. She's at the curb, ready to cross. The light changes, but before she steps out onto the street, she turns and calls out to Graciela, 'Jacob Lander! Woo woo. Good score, girl!' She gives Graciela a thumbs-up and waves.

In a matter of seconds, Graciela makes a calculated move. She smiles, waves at Nicole, and watches her cross the street. Then, still smiling, she turns to Daryl and shrugs. She holds out the water bottle. 'Thirsty?'

He looks at her without responding, and she sees that cold, wild look again. 'Who was that?' he asks.

'Yoga teacher. I took a class with her yesterday. It seems like a long time ago.'

'So what was that supposed to mean? What she said?'

'I have no idea. Jacob Lander's a baseball player, right? Maybe she's a fan.'

'You think that's it, huh?'

'I told you, I have no idea. You know I don't care about sports. Let's go into the park. I want to show you the lake and Bethesda Fountain.'

'Yeah, right,' he says. 'Like I give a fuck about a fountain.' He grabs her by the upper arm. 'We're going back to the hotel.'

'We just left, Daryl. It's a beautiful day.'

'Don't argue with me,' he says, sounding almost as if he's on the verge of tears. 'We're going back *now*.' Her arm is pinched, but she's beyond feeling it. 'You fucking slut,' he starts to murmur. 'You fucking *slut*.'

Graham offered to pick Lee up at the studio and drive her to the restaurant, but that sounded too much like a date to her, so she insisted on meeting him there. It's best not to have to rely on him for a lift, and she'll be more in control of when she leaves. The only thing she has in her little office closet is a belted cotton sweater, but with a pair of leggings and a leotard top underneath, she can make it work. Best to keep it totally casual anyway.

And best not to be too early and appear eager. While she waits to leave, she starts going over the teacher bios Lainey wants her to revise for the updated studio website. In preparation, she's been perusing other studio websites. Reading dozens of teacher bios one after the other is a fairly depressing experience. Most start off with a litany of misery.

'Sabrina came to yoga after being diagnosed with . . .'

'Brian was a competitive skier until an automobile accident left him . . .'

'I was an angry, violent teenager who was told by several of my parole officers that it would be a miracle if I lived until the age of . . .'

'Shortly after 9/11 . . .'

'After Crystal's second suicide attempt in less than six months . . .'

'In 2002, I was legally dead for almost three minutes. . . .'

Lee's own teacher bio, if written in complete honesty, wouldn't be any more uplifting.

'After becoming disillusioned with medical school, suffering depression, losing twenty pounds she didn't need to lose, and hiding in her apartment for three months, Lee was dragged to a yoga class in a church basement on Manhattan's Upper West Side. . . .'

And then the portraits usually turn vague and slightly loopy after the discovery of yoga.

'Yoga has taught me to live in the abundance of the future's present.'

'Crystal tries to bring her understanding of the importance of creation into her classes.'

'Brian's journey, which began on the mat, ends on the mat with every beginning.'

'Sabrina calls her yoga classes "Not Yoga" because they *are* yoga.'

Lee shouldn't be so judgmental, because whenever she tries to describe what she wants to accomplish in class or how she defines her yoga, she gets equally nonspecific:

'My goal is to help people experience a greater connection to their bodies. So they feel rooted to the ground and balanced. So they know the difference between needs and cravings. So they can tap into their own potential to heal their physical and emotional wounds.'

Maybe it would be most interesting, and somehow most relevant, to find out what kind of music a teacher likes, what their three favorite movies are, and the title of the last book they read. Come to think of it, Lainey might go for that after all.

David Todd's bio, which she finds on the website of an obscure studio in Venice, at which, it appears, he no longer teaches, is pretty rudimentary: 'David has been studying yoga for almost fifteen years. He came to the practice through martial arts. He tries to be as open and honest in his classes as possible, and to encourage his students to be as honest with themselves as possible.'

It sounds good, but she's beginning to wonder how completely honest he's being with her.

Katherine spots her as she's leaving the studio and says, 'Nice sweater, Miss Lee. Going out?'

Katherine is too tactful to say so, but Lee knows she thinks Lee should be dating. She once said to Lee she wished she could fix her up with someone. *I've got a lot of ex-boyfriends floating around out there, and for some reason, they all stay in touch. But I'm guessing you're not into sleazebags and junkies.*

'I'm meeting Graham,' Lee says. 'Business dinner. Honestly.'

Katherine reaches out and adjusts the collar of Lee's sweater. 'I like Graham. He's smart. There's something trustworthy about him. Maybe it's the starched shirts.'

'We'll see how trustworthy he is when we find out the date he actually finishes the renovation.'

Katherine busies herself with her appointment calendar behind the desk, and without looking at Lee, she says casually, 'So what's with this David Todd?'

The casual tone is so studied, Lee almost laughs. 'There's nothing with him. He's an amazing teacher, and I'm trying to get him to teach here. Unfortunately, he's not looking for a job.'

Or, it would seem, anything else. After Lee left her message for David, he sent back a text, after midnight, saying he loved her class and would be in touch. But that was days ago. She keeps fluctuating between reminding herself that she should take the hint and realizing that he really is a busy guy.

'What did you think of him?' Lee asks.

'Nice hair, beautiful body. He looks like one of those guys who's trying really hard to be a good person.'

'But isn't?'

'I don't know him. And I give anyone points for trying. Hopefully, it's what we're all doing. I think a lot of guys who do yoga seriously are trying to keep the demons at bay. Anger, aggression. That and hoping to hook up.'

'That's a pretty cynical point of view,' Lee says.

'I'm just telling you what I think. You know I have a lot of experience with demons, so I'm not putting it down. What time's your dinner?'

The restaurant is off Hyperion, and as soon as Lee walks in, she wishes she'd worn something a little less casual and maybe a little less revealing. It's a small Italian place with the kind of low lighting that's inappropriate for a business meeting. Graham is in a booth near the back, and as the hostess leads her over, he gets up, all smiles and gleaming white shirt.

'You're looking as beautifully Zen as always,' he says.

'And you're looking as . . . clean.'

Fortunately, he laughs at this and actually remains standing until she slides into the booth. He has a habit, she's noticed, of holding doors open for her and making other chivalrous gestures that seem outdated but appear so genuine, she finds them unexpectedly appealing.

'It's a character flaw,' he says. 'One of many, I hate to say. I'll tell you two more.'

'You're always trying to talk people into some gummy, rubbery flooring?'

'No, that's one of my few virtues. First is, I'm a terrible wine snob, and another is that I love veal. You're not going to storm out of here, are you?'

'I'll tell you after I taste the wine,' she says.

'I'm relieved. It should be here any minute.'

'I'm sorry if I was a little late.'

He shakes his head. 'You're exactly on time.'

He has a serene half smile, as if he's savoring a private joke, and despite his comments about Lee looking Zen, he's the one who appears calm and relaxed. He has the lean, tanned face of a runner, somewhat reminiscent of a marathoner her college roommate dated. Lee realizes that she doesn't know a whole lot about him, outside of work. She's tempted to ask more, but that might send the wrong message.

Graham folds his hands on the table in front of him. 'Before the wine does get here,' he goes on, 'I want to tell you how great it's been working for you. It's been the highlight of my spring.'

'It must have been a bad spring. I've done nothing but try to keep costs down and bombard you with questions about when the work will be done.'

'That's what people do with their architects. Across the board. Here's the thing, Lee, you do it really nicely.' He reaches across the table and puts a hand on top of one of hers. 'So thank you for that.'

It would be rude to slide her hand out from under his, so she just pats his knuckles with her free hand, a gesture she hopes is neither encouraging nor too 'good dog'-ish. 'Thanks for saying that,' she says. 'Everything turned out so much more beautiful than I imagined, I feel as if I owe you a huge thanks. And we're still on schedule?'

He pulls his hand back, just before it gets awkward and Lee wonders if maybe she's assuming too much about his interests. 'Absolutely on schedule,' he says.

'So I guess that's your cue to take out the floor samples . . .'

He holds up a hand and says, 'That can wait until *after*

the wine gets here. Anyway, that's not why I suggested we have dinner.'

Here it comes, Lee thinks.

'I know we've run over the estimate. That's pretty much the norm, but I understand you've got a lot less room for error than some people I work with. So I'm going to drop most of my fees. You'll still be a little over, but not by as much.'

Lee tries to say something, but he cuts her off.

'And another thing, the contractor and I are throwing you a party for the reopening. Don't consider saying no. I've been working on this with Lainey, and we both know she's the one with the final say.'

Lee looks off across the dark restaurant and sees that the vast majority of other diners are couples, talking quietly and contentedly in the flattering light. Ultimately, it's what you pay for in restaurants like this – edible food and fantastic lighting. The waiter comes over with the wine and pours for Graham to taste. He sips and then indicates for the waiter to let Lee taste.

'I'll trust your opinion,' she says.

He winks at her, which only makes her feel more miserable.

After the waiter has left and Lee has sampled the wine, she settles herself back into the booth. 'I can't let you do that, Graham,' she says. 'The party or the fees. Don't think I don't appreciate it. I just can't. It wouldn't be right.'

Graham is still wearing his serene smile. 'I know why you feel that way. But you don't have to worry about that. I hope you think I'm a good architect, and I hope you love the new space. Beyond that, I'm not expecting anything.

I'm not stupid enough to deny that I think you're an attractive woman, but that's not what this is about. I've seen how you are with people – your students, your kids, everyone – and I just want to give a little something back. Good karma, how about that? Which I really need right now because I'm about to order the veal.'

It's beginning to sound like one of those offers you can't refuse. And so Lee doesn't refuse it. She thanks Graham for his kindness and for being so understanding. She picks up the menu and reads the pasta dishes, wondering if David Todd is a vegetarian.

Katherine finds it both touching and an example of L.A.-celebrity overkill that Imani bought Renay a brand-new, top-of-the-line sewing machine that probably cost somewhere in the neighborhood of five hundred dollars. She's seen these in stores and online and has coveted them, without the hope of ever being able to afford one – or being able to use it if she could afford it. Imani had it shipped directly to Katherine's house – overnight delivery, of course. 'Aunt Harriet' is certainly being good to her niece.

Katherine took it out of the box and set it up on a table in the sewing room, and when she showed it to Renay, the girl looked a little dumbfounded.

'I get to use *that*?' she asked.

'Last I heard,' Katherine said, 'it's yours. To do with as you wish. Which hopefully is sew.'

Now the two of them are sitting side by side at Katherine's sewing table, trying to figure out some of the programming on the machine. Allegedly, there are three hundred stitch patterns programmed into it, which is about 295 more than Katherine knows what to do with.

'This is all pretty new to me,' Katherine says. She points to the 1950s Singer she got at a stoop sale years ago and adds, 'I'm kind of old school, as you can tell.'

'I think you're great,' Renay says, with surprising conviction.

'Don't pin that on me, Renay. I tend to turn into a real bitch as soon as people start liking me. Just ask my boyfriend.'

'He doesn't think you're a bitch. He loves you.'

'Oh really? You could tell that just from that short drive?'

Renay smiles and nods. 'I could.' She took off her shoes when she entered the house and is now sitting with her feet up on the chair and her knees tucked under her chin. She looks like a leggy but graceful bird.

'He's a fireman,' Katherine says. 'They're loyal by profession. Have you ever done yoga, Renay?'

She pouts and burrows her chin into her knees. 'No. I'm not really the yoga type.'

'What does that mean?'

'I just mean I'm kind of clumsy. My balance isn't great, either. Mostly, I like to hang out and read.'

'From that position on the chair, I think you'd be a natural. If Conor can do it, anyone can.'

'*He* does?'

Maybe Renay has a little crush on Conor. 'He's an all-around good sport. What about you? Do you have someone?'

'Not really.'

'"Not really", usually means yes.'

'It means not anymore. That's why I'm here.' She stops and gazes off through the windows. 'My mother and his parents didn't want us seeing each other. He probably would have broken up with me anyway.'

'Why do you think that?'

Katherine can see that Renay is struggling with something, debating whether or not she wants to talk about this with her. 'We don't have to talk about it if you don't want to.'

'I do want to. I promised my mother I wouldn't.'

'Then I think we shouldn't discuss it,' Katherine says. One way or another, they'll get to it. But it's up to Renay, and there's no point in pressing her now. 'We've got enough to worry about with sewing.'

Katherine drops a bobbin into the magic machine, and the needle very obligingly threads itself. Yesterday, she biked down to a thrift shop connected to a Unitarian church not far from the last apartment she and Conor looked at with Carolyn. She rode past the apartment building, trying to find something to like about it, and ended up deciding that what was best was that it looked so insubstantial, it would probably be torn down in the next ten years. She did like the neighborhood more, and she loved the thrift shop. She picked up a couple of cute little cocktail dresses she thought might work. Renay isn't exactly the cocktail dress type – maybe a little too tall and gawky – but Katherine's planning to show her how to take in the skirt, shorten it, and make it look more chic and, hopefully, a little Audrey Hepburn. She hands Renay the scissors and tells her where to make the first cut. 'Just have fun with it. The dress cost four dollars, so if something goes wrong, it's not a big loss.'

Initially, Renay handles the scissors awkwardly, but once she gets going and finds her own rhythm, she turns out to have a steady hand and a surprising amount of patience. She even has an idea about cutting a small slit in the back that strikes Katherine as a sign of nascent fashion sense.

'So you read a lot?' Katherine asks as they work.

Renay shrugs. 'Just the average amount, I guess.'

This makes Katherine laugh. 'The average amount for me is one book every couple of years.'

She says this jokingly, but it's true, and not only true, but a source of embarrassment and frustration. When she was a kid, she used to gobble up books, mostly as a way to escape the chaos of home and her mother. But once she started to do drugs and get involved with the wrong kind of men, she lost her ability to concentrate. It's not something she tells people easily.

'That's *all*?' Renay says.

'God, Renay,' she laughs. 'Don't make me feel worse about it. I have no concentration,' she admits.

As Renay is very slowly feeding the hemline of the skirt under the needle, she says, 'It takes less concentration than this. I had a teacher who told me to read for just ten minutes as soon as I got up. That's how I started.'

By the time they finish with the project, the afternoon sun is glinting off the reservoir in the distance, silver, as it's supposed to be. This and dawn are Katherine's favorite times in the house, when the light is warm and soft and there's a sense of calm and quiet that infuses

166

the neighborhood. The dress doesn't look as good as Katherine imagined, but Renay seems to like it, or at least the fact that she made it.

'You think I can wear it home?' she asks.

'I think you have to. It's practically the cocktail hour anyway.'

'You think Aunt Harriet will like it?'

'I guess we'll find out.' Katherine examines Renay from a different angle, then goes to her closet and pulls out a pair of purple high-top sneakers. 'See if these fit you. Not appropriate for the dress, but they make the whole outfit seem nutty and ironic. It's always a good idea to make a little fun of yourself.'

The sneakers look ridiculous with the dress, but in the best way possible. 'Does Imani want you to call her Aunt Harriet?' Katherine asks.

'My mother does. She says Imani isn't her real name. It's a lot prettier, though.'

'Maybe you should ask your aunt what she'd rather be called. She might appreciate that.'

Renay bites her lip and nods. 'I can do that. When can we meet again?'

'Unless something comes up, the day after tomorrow is good for me.'

'I'll bring you a book,' Renay says. 'Something easy to start out with.'

Lee is talking with Alan about the kids' phones. It's a discussion she didn't want to have, but she can't pretend she doesn't know. They're standing in the living room of the bungalow they bought together and lived in for most of their marriage, and everything about the conversation feels awkward and wrong, starting with the fact that Alan keeps looking around distractedly, as if he's trying to see if Lee's pawned any of their furniture.

'It's a safety issue,' he says. 'We need to be able to keep in touch with them.' This has a familiar ring: Kyra's words as reported by the twins. 'That's why I got them the phones, Lee. Don't tell me you can find something in that to complain about, too.'

'We had an agreement,' she says. 'We should have talked about it first. And then telling them to keep it secret from me? I would never do something like that to you. It just wouldn't happen.'

And you're not the one who bought the phones, she decides not to say.

Alan throws himself onto the sofa, arms folded across his chest, exactly like a petulant child. The one pleasure she gets out of seeing Alan these days is being reminded of the fact that she's not susceptible to his physical charms. He's in his trademark Lululemon pants and tank top, and even though it's clear he's been working out more than ever and his hair is amazingly shiny (new products Kyra is giving him?), the thought of touching him makes her shudder. It's a blessing to know that that part of her involvement with him is safely and happily in the past.

'Let's be honest about this, Lee, okay? I know the kids told you I've been seeing Kyra Monroe. That's what you're really upset about, so just come out and say it.'

'You know what, Alan? I'm *glad* you're seeing Kyra.'

'Why's that?'

'Because I think you're probably a good match. And what difference would it make to me anyway? You're free to see anyone you want.'

'If you're worried that I'm going to repeat to her any of the hostile things you've said about her over the years, you can stop worrying. I wouldn't do that. It wouldn't be fair to her.'

'That wasn't keeping me up nights. Can you at least promise me that you're not going to tell the kids to lie to me anymore?'

'Why should I promise you anything when you don't trust me? It would be wasting my breath.'

It's a reasonable point. She doesn't trust Alan, and extracting a promise from him wouldn't mean much of anything. 'You're right,' she says. 'Forget I asked.'

Alan seems to be getting comfortable on the sofa, usually a sign that he has a favor to ask her. 'Is there anything else you wanted to talk about?' she says.

'You know, maybe if you started dating someone yourself, you wouldn't care about Kyra so much. You wouldn't be so frustrated.'

'You can leave anytime you like,' she says. 'And I'm hoping that's right now.'

'Look at all this space, Lee. I mean, look around. All this for one person, while I'm crammed into a little apartment. You call that fair?'

Lee looks at him and tries to figure out what's really going on. He can't possibly think she'd leave the house. In the current market, it would be insane to sell it. Eighty percent of the down payment was her money, and she's in the process of buying him out.

'Are you and Kyra planning to move in together? Is that it?'

'Her place is too small.'

'Well, I've heard it's a buyer's market out there, so maybe you should start looking for someplace bigger.' She's curious about how long this relationship has been going on, and maybe more to the point, how long it will last. The real surprise is that someone as ambitious as Kyra, someone who was married to a music promoter, someone who is committed to the idea of yoga as just another branch of show business, would be interested in Alan. Maybe she needs a handsome male companion for PR reasons.

'I drove Kyra up to the house,' Alan says. 'She loves the look of it and loves the location. And no, I didn't bring her in and show her around.'

'Do you really think I need Kyra's opinion to tell me it's a beautiful house?'

'I don't know how you think you're going to afford it, Lee. All the bills at the new studio. Do you have any idea how much Kyra makes for her appearances?'

So finally they come to the real issue. Kyra loves the house and wants to buy Lee out of it. Not exactly what Lee had in mind. 'I'm doing my best, Alan. If all goes according to plan, the festival should help bring me some new students.'

'Just out of curiosity,' Alan says, 'how *did* you get invited to teach at Flow and Glow?'

'We've been over this. The real question is why you find it so hard to believe.'

'Do you know how many teachers want to get in on

that? Do you have any idea how hard it is to get assigned classes? I could see if you had a huge following on Facebook or Twitter, but you haven't cracked that market.'

'If it's any consolation,' Lee says, 'I'm humbled and flattered I got asked.' Best not to say she debated for almost a week about whether or not to accept it.

'It's for stars, Lee. They turned down thousands of teachers who applied, including two who'd been on the cover of *Yoga Journal*.'

'You seem to know a lot more about it than I do.'

'No kidding. So why do you even want to go if you're so laid-back about it?'

Whenever Lee starts to get angry, she tries to breathe deeply and work through it. But with Alan, she's been finding it a lot more therapeutic to simply let her feelings out.

'I'm expanding the studio. I need to grow the business. It's good for my reputation. I'm getting paid. I'm trying to build up a reserve for the kids' education. I'm trying, I'm trying, I'm trying. I don't want to go; I need to go. I couldn't afford to pass up the opportunity.'

Alan holds up his hands. 'Sorry I asked.' As he's getting up off the sofa, he says, 'You're not sleeping with Krishna O'Reilly, are you?'

'Who?'

'He does all the bookings for the festival.'

'Get the fuck out, Alan. *Namaste*.'

'I never thought I'd tell you this, but your negativity brought me down spiritually the whole time we were together.'

She's still feeling the low, quiet hum of anger in her gut when, half an hour later, Stephanie phones her.

'I thought you were in New York,' Lee says.

'I am. We're leaving tomorrow. I'm calling about Graciela. I've been trying to get in touch with her for the past two days. Her phone is shut off, and she hasn't answered any of my messages.'

'Are you sure she's still in town?'

'I'm pretty sure,' Stephanie says. 'Her boyfriend was on our plane on the way east, so it doesn't make sense they'd just turn around and go home.'

'Daryl?' Lee asks.

'The only one I've ever seen her with.'

All of her annoyance with Alan evaporates, replaced by a gnawing uneasiness. Graciela never opened up to her about Daryl, but it was obvious to her that something wasn't right in the relationship. She suspected there was some kind of verbal or emotional abuse. And possibly more. When Graciela called her from the sidewalk in New York, Lee had the impression she was about to do something totally uncharacteristic. Sweet, faithful Graciela had obviously met someone. Then Daryl showed up unannounced?

'Best-case scenario,' Lee says, 'she and Daryl are having a great reunion and don't want to be interrupted by the phone.'

'I thought of that,' Stephanie says. 'But how great could it be? Did she give you the name of the hotel she's staying at?'

Lee thinks back to the phone call she had from Graciela. She doesn't remember the particulars, but she knows she commented on the neighborhood. 'I think she said it was a small hotel in the West Seventies. She didn't give me the name.'

'We'll find it,' Stephanie says. 'Roberta's a big fan of Google Earth.'

Roberta insisted on narrowing down their search to a list of five likely hotels. Thank God Graciela chose to stay in the neighborhood she did, since the hotel choices there are more limited than in a lot of places in the city. Within an hour of leaving the Regency, they've visited two of the top five possibilities. When they asked to be connected to her room, they were told that Graciela was not registered.

As they leave the uninspiring lobby of the Lucerne Hotel, Stephanie feels her confidence in the outcome of the search starting to fade. 'What if Lee was wrong about the address? Or maybe they moved? Or it's some place that wasn't listed? It's starting to feel like a needle-in-the-haystack hunt.'

Roberta stops on the street and puts her hands on Stephanie's shoulders. 'We're going to find her. Trust me on this. What's the next place on the list?'

'Beacon Hotel.'

'The one next door to the theater?' Roberta asks. 'Let's save that one. Graciela spent the past year in theaters. My guess is she'd want to get away from them a little.'

'That leaves the Woogo and the Belleclaire.'

'My money's on Belleclaire,' Roberta says. 'I don't see her in a place with a joke name like Woogo.'

From across Broadway, the Belleclaire looks majestic and slightly out of place, surrounded by a couple of more recent and bland buildings. With its pilasters, curved towers, and asymmetrical windows, it's one of those arresting art nouveau buildings that manage to convey whimsy and a touch of malevolence at the same time. The lobby is small and unassuming and smells faintly of the diner next door. Stephanie gives the desk clerk Graciela's name and asks to be connected on the house phone.

The clerk, a small woman with a faint mustache, looks back and forth between Stephanie and Roberta and frowns, then she hands her a phone. Roberta smiles. 'I told you, babe. Was I right?'

'You were right,' Stephanie says.

There's no answer in the room. Stephanie leaves a variation on the message she's left half a dozen times on Graciela's voice mail and passes back the receiver.

'Have you seen her in the lobby in the last few days?' Stephanie asks.

The clerk looks at Stephanie and frowns, and Stephanie has the feeling she disapproves of Roberta and what she assumes about their relationship. 'Do you have any idea how many rooms we have in the hotel, miss?'

'One hundred and ninety-seven,' Roberta says. 'What's your point?'

The clerk begins typing on her keyboard. 'If you'd like to leave a written message for her, I'd be happy to help you.'

'We'll pass on that,' Roberta says.

Stephanie's spirits sink as they're leaving the lobby. The news about Sybille's illness has left her with the haunting feeling that bad news is lying in wait around every corner. If bad things can happen to Sybille in her Beekman Place aerie, she doesn't even want to think about what might be going on here. Out on the sidewalk, she leans against Roberta and sighs.

'At least we have the right hotel,' Roberta says. 'We can come back later this afternoon.'

'There's no point,' Stephanie tells her. 'She's not going to answer the phone; I can feel it.'

'That doesn't necessarily mean it's bad news.'

Looking up the ornate face of the building, all those looming stories, Stephanie feels a shudder run through her. Graciela is in that building somewhere. She's with Daryl.

They decide to indulge in something greasy from the diner, but before they make it inside, they're approached by a small, blond man who introduces himself as Lyle.

'I work at the Belleclaire,' he says. 'Desk clerk. I'm going off duty, but I heard you asking about Graciela. Are you friends of hers?'

'From L.A.,' Stephanie says. 'You know her?'

'We talked a lot at the desk. Her boyfriend showed up a couple days ago. I saw them coming and going during my shift.'

'And everything was fine?' Roberta says it as a question, but it's clear to Stephanie she wants Lyle to confirm that there's nothing to worry about.

'I guess. At first. Then on Saturday, they came in in the middle of the afternoon, and I haven't seen them since. I sent the housekeeper up, but they have the deadbolt thrown. It's not a big deal. You'd be surprised how many people don't leave their rooms once they check in.'

'So why do you sound worried?' Stephanie asks.

'Not worried, exactly,' he says. 'Except . . . when they

came in on Saturday, I was at the desk and the boyfriend had her arm. She didn't look at me. Like she hoped I didn't see. It looked like he was dragging her.'

'That settles it,' Roberta says. 'Give us the room number. We're going up there.'

Imani knows that sooner or later she's going to have to call her sister and tell her that Renay didn't work out as a babysitter, but it's not a conversation she's looking forward to having. Gloria will undoubtedly find a way to twist it around so that Imani ends up feeling as if she failed her niece, failed her sister, and ought to just pack it all in and move back to Texas. She was planning on sending Renay home as soon as possible, but she's started to notice a change in her. Maybe the pressure of taking care of Daniel was too much and now that that's lightened up, she's calmer. Or maybe Katherine's generous offer of sewing lessons is paying off in some way.

Certainly not in the way of clothes. So far, the two of them have made two pieces of clothing, and they're among the less attractive things Imani has seen in a while. A hideous top they made out of a dress and that looks (big surprise) like half a dress, and a cocktail dress that actually is kind of cute in a vintagey sort of way. What is most striking is how much Renay seems to love the clothes and how excited she is about going to meet Katherine for the lessons.

Miraculously, she's also started to talk to Imani. Brynja, the new babysitter, started working shortly after the incident with the stroller. She's Icelandic and madly efficient.

She makes up in professionalism what she lacks in humor. Renay leapt into helping Brynja get settled and familiar with the household routine, all in a way that made it clear she'd been observing and absorbing a lot more of what went on in the house than it seemed. Two days ago, Renay even started calling her Imani. What brought about that break-through is still a mystery, although she suspects Katherine is behind that as well. Today, Katherine took Renay out for a haircut and some yoga clothes. Clearly, Katherine has taken on the role Imani hoped she'd play in her niece's life. At least someone is making progress with her.

Imani's on the set and has a few minutes before she's called for the next scene, and she dials Gloria. Her sister answers with characteristic warmth.

'Hold on, Harriet. I'm in the middle of something.'

'I can call back,' Imani says.

'Oh, well, I'm sorry if you're too busy to wait for thirty seconds while I finish this sandwich.'

'I'll wait,' Imani says.

'To hell with it. Now that you've made a big deal about it, I'd be too self-conscious. I know you don't ever eat so you can stay anorexic.' From the sound of it, Gloria takes a big bite of the sandwich. 'How's Renay?' she manages to get out around her chewing.

'I think she's starting to settle in,' Imani says. 'She loves Daniel, and she really is sweet with him.'

'In other words, it's a big surprise that a kid of mine would actually know something about babies? I might not be a *movie star*, but I taught her something. I might not be *Imani Lang*, but then again, neither are you! And don't forget it.'

This is the moment when Imani usually lashes out at Gloria and the whole conversation spirals down into a debacle. Instead, she starts an approximation of a rhythmic breathing exercise Tara tried to teach her.

'Renay's started taking sewing lessons from a friend of mine,' Imani says.

'Sewing lessons? I tried that with her. The girl can't sew. She's too impatient.'

'Well, she seems to be liking it. Katherine says she's doing a great job.'

'We'll see how far that goes. Anyway, she shouldn't be taking *sewing lessons* when she's there to do a damn job.'

Imani's dressing room is a makeshift affair carved out of a former classroom, but she does have some privacy, and she's grateful for that. The makeup girl sticks her head inside and points a brush at her, and Imani waves her in.

'We've changed her job description a little.'

'What's that mean?'

'We decided she deserved a little more free time since she's out here in a new place. So she's more like the assistant babysitter now.'

'That wasn't the deal, Harriet! If you fired her, tell me and she's coming home. She's not getting a vacation when I haven't had one in ten years.'

Imani cracks a nonchalant grin at the makeup girl, who, she knows, has overheard every word of this rant.

Mimi is a large, pallid woman with enormous hips and bad skin. She's always on the set in too-tight blue jeans and sweaters, and it looks as if she's never put a drop of anything on her own face. She's young, and a little too loud, but she knows her business well. She's using a sponge to blend in Imani's makeup, and Imani can tell it's tough for her not to be chatting as she usually is, although it's probably paradise to be gathering all this gossip she can later spread around.

'She's not on vacation,' Imani says. 'She's learning new things and she's helping out a lot. As soon as I finish this shoot, I'm taking her to yoga with me. That'll be good for her.'

'Yoga! Listen, if you want to marry a white guy and do *yoga*, and hang out in that fake world and pretend you're someone you're not, you do it! But it's not what I want for my daughter. She needs to know who she is, and that's not some skinny blonde in a leotard with her legs up in the air.'

Imani is using every bit of restraint she has to keep her anger bottled up. *Breathe, breathe, breathe*, she keeps reminding herself. Her sister's arguments make her so angry, she decides on the spot that Renay is *not* going home anytime soon, not if she can help it.

'It would be tough to change the ticket now,' Imani says. 'If she makes a lot of progress with the sewing, she'll leave with a good skill.'

'Oh, sure. *My* daughter is only good enough to be a seamstress. Jesus, Harriet, you really take the cake. You get everything handed to you on a platter – looks, money, fame, everything – and then you treat the rest of us like dirt. Believe me, if I'd had even half your luck, I wouldn't be insulting *you* the way you do *me*.'

'I have to get back to work,' Imani says. 'Give Renay another few weeks and then we'll look at it again.'

She can hear Gloria fuming into the phone as she clicks hers off.

Rusty comes into her dressing room and plops his body down on the ratty sofa. This is all she needs.

'You look fantastic,' he says. 'Mimi is a miracle worker.'

Do not engage! 'She is,' Imani says. 'You should let her take a crack at you.'

He laughs, a little too exuberantly. She just hopes that whatever he's on doesn't wear off before the end of the shoot. Ten days and counting.

'I had an idea I want to run past you,' he says. 'You up for it?'

'Go ahead.' This is the seventh take of this scene, and it's clear to everyone, Imani included, that something's not right.

'You've been playing it as if Dina doesn't know what's going on with her husband. How about we try it where you do know, but you're not letting on? To him or anyone. And when you slap him, you put everything into it – what he says to her, what happened over the weekend, and all this anger she's been keeping bottled up inside since she found out about him. Fuck the actor; you put everything into it and mark him up.'

Mimi finishes up with Imani's makeup, and whips off the bib. This idea, which they've never discussed before, sounds so absolutely right, Imani feels a thrill run through her body. Once he's said it, it seems so obvious, she's amazed they didn't try it that way in the first place. And then there's the relatively polite way he's asked it. Maybe with the shoot winding down, Rusty is becoming a human being. She's heard that this can happen to people.

'What do you think?'

'I think you're brilliant. It changes everything in the right way.'

He puts his hands over his head and stretches. 'You see? Once you come off your diva cloud and listen to your director, girlfriend, things get better.'

Maybe it was too much to expect he'd turn into a different person, but it was nice for the two seconds it lasted. Mimi, who senses the chill in the air and has been around for most of their storms, starts putting her brushes and tubes into her kit quickly.

Rusty lets out a big, exaggerated yawn, leaning back on the sofa with his arms overhead and his pale, flabby gut peeking out from under his grimy T-shirt. 'I knew you and I would get along as soon as we got that dyke off the set.'

'O-o-o-o-kay,' Mimi says. 'See you in five.'

Imani gets up from her chair and slowly walks toward Rusty. 'I love your idea,' she says. 'But I'm not your "girlfriend", *Rusty*, and I'm not a diva. I'm Harriet. From Texas. Just another black chick with a good face who got a few breaks. Lucky me, right?'

He's looking at her with a combination of bemusement and disdain. Homely guys like this should learn to lighten up and smile more. *If you weren't a director*, she feels like telling him, *you'd have zero chance of ever getting laid.*

'Let's get one thing straight, though,' she says. 'Becky Antrim told me you got fired off your last picture before shooting even started because you were such an arrogant, impossible asshole to work with. The producers didn't feel like dealing. You're not slumming it on this movie,

Rusty, you're trying to save your career. And if it works, you can thank Stephanie, because we both know *that dyke* is the brains behind this whole movie. And more than that? She's my friend.'

She puts her hand on his shoulder. 'So I'm going to do it like you want and put everything into it and let out all the anger I've been keeping bottled up inside all along; I'm going to mark him up good.'

And then she hauls back and slaps him across the face so hard, her palm goes numb. 'Just like that.'

Stephanie, Roberta, and Lyle are standing in the hallway of the ninth floor, knocking on Graciela's door. There's no answer, but when Lyle knocks again, louder this time, there's a muffled sound from inside.

'They're definitely in there,' Roberta says.

Stephanie starts pounding on the door harder, seized by panic. The hallway is hot, and it gives the place a claustrophobic feeling that isn't helping matters any. 'Graciela!' she shouts. 'It's Stephanie. Open up, we just came to say hello.'

There are more noises from inside, this time the sounds of furniture being moved.

'Do you have your keys?' Roberta asks Lyle.

'I do, but they'll have the chain on anyway.'

Roberta frowns, and Stephanie can see her going into problem-solving mode. She leans against the door and says, 'Listen, Graciela, it's Roberta. We know you and Daryl are in there. You haven't come out in days and everyone's worried. Either you open the door right now, or we're calling the police and things are going to get ugly really fast.'

They wait another minute, and they can hear the sound of voices, and then Daryl shouting, although it's not clear what he's saying.

'I'm calling right now,' Roberta says.

There's some sort of crashing sound and then a door slamming loudly and then, very slowly, the door to the hallway opens. Graciela is standing there, and it's immediately clear that it's worse than any of them suspected. Stephanie starts crying and reaches for Roberta's arm. Graciela's face is gaunt and pinched, and her skin has a sickly yellow pallor, except where it's bruised. Her eyes have the dull, unfocused look of someone who is far, far away and has been for some time. But what upsets Stephanie the most is that she has a jersey or a T-shirt wrapped around her head like a crazy, filthy turban.

'Graciela,' Stephanie says softly. 'Is Daryl here, honey?'

Graciela nods slowly, and Stephanie reaches out and touches the turban. That's when it falls off, and Stephanie sees that Graciela's amazing jet hair has been hacked off roughly, almost as if it was done with a knife. Stephanie pulls her into her arms.

'Fuck!' Roberta shouts. She pushes the door open and storms into the room. 'Where is he?'

Someone has come out of a doorway across the hall, and Stephanie tries to lead Graciela back into her room. As soon as she does, Graciela starts to tremble. Her head is against Stephanie's face, and she says into her ear, 'He went into the bathroom. I think he ran down the fire escape.'

Stephanie repeats this to Roberta. She runs to the bathroom and confirms that it's empty and that the window is open. Lyle takes Stephanie aside and very quietly says, 'There are no fire escapes on the bathroom windows on the ninth floor.'

PART THREE

Lee has never been much of a list maker, but since she's leaving for the festival in a week, she's taken to jotting down notes about what she has to do before she and Katherine actually board the plane. Unfortunately, she keeps losing the scraps of paper with all those important to-do items scrawled across them.

She's sitting at her desk in her office talking with Valerie, nursing . . . is it her seventh? . . . cup of coffee today. She doesn't know if it's more alarming that she's had seven cups or that she's not entirely sure how many she's had. Valerie has been eyeing the cup, but with more interest than judgment.

Call Mother to check on arrival time, Lee scrawls.

'I have to tell you,' Lee says, 'I really loved your class.'

'I'm so glad to hear that,' Valerie says. 'I was a little nervous, and I was *praying* it didn't show.'

'Your prayers were answered. You were composed and strong.'

Find out about opening party costs, Lee scrawls, and then, realizing she's being rude, tosses the list into her drawer.

Valerie is a tall, angular woman with light hair pulled back into a ponytail. As part of her interview this morning, she taught an hour-long class that was one of the best any of the prospective teachers has led. She was exuberant and precise, and showed an admirable knowledge of

187

alignment and anatomy. She's clearly not beholden to any one school of practice, but influenced by many. Like a lot of yoga teachers these days – David Todd, for example – she blends in interdisciplinary elements, including balletic leaps, lunges from martial arts, and a few expressive gestures that seem to have come from Martha Graham. She has a sense of humor, too. At one point, when the class was in reverse triangle, she had everyone drape the back of their hands across their foreheads melodramatically, a pose she called 'soap opera asana'.

Maybe what she liked about Valerie's class is that it reminded her a little of David's. One of the side benefits of being so busy has been a complete inability to focus too much on DT and the fact that she hasn't heard from him in weeks. She's gone through several stages of disappointment and anger, and has ended up feeling that she was just projecting onto him a lot of her own hopes and desires. Thinking back, she realizes he never promised her anything, never made any pronouncements. There's nothing she can blame him for. Alan was right. She's probably just frustrated and lonely and beginning to imagine flirtations.

Finally having found a good teacher in Valerie, she feels a little less bereft, at least about that part of what she wanted from DT.

'This is awkward,' Lee says, 'but there are a lot of things that can come up in class. I don't want to put you on the spot, but . . .'

'Questions about ethical behavior?' Valerie says. 'I am totally in support of that, Lee. Let's face it, we're dealing with students' bodies and well-being. It matters.'

'Thanks for making it easy,' she says. 'Some people get a little bent out of shape.'

'That's a clue that they've got issues.'

Lee has a sheet of twenty questions she asks of applicants. She pulls it out of her file cabinet. It's rare she needs to ask more than a few in order to get a good sense of someone's character. 'You ready?'

'Fire away. Suddenly, I feel as if I'm in a pageant.'

'If you thought one of your students had an eating disorder, how would you handle it?'

'Good question. And let's face it, it's a big problem in the yoga community. Especially in L.A. I once had a student who was clearly anorexic. She took at least two classes every day and you could see every bone in her back and chest. It was really disturbing. You could see other students looking at her with horror.'

'What did you do?'

'I took her aside after class, and I told her that I knew she had a problem, and that I didn't want to force myself on her, but that I was there for her and would give her whatever help she needed to find outfits that disguised her body better. Long sleeves, high necks – a burka, more or less. She really appreciated it.'

'I'm sure she did.' Strike one. 'Let's say a student frequently brings you expensive gifts. What would you do?'

Valerie squints and smoothes back her hair. 'Gifts are always a touchy subject. You never want to hurt someone's feelings by making them think you don't like their taste. I would thank them and then very nicely suggest they buy me gift cards instead.'

'You think that would be better?' Lee says.

'I do. As long as you don't tell them which cards to buy. That makes it sound more like a request. You could just say something like, "Oh, everybody loves Nordstrom".'

Well, she does have a point.

'You have a huge crush on one of your students. What do you do about that?'

Valerie throws back her head and laughs. 'I'm sorry, it's just so relevant! You have no idea. I truly believe you have to treat every student exactly the same. And honestly, I do. My boyfriend said that he had no idea I had a crush on him when he was a student in my class. He said I was so flirtatious with *everyone*, he would never have guessed.'

Lee walks Valerie to the door of the studio and tells her she'll be in touch in the next day or two. It will almost certainly be an e-mail. She feels a crushing kind of disappointment that this isn't going to work out, and then, just as suddenly, a wish that David would get in touch. She takes out her phone and, without thinking about it too much, sends him a text message: *It's been a while. Lee.*

Lainey is sitting at the front desk, sipping from one of the gigantic Big Gulp cups she carries around with her throughout the day. Lee has never had the courage to ask her what it's filled with, and since her own coffee problem is so out of control, she's not in a position to pass judgment on anyone's soda consumption.

'Promising teacher?' she asks Lee.

'Great teacher,' Lee says, 'but some really weird answers to the ethics questionnaire.'

Lainey shrugs. 'Hire her as a substitute for the days you'll be away. Not many of those situations are likely to come up. I'll keep an eye on her. It will probably be a slow period anyway. As far as I can tell, half the yoga students in L.A. are going to Flow and Glow.'

Lee can't tell if Lainey is hinting that she wants to go. Given her lack of interest in yoga, it seems unlikely, but since she's responsible for making it happen, Lee figures she might as well make an offer.

'Do you think it might be fun for you to go?' she asks.

'Oh, the yoga part sounds like hell to me, but there's also a ton of music, and I figure I could get a lot of signatures for the campaign.' This has something to do with legalizing pot, but Lee doesn't feel inspired to press for details. 'But you need me here. The new studio's opening twelve days after you get back, so there's a lot to work out.'

'I have a question for you,' Lee says. 'And I'd appreciate if you'd answer honestly.'

'Not my strong suit,' Lainey says, 'but I'll try.'

'How much is Graham spending on the opening?'

'I have no idea. Ask him.'

'I've asked him. He was vague. Said it would cost him about the same as his monthly mortgage payment.'

Lainey goes wide-eyed over the rim of her cup. 'Wow! He has a big mortgage.'

'Come on, Lainey, out with it. Two thousand?'

Lainey gestures with her thumb to indicate more.

'Not three?'

'Close to five,' she says. 'But he'll write a lot of it off.'

'That's ridiculous!' she says. 'It's out of the question. What's he planning?'

'It's all tasteful,' Lainey says. 'Assuming you have expensive tastes.'

Lee pushes her way through the plastic that's still taped

191

up to cover the entrance into the new studio space. Graham has promised her it will all be done by the time she gets back, and she knows she can trust him. Every time she walks into the new studio, she's overcome with a sense of pride. She made this happen, this beautiful space. And it is beautiful, with the rock wall behind the desk, the oversize black-and-white photos of students near the changing rooms, and, yes, the gleaming hardwood floor in the studio itself. Everything is a little dusty still, and there's a lingering smell of polyurethane, but that will fade before the opening. Standing on the new floor, gazing at the shelves Graham designed for the props, Lee is so overcome with happiness and gratitude that she pops up into a handstand, then drops her feet down into an inverted V-shape.

'Ouch!' she hears. She can see Graham leaning in the doorway, grinning, and she pops up to standing. 'That looked painful,' he says.

'Actually, it felt great.'

'You'll have to teach me.'

'It might not be the best place to begin.'

'I might be a lot more flexible than you'd think. And don't worry, by the time you come back from your festival, this will all be cleaned up.'

'I'm not worried about it,' Lee says. 'But you and I need to talk.'

'I'm always happy to do that.'

They're standing on opposite sides of the studio, speaking loudly across the empty space. He looks tall and lean and oddly incongruous standing there in his white shirt and pressed black jeans.

'What I'm worried about is the opening party,' Lee says.

'It's all arranged. You've got nothing to fear. Just a few people and some wine.'

'I managed to pry some information out of Lainey, and it sounds like it's going to be some mighty expensive wine.'

'I have a few choice bottles lying around my basement.'

'It's crazy, Graham. I can't have you spending all that money. I can't.'

He walks toward her, his polished shoes squeaking against the shiny new floor. It's a ridiculous sound, and they both start laughing about it. After the stress of the past few days, it's a huge relief to laugh, and Lee starts to do so even harder, mainly because it feels so good. When Graham comes up to her and puts his arms around her, both of them still laughing, she doesn't think anything of it. 'You *can*,' he says quietly. When he leans down and starts kissing her on the mouth, it feels as if it's just another part of their private joke. It isn't until she realizes that she's kissing him back that she stops laughing.

'Lee,' he says, 'you can.'

She feels her phone buzzing in the pocket of her pants and, relieved to have an excuse to pull away, she checks it. A text message back from David Todd: *I was in Chicago for family. Back tomorrow. Will call when I get home.*

'I'm sorry,' she says to Graham.

'From my point of view, you've got nothing to apologize for.'

'I didn't mean to do that.'

'I wouldn't have guessed.'

She walks away from him, back toward the entrance to the old part of the studio. 'I have to get the kids,' she says. 'I shouldn't have done that.'

'I disagree.'

'Please, Graham. Let's say it didn't happen.' And then she walks through the stiff plastic covering up the hole in the wall.

Katherine is setting the table in the dining room of her little house. She lays out a couple of vintage Fiestaware plates that she got at a garage sale a million years ago and almost never uses, and some jaunty cutlery with red Bakelite handles. She's not sure where she got those, but she loves their jewel-like appearance and their weight.

She's expecting Conor to arrive any minute, and she's prepared an elaborate meal – a vegetarian onion soup with butter dumplings and a savory cheese tart, made from scratch. She's stepped outside a couple of times just for the pleasure of walking back into the house and smelling the warm scent of butter and cheese and flaky pastry. Conor's idea of a perfect meal is more along the lines of bloody meat and a mandatory vegetable boiled into submission, but he's always enthusiastic about her cooking. He's always willing to give it a try.

She dreamt up this particular dinner as a distraction. Maybe if he loves the food enough, he won't care so much when she tells him she just can't sign the lease on the cramped apartment Carolyn showed them. Maybe he won't feel they're back to square one, and he won't take it all so personally. Maybe he'll understand that she can't envision sharing six hundred square feet with him. Not because she doesn't love him, but because she's worried that it will upset the balance of their relationship. It would all be so much easier if she didn't love him so much.

And maybe, *maybe* if he does understand all that, she'll be able to tell him her other news and the decision she's made about that. And maybe he'll understand that, too.

She's surprised to hear the doorbell ring, since Conor always uses his key, but when she gets to the door, it's being opened by True, the real estate agent hired by her landlord. He's a fidgety, handsome guy, probably in his late twenties, who seems to be trying so hard to appear hip and cool that he comes off as desperate. And 'True'? Did he really think this was a good name for a real estate agent? (Surely it isn't the name his parents gave him.) It's like hanging a big sign around your neck that says you're a hopeless liar.

'Katherine,' he says. 'I didn't know you were home. Smells great in here.'

'I'm having a friend for dinner,' she says. 'Any minute now.'

'You didn't get my message?'

There's a couple standing behind him, both tall and tanned, and the wife so pregnant, it looks as if she's about to give birth on the walkway leading into the house. Katherine can see where this is going.

'I didn't get any message.'

'I had my assistant call about showing the house. Bruce and Charlotte came all the way up from San Diego.'

Katherine has made sure she's been out of the house for every showing; the thought of strangers traipsing through her house with the intention of moving in makes her a little sick to her stomach. Bruce and Charlotte look

195

like annoying types to begin with, with their perfect sun-tans and big grins. But what can she do about it? They've come *all the way* from San Diego.

'I never got the message,' Katherine says. 'You're sure your assistant called the right number?'

'You can't trust technology,' True says. 'Can we come in anyway? I promise it will only be for a minute.'

Katherine glances out at the couple. Charlotte has her arms encircling her belly, as if she's presenting it to Katherine. One more irrefutable piece of evidence to prove to Katherine that she can't deny them entrance, that they deserve to be living in this house more than she does.

Katherine steps aside and waves them in.

'We really appreciate this,' Charlotte says. 'I promise we won't ask to stay for dinner. It smells yummy. Well, what doesn't at this stage?' She pats her stomach. 'I wouldn't say no to a glass of water, though. Oh my God! Look at that view.'

'You wouldn't guess from the street side, would you?' True says. 'You're looking at the money shot. The rest is reparable.'

'I'm not so sure,' Bruce says. 'I'd say we're looking at a teardown.'

'That's a *little* extreme,' Charlotte says. 'As long as we could rip everything out, I'd love to keep it as is. I can't believe we didn't have time to stop for water. I'm so parched. The air is dry up here.'

Katherine takes her cue and goes into the kitchen to get her a glass of water with ice. And then, because really, it isn't their fault the house is for sale, she adds a slice of lemon. She follows the sound of their voices into the sewing room, where Charlotte is examining Katherine's old machine as if she's looking at a relic from an archaeological dig. Katherine hands her the glass of water.

'So sweet of you to add the lemon,' Charlotte says. 'I really hate to ask this, but I heard you running water in the sink. Is this from the tap?'

Katherine looks at her as if she must be joking, but apparently she's waiting for an answer. 'I have a filter on the faucet.'

Charlotte gives her an apologetic grimace. 'If it weren't for the baby, I'd risk it, I really would.' She hands the glass back as if it's emitting toxic fumes. 'But I just can't. You'll understand when you're pregnant. I just *love* that you sew. It's so cute and old-fashioned.'

Katherine brings the glass back into the kitchen, takes a big sip, and pours the rest down the drain. The best thing to do is get out of the house right now. She turns off the heat under the soup and takes the tart out of the oven. They can eat it tomorrow. She slips out the front door and sits on the walkway to the street, letting a warm breeze blow over her.

Did she believe that the house wasn't going to sell? Did she think that Tom was suddenly going to change his mind? Or that suddenly she was going to come into a couple million dollars? Maybe Bruce and Charlotte are the best things that could have happened to her. Reality check, lemon slices and all.

When Conor arrives, she waves to him and runs down to the end of the walkway. 'Couldn't wait to see me?' he asks, taking her in his arms.

'Change of plans,' she says. 'Let's go out for dinner.

There's a sushi place down by the new apartment. We should probably try it out.'

'Because?'

'Because we're probably going to end up eating there a lot once we move in.'

One virtue of interviewing so many prospective teachers is that Lee has been forced to take a huge variety of classes in the past few weeks. Today's interview started off unpromisingly. The teacher told Lee he didn't want to be judged by the class he was about to give. It was a confusing comment, since that was, of course, the whole point of having him offer a class at Edendale as part of the interview.

'Are you sick today?' she asked.

'Oh, no. I never get sick. It's just that the class I'm doing today is going to be really standard. Usually, I have a completely original flow. It's not like anything anyone else teaches.'

'I'd love to see that,' Lee said. 'It's what you'd be teaching at the studio, isn't it?'

'It depends. I have a lawyer friend who's been trying to help yoga teachers around the country get patents for their poses. He told me I should hold off teaching them in class until we see how it works out.'

Lee has heard that in the increasingly cutthroat jockeying for jobs at good studios, some teachers have tried to get a legally binding patent on their poses. When she first heard it, she thought it was urban legend. Apparently not. The teacher's name is Craig, and he's a short, solid man, probably in his early thirties. He was recommended to Lee by a student who said he has a powerful and original teaching style. Too bad it's so original it has to remain secret.

'But the whole spirit of teaching is learning and sharing knowledge with others. That's how we all learned, isn't it?'

'A lot of teachers go around to different studios specifically to learn new poses. They hear about someone like me, and then they come and steal the poses, names and all, pretend they made them up. It's self-protection on my part.'

'Can you give me some idea of what your style is like?'

Craig has an appealingly open face, surprising for one who is so closed off.

'I spent a lot of time in Europe when I was in college. I originally thought I wanted to be an architect. Last year, I had a realization that a lot of my teaching and the poses I've invented are based on Gothic architecture, which is what I really love. I used the Reims Cathedral as my inspiration and named poses after various details you find throughout the church, the ones that are beautiful and look fluid, but are also the foundation of strength in the design. The "flying buttress", the "newel", the "equilateral arch." And so on.'

'It's an interesting idea,' Lee said. 'When will you find out about the patent?'

'Hopefully soon. I can give you a private demonstration, if you like.'

Craig did have a strong practice, but the flying buttress looked suspiciously like warrior 2, and how the newel was different from mountain pose was unclear. The day before, she had interviewed a teacher who told her he and a yoga friend had gone to the Caribbean to dissect corpses to have a better understanding of anatomy. She should have been impressed, but there was something in the way he discussed it that gave her the creeps.

After Craig has left the studio, she calls her mother to confirm that she will be arriving in two days.

'Oh, Lee,' she says. 'Don't tell me you think I'd cancel at the last minute and leave you high and dry? I am so looking forward to coming out there and being a help to you for once!'

'I know you are, Mom. And I'm looking forward to seeing you. So are the kids.'

'I wish I could prepare meals for everyone, but I know you don't trust my cooking, so I'll let you do that before you leave. Just put up a few days' worth of meals in the freezer, and the rest I can have delivered. The kids aren't allergic to MSG, are they?'

'Whatever works for you, Mom. We'll talk about it when you get here.'

'No, honey, this is about *you*. Just make sure to leave your credit card or cash. I told Lawrence you're going to this festival, and he was on cloud nine. He said the teachers who go there become real stars. Not that you aren't already. You know I never watch TV, but I saw *The View* the other day, and they were talking about the festival! I practically fell out of bed! Some teacher was on showing off. Kyla, or one of those made-up names you all have.'

'I have my own name, Mom.'

'Oh honey, did you really think I forgot what I named you? I wish I wasn't afraid to drive in L.A., but you know my hypertension. We'll just make sure you stock the fridge and the cabinets before you leave. Did I tell you I'm on the South Beach Diet? I've been on it for a week and a half and I've already lost three-quarters of a pound. I'll e-mail you my shopping list tonight, in case you have a chance. Oh, Lee, I'm so glad to finally be able to be *useful* to you, honey, instead of a burden.'

'I have another call coming in, Mom.'

'Oh, I know you don't, honey. You're just trying to cut me off. It's okay. I'll see you soon.'

The other call is from David Todd, and as soon as she hears his voice, she forgets her anxiety about seeing her mother.

'Lee,' he says, 'I owe you a big apology.'

'I got your message,' she says. 'What's going on with your family?'

He explains that his father had a stroke, and he had to rush back to Chicago for two weeks to help take care of him. 'He's going to be all right, but when you go through something like that, it makes you look at your own life a little differently, reevaluate some of your choices.'

'I'm sure it wasn't easy.' When Lee lost her own father, it threw her whole life into upheaval.

'I thought about you a lot when I was away,' he says. 'I feel terrible I didn't call you sooner, after the class.'

'You needed to take care of your family. I know you go into a tunnel when that happens. Anyway, I'm leaving for the Flow and Glow Festival in a couple of days, so I'm glad I heard from you now. I'm teaching there. The opportunity came up, and I couldn't turn it down.'

'I know you're going,' he says. 'I decided to go, too. I'm

driving up at the end of the week. I've already signed up for one of your classes. I have to get going, but I'll look for you when I get there.'

'But there's supposed to be ten thousand people,' she says.

'You'll stand out.'

For forty-eight hours, Stephanie has been trying to convince herself she's looking forward to the wrap party for *Above the Las Vegas Sands*. The shoot is over, and even though she's not naive enough to think there won't be calls for reshooting a scene or two of additional footage somewhere, the daily grind of this portion of the process is finished. Two days ago, she got a call from an agent at ICM telling her he'd heard about her work on the film and asking about her next project. 'I'd like to represent you,' he said. She had enough confidence and presence of mind to tell him she would get back to him. It was the most concrete piece of evidence she's had that her career has entered a new phase. She's been launched. She wanted to call Roberta and tell her, but she has sensed that Roberta, while happy for her, is worried about the turn her life is starting to take. As for Sybille, how could she call her with her own happy news when Sybille is in the middle of chemo?

Part of her wishes she could just stay home and start working on her new project, the original screenplay she had to put aside as soon as they started shooting this one, but part of her job is to show up and look as if she's happy to be there.

The party is being held in a converted loft downtown,

one of those amorphous spaces people are always renting for parties, despite the fact that there's something chilly and off-putting about them. There will be halfway decent food and way too much alcohol. It's not as if she's tempted by alcohol anymore. She still thinks about it sometimes, but mostly because she can't quite believe how out of control she was, and how rotten she felt all the time back then. The worst thing about having given up drinking is that she now can tell how sloppy and unattractive everyone else looks when they're on their fifth plastic glass of vino.

As she's driving on the 101 toward downtown, she sees the lights of the city burning all around her with the excitement and intensity of fire. There's no real nighttime in this city, just different shades of day. She hasn't gotten used to that after all these years, and she's not sure if she loves it or hates it. Sometimes she longs for a perfectly dark sky and deep silence. Does she even know what those are like anymore?

She's swamped by a feeling of loneliness and insignificance. Who is she in the middle of this sprawling hive of power and ambition and talent? And what if, thanks to the movie, thanks to the agent, she turns out to be somebody? Not a major somebody, not a marquee name, but somebody who pulled herself out of a bad situation and proved that she has talent and wasn't a fool to pursue her dream?

If that happens, the person she's come to think of as her godmother will probably be gone. It's late back east, but Sybille still seems to be up at all hours, and Stephanie can't resist calling.

'I thought you were at the party,' Sybille says, her voice weak but surprisingly cheerful.

'I'm headed that way. I just started to miss you. I wish you were here. You're the one who should be celebrating.'

'If it's any consolation, dear, I probably wouldn't have gone to the party even if I'd been able to. No matter how I presented myself, I'd still look like Lady Bountiful, and people would only let their hair down once I left. It's much better for me to appear aloof. That way people can be openly resentful instead of straining to be polite.'

There's an unspoken rule that Stephanie is not supposed to ask Sybille about her health. Sybille is completely private about that – and everything else – but two days ago, she sent Stephanie an e-mail with a phone number in it, telling her she should feel free to call it if Sybille is 'unavailable'. It wasn't hard to figure out what that meant.

Sybille coughs a little, a rattling sound to clear her throat, completely incongruous with her usual poise and demeanor. 'And how is your friend, the dancer?'

Her friend, the dancer. Stephanie has started to wonder if Graciela will ever dance again. 'She stayed at my place for a couple of days when we first got back. I told her she could stay as long as she wanted, but she decided to go stay with her mother. She couldn't even think about going back to the apartment she shared. With him.'

'That's probably a good plan.'

'I'm not so sure. She and her mother have never gotten along. She's still in shock. I don't think she's in a position to decide anything, but I couldn't stop her.' Stephanie tried, but it's clear that Graciela's problems aren't going to be solved by a little comfort and girl talk, and Stephanie wasn't sure she wanted to take it on.

'Have you talked with her?'

'She's called a couple of times, but mostly she wants to be left in peace.'

'And Roberta? Is she with you?'

Stephanie doesn't say anything for a moment, and then she says, 'She couldn't take the time off to fly down. She's coming in a few weeks to visit her mother.'

Stephanie and Roberta met through Roberta's mother. Billie lives across the hall from Stephanie and is one of those overdone elderly women you see often enough in L.A., a suntanned character who's always decked out in too much jewelry and lives in her own private world, a world in which she is a Big Star. Billie claims to be in her fifties, even though, according to Roberta, she's close to eighty-five. To her credit, she still goes to yoga classes and – more power to her – has started dating a man in his seventies, a relationship she explains by saying, 'I always liked older men.' She's supportive of Roberta, as long as Roberta goes along with Billie's story that her daughters are all in their late twenties.

As Stephanie was leaving the house tonight, dressed up, she bumped into Billie and her new boyfriend coming home from an early dinner.

'Pretty dress,' Billie said. 'Going out?'

'Just meeting a friend,' Stephanie said.

'Anyone I know?'

'I don't think so. Someone from the movie.'

She hadn't invited Roberta down, hadn't even mentioned the party to her. It wasn't fair to ask her to spend all that money on a ticket from San Francisco, to take yet more time off from work after the New York trip. At least that's how she rationalized it. But really it's more about the fact that with this new success looming, Roberta is something of a liability. It isn't that she's ashamed of her or their relationship; it's just that she doesn't want to be labeled by anyone now. Success has been so long in coming, she doesn't want to upset what feels like a delicate balance. If she can get set up for her next project, sign with the best possible agent, maybe sell a few ideas, then she can be completely open and to hell with everyone. But not yet.

She and Sybille chat for another few minutes, and then Sybille says, 'If there's anything I can do to be helpful, let me know. Now I think I'd better get off.'

'Are you tired?'

'Not at all. I can hear your GPS chattering on, and I want you to get to the party in one piece. And Stephanie, you've earned a very good time, so please, have one.'

Stephanie leaves her keys with the valet. She can hear the party from the street, and see the tall, third-story windows lit up. She's never felt quite so alone as she does walking into the building, but she's determined to have a good time. If not for her sake, then at least for Sybille's.

Imani thought about bringing Daniel to the party with her, if for no other reason than to annoy Rusty. Then, as she was getting ready, she looked in the mirror and decided that the best way to annoy him would be to show up at the party looking her best and *not* carrying her baby. Solid, reliable, humorless Brynja will have the pleasure of Daniel's company for the evening. Imani goes into his bedroom and lifts him up out of his crib. She holds him out at arm's length and makes his legs dance a little. His old man's face splits open in a wide smile, and he starts laughing. He looks so much like Glenn at these moments, it's almost comical.

'After tonight,' she says, 'you and I are going to be spending a lot more time together. Did you know that?'

His lips start to move, and she feels certain that he's trying to talk to her. She holds him against her chest and squeezes him and feels a moment of perfect happiness. If only she could stop everything right now and savor this for another week or day or hour. Then stern Brynja enters, and Imani lays him back down in the crib.

'You look fantastic,' Brynja says in her eerily flawless English.

'Thank you,' Imani says. 'I feel adequate.'

Not true, but humility never hurt anyone. Imani knows she is looking better than she's looked in months. The day after the shoot ended, she called Tara Foster, her private yoga teacher, and told her she wanted double sessions daily, and she wanted her to kick her ass. 'Pretend it's boot camp,' Imani said. 'Be ruthless. And if I ask you any questions about any of your other clients, ignore me.' She's amazed at how much flexibility and strength has come back in the past week. Already, she can feel her body firming up again, and her arms have started to get stronger. Strong and firm enough to influence her decision to wear a sleeveless dress tonight. Not that doing yoga has *anything* to do with vanity.

She knocks on Renay's door, and her niece opens it, ready and looking pretty amazing herself. She's wearing some kind of 1950s cocktail dress with cherries on it and a red belt in what appears to be patent leather. The belt is about four inches wide, and it gives Renay an hourglass shape Imani would never have guessed she had. Then there's the short, sculptural haircut she came home with last week. She can't imagine how much Katherine paid for that, but whatever it was, it was worth it. How could she have missed Renay's long, graceful neck and the beautiful bones of her face?

Imani suddenly feels a surge of regret that it's Katherine who has been able to bring this out in her niece and not her. In the past several weeks, she's sensed that the two of them have become fast friends. Or maybe it's more that Katherine has become a surrogate mother to Renay. Renay mentions her in passing often enough, but she's circumspect about their conversations, and Imani has a suspicion that the two have started sharing secrets. But what would those be? How much of a secret life can Renay have at this stage of her life?

Imani wraps her arms around Renay and says, 'I wouldn't have recognized you.'

'Is that a good thing?'

'I just mean you look even more beautiful than usual. Is Katherine coming to the party tonight?'

'I invited her. She said she had to talk Conor into it.'

'They'll be there,' Imani says. 'Conor would never turn down an offer from Katherine. Let's get going. Glenn has been waiting downstairs for half an hour.'

Katherine has noticed that no matter how far people go in life, they have a way of reverting back to their junior high selves in certain social situations. The wrap party, for example. Shortly after she and Conor arrived, it became obvious that the crowd had formed into two neat groups: the actors, glowing and groomed, on one side of the room, and then the much larger group of tech people bunched together on the other, near the food. You wouldn't call the latter group glowing or groomed. Most of the men and women have a scruffy, unkempt, asexual appearance, with long hair that looks as if they haven't run a comb or water through it for a few weeks.

'Recognize anyone?' Conor asks.

'I was hoping Stephanie would be here by now, but I don't see her. I guess we should get some food.'

'You work on that while I grab a beer.'

Katherine watches Conor amble away, and she feels an ache at being left alone. She can still see that young couple in her house, walking around it as if they owned it already and as if she should have no feelings of ownership or pride about the place. She, after all, is just the tenant, and undoubtedly they were told that she's ready to leave the minute they want to close and start tearing apart the beautiful, perfect house that has been her shelter as the roughest time in her life turned into the happiest. And there was the wife, displaying her huge bump to Katherine as if it meant she should run around serving her drinks and mopping her brow, because Katherine is clearly *single* and a *tenant*, and not suited to own a house or be a mother. And the worst of it is, she's probably right on both counts. She heard from her landlord that the couple has made an offer. Insultingly low, but they're negotiating.

The conversation around the food tables is loud and consists mainly of anecdotes about the shoot. As far as she can tell, everyone believes that he or she is solely responsible for the movie. ('I totally ignored his direction on the lights. Then he took credit for how good it looked.' 'The angle I used on that scene in the club changed the *entire thing.*' 'I'm not saying I wrote the ending, but it was my suggestion they change it.') Occasionally, someone will look toward the actors and make a dismissive joke. This group clearly considers all those glowing and groomed people over there to be mere puppets. Anyone with whitened teeth and colored contact lenses could do the same jobs they do. It feels to Katherine as if she's trying to wedge her way into a tight-knit community that's spent months bonding. Which, she realizes, is pretty much what's going on.

It's with relief that she spots Stephanie walking out from behind a partition, looking a little sheepish and surprisingly tentative. Katherine hasn't seen her in at least six weeks, and she's surprised to see how drawn and exhausted Stephanie looks. She makes her way through the crowd and gives her a big hug.

'Look at all this,' Katherine says, sweeping an arm around the room. 'This is all thanks to your script. I'm so proud of you.'

'Don't say that too loudly,' Stephanie replies. 'There are about one hundred people in this room who think this party is all thanks to them. Bottom line is, it's a team effort.'

'But you wrote it, Stephanie. No one else can claim that.'

'Actually, someone else *is* claiming that.' She nods toward two men locked in a conspiratorial huddle on one side of the room. 'The redheaded tall guy's the director. He showed up tonight with the author of the book I adapted.'

'Is that bad?'

'There was a falling-out about the script. He wrote a horrible first draft, and Sybille ended up buying him out of his contract so I could start from scratch. I just found out tonight he's contesting the screen credit.'

'The director, too?'

'He's stirring up trouble. He's one of those guys who just can't believe a woman could possibly write a decent script. The funny part is, I think he's convinced himself the author really did write it.'

'You look a little wiped out,' Katherine says.

'It's been a long month. You heard about Graciela, right?'

Katherine nods but doesn't say anything. Lee told her the story of what happened in New York, but it sounds so horrible, she can't bring herself to talk about it. Especially not here, in the middle of a party.

'Lee and I are leaving for a yoga festival in a few days. You should come.'

Stephanie scrunches up her face. 'What the hell is a yoga festival?'

'It's a beautiful place in the Sierras at about five thousand feet. You take three or four classes a day, some of the best and most famous teachers in the country. You go for hikes, go swimming, listen to music. Or you just lie around and relax. On top of that, we all get to hang out together. How bad could it be?'

'I haven't practiced in over a month,' she says.

'Then you really do need it. Renay and I have been try-ing to talk Imani into coming along. Don't think about it too much. Just come.'

The director and his writer friend make their way toward them. The director is one of those tall, sloppy men who think their masculinity is defined by how infre-quently they bathe. Or at least that's what Katherine guesses after taking one look at him. The writer, on the other hand, is short and cocky, strutting with his chest puffed out and the air of a schoolyard bully wannabe. He probably believes that if he's arrogant and obnoxious enough, you won't notice his height.

The director gives Stephanie a nudge that knocks her off balance. 'So Stephanie,' he says, 'I'll bet you were sur-prised to see our author here.'

'Not really,' Stephanie says. 'I'm happy to see you, Josh. It's been a while. How's the new book coming?'

Josh throws his head back and lets out a loud laugh that's completely humorless. 'Just so you'll know for the future,' he says, voice dripping with condescension, 'that's the one question you should never ask a *writer*.'

Katherine has met a few writers through her massage work, and she's noticed that there's usually something a little off in their appearance and behavior. She's never heard of most of the writers she's massaged, but they seem to consider themselves important public figures. She always has the impression they're trying to live up to the glamorous image of their author photos and con-stantly falling short. They frequently have a chip on their shoulder, probably because they work so hard and get so little recognition. Within ten years, books will probably be a cultural artifact anyway. Although it is true that since Renay gave her the idea of reading for ten minutes every morning, she's made her way through two novels. And now instead of reading for ten minutes she's up to half an hour.

This guy's pants are a couple of inches too long and the cuffs of his shirt are frayed. Still, he said the word 'writer' as if there was something sacred in it.

'Don't ask about current book,' Stephanie says. 'I'll keep that in mind.'

Katherine knows she ought to keep her mouth shut, but given the mood she's in and how much she'd like to start ranting and raving at the couple who just might be buying her house, at True, the lying real estate agent, and at the nurse at the health clinic who confirmed the news she really didn't want to believe, she can't hold back.

'Just so you'll know for the future,' she says, 'Stephanie *is* a writer. But I guess you know that since she wrote the whole screenplay.'

Both of the men look at Katherine with boredom, as if she's been rambling on in gibberish for the past forty minutes.

'So, Stephanie,' the director says, 'you going to introduce us to your girlfriend?'

There's a mocking tone in his voice that adds an extra spin to the word 'girlfriend', and a cold look comes into Stephanie's eyes. Katherine can see clearly that the past two months have been an extended battle of wills between these two, but to her credit, Stephanie doesn't take the bait. She turns toward Katherine and smiles. 'I think you're right about the festival,' she says. 'It would be nice to be around some decent people for a change. What day does it start?'

Imani is talking with Millie, the girl who plays the ingenue in the film. Millie was on a sitcom for three seasons when she was a kid, and this role is her attempt to make a transition into playing more grown-up characters. She's a strange synthesis of quirks, as so many former child stars are. On the one hand, she has a high voice and a slight lisp, as if she knows that in the minds of millions of people, she'll always be a chubby, too-adorable eight-year-old; on the other, she's wearing a dress that seems to have been designed to show off the breasts she had enhanced to remind the world that she's a voluptuous, nineteen-year-old woman. She and the young male lead had one of those on-set flings during the shooting and, true to form, broke up one day before production shut down. Millie keeps glancing toward him warily, just to make sure Imani knows what's up.

'James isn't looking at us, is he?' she asks.

'I can't tell from where I'm standing.'

'God, he's being really immature about this.' Undoubtedly true, but since it's delivered in Millie's trademark baby talk, it's a little hard to take seriously.

'He's young,' Imani says.

'He's *twenty-one*!' Mille lisps.

Imani knows she's supposed to follow up with a question about their 'relationship' so that Millie can make it clear that while he was attractive enough to hook *her*, she was attractive enough to *dump him*. But at the moment, Imani can't be bothered. Since Millie cornered her a few minutes ago, she's been dousing Imani with the kinds of compliments that make her feel as if she's a dinosaur. 'I've learned *so* much from you.' 'You were my *idol* when I was a kid.' 'It must have been *so* different when you got into the business.'

'I should go find my husband,' Imani says. 'I don't want him getting distracted.'

'I talked to him a few minutes ago. He's not the type of guy I imagined you'd be with.'

'You mean because he's white?'

Mille reels back as if Imani's waving fire in her face. 'He *is*? I guess I didn't notice. Or maybe I just don't even think of you as African American.'

'Do me a favor,' Imani says. 'If you run into my sister, Gloria, don't tell her that.'

'Is she here?'

'God, I hope not.'

Imani can tell that she's gone too far. Poor Millie is just trying her best. No need to take her own bad mood out on her. 'Sorry,' Imani says. 'She and I have a little argument going. I love your shoes.'

Unfortunately, Millie isn't going to be bought off so cheaply. She downs the rest of whatever is in her glass and says, in a miraculously adult tone, 'The main thing I wanted to tell you is that in case you hear any rumors or anything, please don't believe them. My agent is the one trying to get me top billing in the movie. Not me.'

At this point, Imani doesn't really care one way or the other. If Millie gets a career resurgence based on ten minutes of screen time, more power to her. Imani sees Stephanie, Katherine, and Renay hanging out together and sampling the food, and she waves. Glenn has been swallowed up by the crowd. How nice to not have to worry that he would ever be distracted by anything other than a call from the hospital.

'I have to go talk to my friends,' Imani says. 'And Millie, you really were great in your scenes. Just know that and enjoy it, no matter what happens with this movie. Enjoy everything and expect nothing.'

When Imani makes it over to her friends, Renay says, 'Was that that girl from that TV show?'

'Exactly. What's the conspiracy over here?'

'We're plotting,' Stephanie says.

'That's clear. Fill me in.'

'Lee needs a support network at the yoga festival,' Katherine says. 'Alan and his new girlfriend are going to be there. She's an old rival of Lee's from way back.'

'Jesus,' Imani says. 'Alan turned out to be such a lame human being. Poor Lee.'

'I feel worse for the new girlfriend,' Katherine says. 'At least Lee has him out of her life. Except when he isn't.'

'She's a yoga star,' Stephanie says. 'New breed of celebrity.'

'And Lee's not?' Imani asks. 'She changed my crazy life. I call that star quality.'

'More reason to come,' Stephanie says. 'Plus six hours of yoga a day. What could be more fun?'

'Six hours of rest,' Imani says.

Renay turns to Katherine, and in her quiet voice, she says, 'Oh, I didn't think of that. Is it going to be okay for you to do all that yoga?'

There's an awkward moment when the music goes silent

216

and all the conversation in the room seems to stop. It lasts for only a few seconds, and then the thumping of bass and the clatter of voices returns. In that moment, Imani has a better idea of at least one of the secrets Katherine and Renay have between them. Renay clearly realizes what she's done and looks down at her feet apologetically. When Imani sees Katherine looking over her shoulder at Glenn and Conor, who are standing by the huge windows, she knows that poor Conor is in the dark about this development. Which probably means that Katherine is undecided about whether or not to have the baby.

In truth, Imani doesn't want to go to a festival of yoga in the mountains. She hates the mountains. She tends to feel closed in and anxious surrounded by all that towering granite. And she's never been good at high altitudes. As much as she's loved feeling more fit from working with Tara this past week, she's not sure she's ready to sign on for a marathon. But she's not ready to say no. She'd be surrounded by her friends, and she'd be helping out Lee. When she glances at Renay and sees the eagerness in her eyes, she hesitates.

'I'd have to bring Daniel,' she says.

Renay leaps at her and throws her arms around her neck, and Imani knows the decision has been made.

'Lee, honey,' her mother says. 'I want to have a little talk with you, and I don't want you to get upset about what I'm going to say.'

'You know, Mom, there's something about that as an opening comment that isn't very encouraging.'

'You see what I mean? You take everything the wrong way, and I haven't even begun.'

Her mother is sitting on the edge of Lee's bed, observing her while she packs for the Flow and Glow Festival. She has her legs crossed and is nursing a glass of wine. It's her second since dinner, and she's beginning to get a little vague and maudlin, alternating between sentimentality and ambiguously cutting remarks. The one thing Lee knows for sure (okay, *almost* for sure) is that her mother will cut back on the wine as soon as she leaves. She might not be the most emotionally reliable person in the world, but when it comes to taking care of the boys, she is responsible. Hopefully.

The wine and the worry about her legal problems are beginning to take their toll on Elaine's face. She was always a pretty woman, and she still is, with clear blue eyes and once-blond hair that's now a beautiful shade of silver. But she's spent too much time in the sun, and her skin is beginning to get the weathered, wrinkled look of golfers and Kennedy wives.

Lee is tidily rolling her yoga clothes so she can fit as many as possible into her suitcase. Allegedly there are laundry facilities at the accommodations the organizers are supplying, but better to be over-prepared than end up having to wear sweaty outfits.

'Go ahead, Mom,' she says. 'I really do want to hear what you have to say.'

'I know that's not true, but I'm going to tell you anyway.' Sip, sip. 'You should be dating.'

'Okay. Noted. Next?'

'Now wait a minute, Lee. You're a young, healthy woman,

and it's not good for you to be alone. There are studies about that. Especially since you don't have a pet. The kids don't count, apparently. You're in the prime of your life.'

'I'm doing okay, Mom. Honestly.'

'No, you're not. And you're not as young as you think, honey. Certain options are going to start drying up.'

Her mother always did have a way with words. Not the most appealing way, unfortunately.

'All right, Mom, whatever you say. I'll start dating as soon as I get back. Hopefully, my options won't dry up in the next five days.'

'I don't appreciate the sarcasm. I knew Alan was no good before you married him, so I have a proven track record here. I only wish I'd had the *guts* to tell you that years ago.'

Lee can hear emotion starting to well up in her mother's voice. The last thing she needs now is to have to spend the next hour attending to her mother's weeping.

'I wouldn't have listened, Mom. For better or worse, I was in love. We can't go back.'

'I know that. It's all about the future. But my point is, when I tell you that that architect fellow is interested in you, you should believe me.'

'I know he is, Mom,' she says. 'And he's a wonderful man. But I can't say I feel the same about him.'

'You're not giving him a chance. I certainly hope you don't think I loved your stepfather when I married him. I used to shudder every time Bob touched me, even just his hand brushing against mine by accident at a restaurant or in the liquor store. But over time, I started to find him less and less repulsive. So you see how nicely it worked out?'

'I'm glad you're happy, Mom.'

'Oh, Lee, that wasn't a thong you just packed, was it? Those things are awful. Bob wanted me to wear one, and I found it so uncomfortable.'

They have officially crossed deep into the TMI zone. Lee can't think of anything to change the subject, so she says, 'If you want to know the truth, Mom, there is someone I'm interested in.'

'Oh, Lee, I knew it. That's so exciting. Just promise me, *promise* it's not another yoga teacher.'

'As a matter of fact, he is.'

'You didn't learn your lesson the first time.'

'Alan is a musician. He wasn't a yoga teacher.'

'Well, he wasn't much of one, whatever he was. And I'm sure this new one doesn't have a solid income like the architect. And I really wish you'd cut down on the coffee, honey. I don't know how you don't have an ulcer. You've always got a cup in your hand.'

If Lee dared to mention her mother's wine consumption, there would be a battle raging for hours. Instead she says, 'I'm giving it up this week. As soon as I get to the festival, I'm stopping.'

'You see, I knew I was right about you being out of control. Oh, Lee, honey, I wish you wouldn't roll all those horrible stretchy clothes into little balls like that. It's bad enough you wear them, but it just looks so depressing in the suitcase like that. I'd be embarrassed to go through security in the airport.'

'It's a practical way to travel,' Lee says. 'I'm going to be spending a lot of time teaching or practicing, so I need clean clothes.'

'And that's another thing, Lee. You're working too hard. You need to hire someone to help you out with all the teaching.'

'I'm trying, Mom. It's not as easy to find good people as I thought.'

'I know. That's why I'm going to say this, so don't jump down my throat.' Her mother polishes off the rest of her wine and, after a few misses, sets the glass down on Lee's night table. 'I think you should hire Lawrence to teach at your studio.'

'Mom, come on. Lawrence is costing you tens of thousands of dollars in legal fees. For running a sex party at your house.'

'I won't put up with that kind of talk, Lee, from you of all people. It was a yoga class! Those nude classes are very popular now.'

'I know, Mom. But they went on past midnight.'

Her mother gets up off the bed unsteadily and throws her arms around Lee. 'I didn't come here to fight with you, honey. I came to help out. I only want what's best for you. I'm not trying to put any pressure on you. The fact that he'd be out of the state of Connecticut might help me, but don't even consider that. I'm just so proud of you, and all your success.'

Her mother gets weepy, triggered by the alcohol, no doubt, but always a hook for Lee. 'Have a good time with the boys,' Lee says. 'They love you, and they're really excited to have you here. And call me if you need anything.'

Elaine straightens up and dries her tears. 'Just focus on *you*, please. For once, Lee, just focus on you. I know how important this festival is for you, so just put everything else out of your mind and take care of your own needs for once. It's going to help you so much. It's all about you, baby girl.' She looks down into Lee's suitcase and takes out a white muslin blouse Lee bought last week. 'Oh, Lee, wouldn't this be cute with that skirt I wore the other day? Maybe you should leave it here instead of taking it with you. You don't want to get it dirty in the mountains.'

PART FOUR

Conor is taking Lee and Katherine to the airport in his truck. Katherine is squeezed into one of the jump seats while Lee sits in the passenger seat up front.

'You should have let me take that place,' she says to Katherine. 'You look uncomfortable.'

'You're both pretzels,' Conor says. 'It's good practice for the festival. And you should have let me drive you all the way up to Reno. I could have hung around the casinos for a few days while you sweat.'

'No way, Mr Ross,' Katherine says. 'I'm not leaving you on your own in Reno. There's a reason they call it Las Vegas's trashy little sister.'

Lee knows this is a joke. Conor is possibly the most trustworthy man Lee has ever met. Sometimes she wonders if Katherine would like it if he were a little less trustworthy. By her usual standards with men, Conor isn't much of a challenge. Earlier this morning, she gathered together as many of the scraps of paper on which she'd scrawled her lists as she could find, thinking she'd go over them on the flight. It's only now that she realizes it will be too late to do anything about it if she's forgotten something. In some ways, it feels like a wonderful luxury to know she can't fix anything now. She just has to get on the plane and be on her way. She has her notes for classes almost finished, and she figures she can spend a few more hours in the hotel putting on the final touches. After all the hesitation and doubt, she can feel herself starting to get excited. Thousands of yogis gathered in one spot, some of the best teachers in the country, music. At this point, it's hard to know why she was doubtful at all. With any luck, she'll have time to take a few classes. Maybe not Kyra's, but there are at least a dozen teachers coming that she's been curious about for years.

She's ready to start flowing. As for glowing, she's not so sure. She'll have to see how it goes with David.

Graciela is sitting in the little backyard of her mother's house in Duarte, waiting for her mother to come out so she can drive her to the mall. She's smoking. It's too hot out here in the sun and dry wind, but she's ashamed of the fact she's taken up this bad habit again, and she'd rather not deal with her mother's disapproval if she smokes on the porch.

She can't complain about her mother. The most astonishing thing is how nice she's been since Graciela moved back in. When Stephanie drove her to Duarte, her mother ran down to the sidewalk and threw her arms around her. *'Mi bebe, mi bebe',* she muttered over and over, while running her gnarled fingers over Graciela's shorn hair.

Graciela hadn't told her mother any of the specifics of what had happened to her in New York. She can't repeat any of that to anyone. It's still too painful. She can only face it in fragments. She told her mother that Daryl had come to see her and that there had been an accident and he had died. Her mother's lack of curiosity about the accident and the fact that she hadn't asked for specifics made it obvious that she knew there was more to it and that Graciela wasn't able to talk about it. Even after Stephanie had taken her to a salon, her hair was a red flag, an indication of something violent and frightening. The bruises on her face and neck have started to fade, but they were still visible when she moved out to Duarte. Her hair will grow back, her face will heal, but she knows that the experience will always be with her, that her life was changed forever in that small hotel room.

For the first week she was back here, Graciela didn't do much of anything but lie in bed, curled in on herself, trembling and afraid of the light. She's still sleeping weird amounts, more than she thought was physically possible, but she knows she's turned a corner. Every day, she feels something inside her waking up, new feelings sprouting like tender shoots. Memories are surfacing, too. The horrors, of course, but increasingly, some happy ones as well.

She can't will any memories into being; they just come unbidden, connected to a smell or a sensation. The other day, she cut herself while helping her mother prepare vegetables for a stew. She sucked on her finger, and the taste of her blood brought back images so sharp and vivid, she had to go into the other room and lie down until her breathing returned to normal. Her mother came and quietly drew the shades and closed the door for her, as if she understood.

Last night she had a dream about Jacob. They were lying side by side in hammocks, and a warm breeze was blowing over them, and when she woke up, she felt an ache for him so intense, it almost hurt. The dream obviously had to do with the aerial yoga class they'd been to. That afternoon. That last afternoon. The one that seems like a lifetime ago.

Initially, she was so numb to everything, she didn't even think about Jacob, but when she woke up this morning, the dream still fresh and real to her, she remembered that she was supposed to call him that afternoon. The afternoon Daryl showed up. What does he think happened? Did he try to get in touch with her? Did he call the hotel? There were no messages there. As for her phone, she somehow managed to slip it out of her pocket and throw it into the trash as Daryl was dragging her back to the hotel that afternoon, knowing that he would have turned it on and gone through all her messages. She tossed her lifeline into the trash, and she still doesn't know why she did it, why she was so sure that she deserved to be punished.

There's a banging on the back door, and when Graciela looks toward the house, she can see her mother trying to unlatch it. She grinds her cigarette out in the dirt and goes to open it for her.

'You ready, Mama?'

Her mother scowls. 'I've been waiting for *you*,' she says. 'I couldn't wait all day.'

'Let's go, then,' she says and starts to take her mother's arm and lead her to the car.

'You smell of cigarettes,' her mother says. 'Don't do that to yourself. Whatever it is, it's not worth it.'

As they're nearing the Mount Pleasant Vista Shopping Plaza, an ill-named spot if ever there was one, Graciela says, 'Let me buy you something pretty, Mama. Let's go to that dress shop downtown you used to like so much.'

'It's closed,' she says. 'I like Target better.' And then she reaches out and touches Graciela's arm tenderly. 'You keep your money, *bebe*. You worked hard for it. I don't need pretty dresses anymore. Buy one for yourself.'

She helps her mother get a carriage at Target, and then, daunted by the size of the store and the fact that her mother will probably be there for an hour buying things she doesn't need and will never use, she steps into the mall and starts wandering past all the chain stores selling sneakers and ugly skirts and gift items that are made to be discarded. When she spots the logo for her cell phone company, she stops short and feels something pulling at her so strongly she can't resist it.

The store is completely empty, but there's something about the corporate sterility of it that Graciela finds comforting. She feels a vague echo of the hammock in her dream and the warmth of Jacob's body against her skin. She goes up to the desk, and the round-faced girl looks up from a battered paperback, *Gone with the Wind*. The beat-up copy of this old-fashioned book, here in the middle of all this technology, makes Graciela smile for the first time in a long while.

'Need help?' the girl asks.

'I lost my phone,' Graciela says. 'A long time ago. I'm wondering . . . if I got a new one, would I still be able to get my old messages, if there were any?'

The girl gives Graciela a puzzled look, as if she doesn't understand the question.

'I mean, the messages I received while the phone was lost.'

'Yeah, I got it. Of *course* you can get your old messages,' she says. 'It happens all the time.'

'I should have figured,' Graciela says. 'So, can you help me pick out a new phone?'

The girl sticks a pen into the book and closes it. She sighs herself off her stool and says, 'That's what I'm here for.'

Imani can only hear one side of the phone conversation Renay is having with her mother, but based on that, she can guess everything that Gloria is saying.

'It's only for a few days, Mom. It's *not* a religion; it's exercise. I know I didn't used to, but maybe I'll start to like it now. Not *only* white people do it, Mom. I can't name one offhand. But I mean, look at India. No, Imani said that not *everyone's* skinny. What difference does it make, anyway? Because it sounds a lot prettier than Harriet, that's why. Besides, that's what everyone calls her. And guess who's coming with us? Becky Antrim. Of course that one. She and Imani are friends, and she's really nice. Okay, hold on.'

Renay gives Imani an apologetic look and hands her her cell phone. 'She wants to talk to you.'

The truth is, there's no way Imani isn't going to the festival, and there's no way she isn't taking Renay along with her. All she has to do in this conversation is assure her sister that everything's going to be fine. This isn't about winning and losing.

'It's obvious that this is going to happen whether I like it or not,' Gloria says, sounding much more calm than Imani expected. 'Correct?'

'It's a great opportunity for Renay. She's never been to the mountains before.'

'Oh, and I have?'

'I'm not sure what that has to do with it.'

Gloria sighs. 'You're right. It's got nothing to do with it. Is Renay there?'

'Yes.'

'Can you go to another room where she can't hear you?'

Imani goes outside and sits down by the pool. It's a warm afternoon, and there's a dry wind blowing, making her feel as if she's back in Texas. Even though she tries not to think about it, there are certain days, when the weather is like this and the air is hot and dusty, that she starts to miss home terribly. It's not as if she'd go back or as if she was especially happy when she was there, but there's a longing for that familiar world that's probably nothing more than a longing for her mother.

'I'm outside,' Imani says. 'What's up?'

Gloria takes a deep breath and says softly, 'Remember I told you Renay had some problems at school? Well, that's not the whole truth.'

'I figured that. She's read about ten books since she's been here, so the academic problems didn't sound plausible.'

'I never said she wasn't smart, Harriet. And believe it or not, I'm literate, too.'

'So what happened?'

'The whole truth is, we found out she was having sex with her boyfriend.'

That's an anticlimax! Imani is not about to tell Gloria

that she lost her virginity at fifteen, and that while she knows there are pitfalls to this, it isn't exactly a major shocker. 'I know it's not ideal,' Imani says. 'But you're not telling me that's the reason you sent her to L.A., is it?'

'We sent her to L.A. because she wasn't using birth control.'

'I'm not sure –'

'She got pregnant, Harriet.'

Imani looks into the house, where Renay is wheeling around her new suitcase, almost as if it's a toy. She's never looked more like a little girl. 'She's a kid.'

'That's right. She's a kid. So was her boyfriend.'

Imani glances into the house again and thinks about the wide patent leather belt and Renay's slim waist. 'But she's not still?'

She can hear Gloria start to cry. When Gloria cries, she makes a little panting sound, exactly the same as their mother did, and listening to it, Imani thinks back to the horrible year they lost their mother to cancer. It was the only time she and Gloria felt truly close, and Imani foolishly believed they'd had a breakthrough in their relationship and would always remain close.

'No,' Gloria says. 'She's not still. We all talked about it, we fought about it, we got advice. In the end, the boyfriend's family made sure he stopped talking to her.' She's panting more loudly now. 'It was her decision.'

'Why didn't you tell me sooner?' Imani asks.

'I couldn't,' Gloria says. 'Not after what happened to you. It's not even two years ago you had the miscarriage.'

'So why did you send her away? And to take care of Daniel?'

'I don't know. I needed time to think everything over. I was afraid I was going to say something hurtful to her. When I looked at her, I saw a different person. That she could do something like that. How could she decide to do that, Harriet?'

Inside the house, Renay has abandoned the suitcase and is now playing with Daniel. Imani is relieved to see that she looks, to her, like the same person she did a few minutes ago. She doesn't know if Gloria is talking about her daughter having sex or choosing not to go through with the pregnancy. Probably a confused blend of the two.

'She's fifteen,' Imani says. 'We just do the best we can, Gloria. We make it up as we go along, and we make mistakes, but we do the best we can.'

'You don't hate me, do you?' Gloria says. 'For sending her to you? You don't know how grateful I am to you, Harriet. Taking her in. I'm just so afraid you see a pathetic person when you look at me. You don't know what it's like, everybody asking after you all the time, telling me how gorgeous you are. And I know it's true. I'm proud of you, but sometimes I just get sick of it. That's why I say the things I do.'

'If it's any consolation,' Imani says, 'I get sick of it, too.'

'Well, that's just too bad, isn't it? It might be boring for you, but at least you get the ego trip. I get nothing good. You'll take care of her at this yoga thing, won't you?'

'You know I will.'

'Yeah, I do know. But promise me one thing, okay?'

'Whatever you want.'

'Get me Becky Antrim's autograph. On one of her photos, if you can. They're worth a fortune on eBay.'

Graciela sits on a bench outside the mall, studies her new phone, and lights up a cigarette. She swore she'd never again take up this habit once she quit, even though it's so common among the people she's been hanging out with this past year. It's practically expected of dancers, and she was always proud to be the exception. What would Lee say if she saw her smoking? Probably nothing, but she'd somehow let Graciela know that she was there to help if she wanted to stop. She's been smoking for only a few weeks, but already she can feel herself getting winded more easily and quickly. Oddly enough, there's something about the pain in her chest she feels when she breathes too deeply that pleases her. It's easier than feeling this other ache inside that has nothing to do with her lungs.

She glances at the time. With any luck at all, her mother should be done at Target in twenty minutes or so. She keeps turning the phone over and over in her hand. She knows that checking the messages will change everything for her, but she's not sure how. The girl in the store turned the phone on, and she feels the weight of it in her hand and half expects it to start ringing.

From the corner of her eye, she can see a teenager standing on the far side of the bench, watching her. She looks up, and the girl sits down warily, as far from her as possible. She's a funny, pale little thing with legs so skinny, it doesn't seem likely they support her and her hair in a bun on top of her head. Is it possible that, like Lyle (even the name brings back a horrible image of the hotel room door opening), she recognizes her from Beyoncé's concerts? She keeps glancing at Graciela furtively; finally, she says, 'Any chance I could bum a cigarette?'

Not what Graciela was expecting.

'Aren't you a little young to be smoking?'

The girl frowns at her. She has on way too much eye makeup. Without it, she'd be pretty. 'I'm trying to lose weight,' she says.

'Oh, honey,' Graciela says. 'Don't. You're too skinny already, and you're just going to end up making a mess of your body. Twenty years from now, your joints will be aching and your heart rate will be crazy. I've seen it happen. It's not worth it. Look at how beautiful you are.'

'Well, you should talk. You're smoking.'

'It's a temporary situation, and I'm trying to quit.'

The girl lets her head drop and turns her eyes to look at Graciela. 'Do you have cancer?'

'What kind of question is that? And no, I don't.'

'Sorry. It's just . . . your hair.'

Graciela runs her hand across the stubble on her scalp. 'I had an accident,' she says. 'It will grow back. You know, you'd probably feel a whole lot better if you had something to eat instead of smoking.'

The girl looks her up and down. She has that funny, piercing gaze that girls with anorexia sometimes have, as if they're trying to calculate how much of a threat you are to their dangerous, cherished disease.

'I'm a dancer,' the girl says. 'I need to stay thin. They're not supposed to tell us to lose weight at my school, but

235

the skinniest girls always get the best roles. It's just how it is. You wouldn't know.'

'Ballet?' Graciela asks. The bun is starting to make sense. The girl nods.

'You're right, I wouldn't know.'

'I hate my school. I hate the director. The other girls are all bitches. And I don't like smoking.'

'Maybe you should do something else besides dancing.'

'I can't,' the girl says. 'I love doing it too much. I love how it makes me feel when I'm doing it. I think it's just who I am.' The girl moves a little closer to Graciela on the bench. 'So . . . can I have a cigarette or not?'

It comes to Graciela in a flash.

'I'll tell you what,' she says. 'I'll give you a cigarette if you do me a favor. I haven't checked my phone in a long time, and I want to know what my messages are, but I can't really listen to them right now.'

'The accident?' the girl says.

'Pretty much. What I'd like is for you to listen for me. Tell me who each one is from and the basic idea of what they're saying, and then delete it. How's that sound?'

'I could do that.'

Graciela passes the girl her phone. It's a relief to have it out of her hands. She tells her the password and hands her a cigarette. As she's lighting it for her, the girl says, 'You're popular. Fifteen new messages. Do you want me to tell you the time and date?'

Graciela finds that she's too choked up to say anything. She shakes her head no.

'The first one's from Jacob. He says he's in the restaurant and are you okay.

'The next one's from him, too. Where are you, he's getting worried.'

Graciela watches carefully as the girl's red nails delete each message. Her last chances at hearing Jacob's voice are disappearing, one after the other.

'Now he says he's going home. You could at least call him and tell him you changed your mind. He sounds pissed off. Is he your boyfriend?'

'No, he wasn't my boyfriend. Not exactly, anyway.'

Graciela has the eerie feeling that this strange girl understands everything, maybe better than she does herself. Even as she's listening, she doesn't take her eyes off Graciela.

'This one's from somebody named Stephanie. She said she's been trying to get you. . . .'

'It's okay,' Graciela says. The girl is looking at her with big eyes, as if she's worried about her. There are probably a lot from Stephanie. 'You can delete the ones from Stephanie. You don't even have to listen.'

'Okay. Wow, she left a bunch. That's about seven in a row. So, here's one from Jacob again. He says he's in Saint . . .'

'Saint Louis.'

'He says he doesn't understand. He says . . . he says he loves you. Why would you do this to him? He says he didn't think you were like that. Are you sure you want me to listen to them all?'

'If you don't mind. I kind of need to know.'

'Why didn't you call him?' the girl asks.

'Just tell me what else is on here.'

'A bunch more from Stephanie.' The girl reaches out a

hand and puts it on Graciela's knee. She looks as if she's going to cry. 'It's Jacob. He says he's not going to call you anymore.' And now the girl really is crying, so hard she drops the cigarette onto the ground. 'He says . . . he says you're selfish and he never wants to hear from you again. He says you shouldn't treat people like that. He trusted you. . . .' The girl clicks off the phone and tosses it at Graciela. 'Why didn't you call him? Why would you do something like that and be so mean? He loved you.'

'I know he did. I loved him, too. I just couldn't call him.' Since the girl is crying so hard, Graciela finds she can't feel anything herself. She puts her arm around the girl's bony little shoulders. 'It's okay,' she says. 'Don't cry. Sometimes things aren't meant to be. Sometimes they seem perfect, but they're not. You have to let go of things sometimes.'

'But you could call him now.'

'No, I can't. Too much happened. I can't change it back.'

The girl sits up and pulls away from her. 'What was your accident?' she says, boldly, as if Graciela owes it to her to tell her. And maybe she does.

'I was a dancer, too,' she says. 'Or maybe I am. Not ballet, anyway. I'll tell you about it if you let me buy you an ice cream.'

'I don't eat that,' the girl says. And then she pulls herself together and dries off her face, smearing the eye makeup. 'I guess frozen yogurt would be okay.'

'It's a deal,' Graciela says.

*

238

Katherine opens up the blinds in her bedroom and stands back in amazement. In front of her is an uninterrupted view of mountain peaks, gray and purple against the blinding blue of the sky, and beneath that, a line of piney green. She and Lee arrived late last night, and all they could see was a dark horizon and the light in the sky fading to purple above.

Honestly, Katherine can't remember the last time she was in a place this beautiful. Her misgivings about coming, her sadness about the house, her ambivalence about the pregnancy all melt in the face of this. She opens the window and breathes in the clean, chilly air. From somewhere in the distance, she can hear the sound of an accordion playing one of those bittersweet French waltzes and the faint beat of a drum. It's like a dream.

'I don't ever want to leave,' she says out loud.

She puts on a long T-shirt, one of Conor's that he gave her as she was leaving, and goes out into the little kitchen and living room of their suite. The place has a rustic charm that's somewhere between luxury and ski-chalet tacky, but whether it's to her taste or not, it's clear that Lee is being treated well by the bookers of the festival.

She knocks lightly on the door to Lee's bedroom. There's no answer, so she pushes it open and goes to sit on her bed. 'Wake up, Miss Lee. It's a beautiful day here in paradise.'

Lee pulls a pillow over her face and groans. 'Headache,' she says.

Katherine rubs her foot under the covers. 'Maybe it's the altitude,' she says. 'We're at almost six thousand feet.'

'I think it's because I haven't had any coffee since noon yesterday. I'm giving it up.'

'You think this is the best atmosphere for that?' Katherine is thinking more about Alan and Kyra than about the mountains.

'I hope so.'

'Aspirin?'

'I don't think the headache will last that long. I should be okay once I get up and move around. Anyway, a little pain's a good reminder of why I shouldn't be drinking it in the first place.' She pulls the pillow off her face. 'Give me about five minutes and I'll be ready. I have to go to a teachers' meeting.'

'I'm going out to grab some juice,' Katherine says. 'See you in a bit.'

The festival has taken over a sprawling ski area, and their rooms are in a hotel at the base of the mountain. A Winter Olympics was once held here, and a passageway from the side of the hotel leads out into a little Alpine village, replete with stores and restaurants. The entire place has the slightly otherworldly feeling of the few ski areas Katherine has been to, as if a piece of surreal Disney World has been dragged into the crotch of these astonishing mountains on a glacier. It's after eight, and there aren't many people around, just a few tall girls in billowing pants and big sweaters, walking with the kind of poise and confidence she sees around the studio. It's what happens when you know your body well and actually like it. They're teachers, no doubt, since the festival itself doesn't get under way until tomorrow.

She steps into a little storefront that has a blackboard

240

outside advertising 'Breakfast Asana Special'. This turns out to be a costly variation on an Egg McMuffin – there's avocado instead of bacon, and the price tag is $8.99. She gets an orange juice for herself and orders something for Lee called a Greener Cleaner: lettuce, carrots, spinach, kale, cucumber, and ginger. An entire garden. Lee needs all the help detoxing she can get, especially if she's about to bump into her wonderful ex-husband.

She sits down at a little table outside, partly in the shadow of the buildings, and starts sipping her OJ. The scene in the Reno airport was pretty crazy, a disorienting jumble of rabid gamblers hunched over the slot machines that clutter the terminal, cigarettes in hand, and yogis from all over the country arriving in stretch pants and belted sweaters, yoga mats slung over their shoulders. She saw several who were barefoot – oh so affected, but sweet anyway. *I love this*, she thought. She was tempted to join them and kick off her sandals, but she doesn't love athlete's foot.

She and Lee rented a car, and she was the one who got behind the wheel and drove. They were warned that it's a twisty road over the mountains and that it can be danger-ous, especially at night.

'Conor has been giving me lessons,' she told Lee. 'I'm happy to drive.'

When the road got to be challenging, she pretended that Conor was sitting beside her, gently urging her on and convincing her that everything was going to be just fine. As soon as she got into bed, she took out her phone and contemplated calling him and telling him she's preg-nant, but every time she put in his number, she stalled. At the very least, it would be nice to hear his voice now.

'Don't even think about calling. The reception in this part of the village is terrible.'

She turns and smiles at the man at the next table. 'Thanks for letting me know,' she says. 'I was a little ambivalent about making the call anyway.'

'Problem solved,' he says. He winks at her and holds out his hand. 'I'm Jake. Are you here for the yoga?'

'Isn't everyone?'

This seems to strike him as funny. 'Not really. Some of us actually *work* here, girl. Let's put it this way. If you get stuck on that' – he points to the gondola, which appears to be floating up the side of the mountain like a dirigible – 'I'm going to be one of the people that gets blamed for not having done his job.'

'In that case, I hope you're really good at what you do.'

'I'm incredible.'

Jake is a weathered guy in a flannel shirt, obviously a ski bum who figured out a way to live his life on and around the slopes. He's a little more wholesome than the men Katherine used to go for in the days before she straightened herself out and met Conor, but there's something familiar in the haggard, slightly arrogant look in his eyes. What is it, she wonders, that she still finds appealing about this kind of guy? They're unreliable, self-absorbed, and irresponsible. On top of that, they're usually so focused on themselves, they're disappointing in bed. Maybe it's the fantasy that you can actually change them or at least get the upper hand and teach them a lesson.

He's a reminder of how lucky she is to have found Conor. Attractive? She'll give him that, but not tempting.

'I've never been up in a gondola,' Katherine says. 'I'm not really the skiing type.'

'You'll be on one this weekend. Half the classes are being held up at the summit.'

Jake is decked out in full cowboy regalia, including boots and a pair of tight, muddy jeans. She would bet anything he's from some pampered California suburb, or maybe one of those rich yachting towns in Maine.

'Should be good views,' Katherine says.

'From what I've seen so far,' he says with a wink, 'the views will be *excellent* this weekend.'

She laughs at the comment. It's so obvious, so tacky, it's almost charming. And then, feeling a little reckless and giddy in the mountain air, she slaps his thigh. 'On that note, Jake, I think I better head off. I have to get this back to a friend. She's got a headache. Maybe I'll see you around.'

'I'll make sure of it.'

From her place on the ground at the back of the tent, Lee can see a green field and the mountains beyond. There are about a dozen yoga teachers on the stage, many of them such familiar faces that Lee gets a thrill from the sight of them, the same way she got a thrill when Imani first came into Edendale with Becky Antrim in tow. Or, for that matter, the first time Imani came alone. There's a strong, fresh breeze blowing through the tent, making its material ripple and snap. Between this noise and the fact that the sound system, which clearly needs some tweaking, keeps cutting in and out, Lee is having a hard time hearing the welcome speeches. Even so, she's getting the gist of it.

'You're here now, and we are as excited to be . . . as we hope you . . . here in this glorious . . .'

There are about a hundred people gathered under the tent, and from what she can tell, most of them are teachers. She sees some familiar faces from studios she's visited around L.A. and a few that she's pretty sure she saw in the pages of *Yoga Journal*. But whether they're teachers or volunteers, there's no doubt about the fact that she's in a room full of yogis – not a slouch in sight.

'. . . you want to run your classes, we're here for you with . . . and all of the . . . But students love it if you include more nature metaphors than usual. To help bring the spirit of the . . .'

The speaker, the infamous Krishna O'Reilly, if Lee heard correctly, stops talking and storms over to the person sitting at the soundboard. He looks a little red faced as he scolds the poor guy, and then the words 'fire your fucking ass' come through the speakers loud and clear.

'I guess we got that problem solved,' he says, and the audience applauds.

The young woman on the ground next to her says, 'I just signed up for one of your classes. Tomorrow morning.'

'Thank you,' Lee says. 'Are you a teacher?'

'Not yet. I'm thinking about enrolling in a teacher-training program, but I haven't decided which one. I'm here volunteering.'

'From L.A.?'

'Chicago. A friend of mine told me she thought I needed to get my sparkle back, so I figured doing a ton of yoga in the mountains and dancing all night was a good place to start. I was going to go to Burning Man, but I have really dry skin, so all that sand put me off.'

'I hope you like the class.'

'I'm sure I will. I tried to sign up for about six other ones, but they were all sold out, so I was thrilled to get anything. And don't worry, I have low expectations.'

She says this with such openness and lack of malice, Lee starts to laugh, even though doing so makes her headache worse. 'Low expectations are good. And who knows? Maybe I'll exceed them.'

The woman, who appears to be in her early twenties and has a pink face and a boy's crew cut, opens up a green messenger bag she's carrying and takes out a folder of papers. 'If I'd met you earlier, I'd have signed up right away. You have great energy. Here are the class enrollment lists. We have to check off every person as they come in.' She flips through the pages, many of them covered with names in tiny print, until she comes to Lee's. 'You've got thirty-three people enrolled so far for your first class.' She nods toward the stage, where the headliners are sitting. 'They've got hundreds, but, you know, Baron Baptiste has been on QVC a bunch, so what can you expect? I heard from some of the volunteers who've been here before that if you end up teaching in an empty tent, it's really bad for your career. Word gets around, and you get a reputation for being unpopular. So thirty-three isn't too, too bad. More will come if word of mouth is good.'

It never occurred to Lee – or to Lainey, apparently – that there might be a downside to teaching at Flow and Glow.

Krishna O'Reilly is introducing the headliners, and the

room erupts in applause at the mention of each name. She takes a bit of spiteful pleasure in the fact that the sound cuts out again in time for Kyra's introduction, but she bounds out of her chair with such exuberance that Lee gets caught up in the excitement and applauds loudly. She's more beautiful than Lee remembers. She has on a pair of white yoga pants that look as if they were stitched onto her body, and a long-sleeved scoop-necked top in a color that so closely resembles her skin tones, she appears at first to be topless. Maybe she overdid it a little with the blond highlights, but when she tosses her hair over her shoulder, it creates a pretty striking effect.

What is she thinking getting involved with Alan?

'I love Kyra,' the girl with the papers says. 'She has such a beautiful aura. Especially since she became a priestess. I heard she's with a really hot guy. An amazing musician. He and a band are going to be playing at her classes. Will you have live music?'

'I'm afraid not. Unless something comes up.'

'You should try to arrange something. They've got you teaching in the big tent on the last day. It might get more people in. You've got . . . thirty-seven signed up for that class.'

'How many people does the tent hold?'

'Three hundred. Four if they put people in the sun.'

Lee feels her headache start to throb. Four hundred people? And she has only thirty-seven signed up?

When the meeting ends, Lee races off to the back of the tent and leaves a message for Lainey. 'What have you gotten me into?' she says. 'I hope this plan doesn't backfire.'

As she's finishing up on the call, she looks up and sees

246

Kyra coming toward her, hair flying in her face in the warm breeze.

'Oh my God, Lee,' she says. She wraps Lee in a tight, geranium-scented embrace. 'I was so excited to hear you were coming. I didn't think this was the kind of scene you liked. I thought you were so low-key.'

Maybe it's the smell of the geranium oil Kyra's wearing, or maybe it's just that they've finally had their dreaded encounter, but Lee starts to feel some of her tension dissipating. When all is said and done, Kyra is just another teacher, and if she weren't a good one, she wouldn't be where she is.

'I have a few surprises,' Lee says.

Kyra laughs. It's one of those high, musical laughs that people give when they know they're being watched and want to appear good-humored. 'I just want to make sure this isn't awkward for you in *any* way, Lee. There's no reason it should be. I know we're really different people, but we have more in common than you probably think. When Alan took me in to see your house, I loved your taste. Honestly, I was surprised at how much I loved it. That little couch thing in your study? So cute!'

'To tell you the truth,' Lee says, 'this probably isn't the best time to talk about it. I'm giving up coffee, and I've got a bit of a headache.'

'Oh, that explains it,' Kyra says. 'When I saw you, I was afraid there was something really wrong with you. I just wanted to say, if you ever have any problems with the house, let me know. I would love to buy it. And the kids would be able to stay there instead of the trauma of seeing it sold to a stranger.'

'That's kind of you,' Lee says.

Kyra gets dragged off by a fan and Lee steps out into the bright light. Although she can feel the sun burning on her skin, the air is still cool and filled with a piney sweetness. She looks up at the mountain and sees the gondola making its way up the steepest part of the ascent. From this angle, it looks as if it's going to smash into the rock face of the peak. Then it lifts into the air and disappears over the top of the mountain.

The narrow pedestrian streets of the village are beginning to fill up with people, and there's a feeling of excitement and anticipation that's building. Men are setting up tables in little tents, getting ready to sell. Corporate sponsors. Not what she imagined when she was studying with her teacher on Long Island, but if this is the future, she's going to have to adapt.

She feels a tap on her shoulder, but before she can turn around, a pair of hands is clamped over her eyes. 'Guess who?' she hears.

She doesn't have to guess. She's been waiting to hear DT's voice since she arrived.

It was Becky Antrim's idea to rent a minivan and drive to the Flow and Glow Festival instead of flying, and Stephanie has ended up spending the entire seven hours behind the wheel. Becky is a fast, erratic driver who tends to take chances while talking with excitement and gesturing with her hands; Imani is hesitant and a little too cautious, often staying dangerously below the speed limit; and Renay doesn't have her license. It makes Stephanie feel like an outsider to be in the driver's seat, like the hired hand, but there's a certain amount of pleasure in being in control and watching the scenery fly past. According to her GPS, the house they've rented is about twenty minutes away, and after being cooped up for so long, everyone is starting to get giddy in anticipation of arriving.

'If this place turns out to be horrible, don't blame me,' Becky says. 'One of Chelsea's friends who comes here in the winter recommended it to me. It looked nice in pictures, but you never know.'

'We're spending most of our time at the festival, anyway,' Imani says. 'If we were going to hang out in the house, we could have had a sleepover at your place, Becky.'

'I saw the spread they did on it in *Architectural Digest*,' Stephanie says, a comment that leaves her feeling more like a fan than a friend.

'You are going to love the classes I signed us up for,' Becky says. 'I pulled a lot of strings to get us in at the last minute. In four days, we're going to sample most of the superstars in the business.'

Imani and Renay are sitting in the backseat with Daniel in his car seat between them. Stephanie has caught Imani in the rearview mirror looking tenderly at her niece, as if something has changed in a big way over the past week or two since the shoot ended. Even Renay has started to look more beautiful and relaxed.

Becky's in the passenger seat with the window down and her famous hair blowing all over her face. The thing about Becky is that, in addition to being gorgeous, she always smells good, as if she's just rubbed herself with lemons and peonies. When they made their most recent bathroom and fuel stop, she beckoned to Stephanie from the side of the gas station and asked her if she wanted to share a joint.

'Designated driver,' Stephanie said.

'I understand,' Becky replied, inhaling deeply. 'But if you get tired, just ask me to take over. I love driving when I'm stoned. I space out and pretend I'm flying a jet. Especially up in the mountains.'

'I'll let you know.'

'And listen,' Becky said, 'I heard they're making threats about the screen credit. Nothing to worry about. If it comes down to it, they count words to determine, and it sounds like you're covered. I've got a lot of people who could help you out with this. The director is just stamping his feet like a brat.'

'He has been from the start,' Stephanie said. 'I don't know what he has against me.'

Becky took another drag off the joint, this one so powerful that the whole thing, paper and all, seemed to morph into a glowing ember.

'One of the great things about doing so much yoga,' she said, 'is that it increased my lung capacity amazingly. What were we talking about?'

'Rusty Branson. The director.'

'Right. From what I hear, he's a misogynist and a homophobe. A friend of mine, gay, who was in his first movie – totally overrated, by the way, in my humble opinion – got a creepy vibe from him. So, who knows?'

Stephanie gave a noncommittal shrug. What she wanted to ask Becky is what makes her think that Rusty being a homophobe would have anything to do with her.

The road has become winding, and they make one dramatic turn and see in front of them the expanse of the lake, shimmering in surreal tones of electric blue and green, surrounded by mountains. None of them has been up here to the Sierras before, and they all give off oohs and ahs, as if they're watching fireworks. Even Becky, who's pretty much seen everything, is impressed. Then the road turns and the lake disappears.

'I love a good tease,' Becky says.

'It's the second-deepest lake in the country,' Stephanie tells them. 'And one of the biggest. The water quality was so good, you used to be able to see down hundreds of feet.'

'Somebody did her homework,' Imani says.

'I'm a map freak and information nerd,' Stephanie replies. 'Don't get me started.'

A few minutes later, they pull into a steep drive and enter the deep, fragrant shade of pine trees. As the drive continues, it brings them down to the lakefront and then the house. As soon as Stephanie stops the van, Becky leaps out. 'I'm sorry,' she says. 'It's smaller than I thought.'

Renay has already dashed out of the car and up onto the deck, and seems to be whooping out at the water.

'I think that means she likes it,' Imani says.

'Have you been to Flow and Glow before?' Lee asks David.

He laughs at this. 'No!' he says with such vehemence, it's almost as if she's accused him of something. 'This isn't exactly my scene, Lee. I'm an off-the-grid kind of guy, and this is about as mainstream as it gets.'

Is she supposed to understand, then, that he really did come solely to see her?

They are strolling around the grounds of the festival, and as more and more vendors are setting up their tents and the alleyways through the mock Alpine village are filling with people, it is beginning to feel like a true gathering. Street musicians are playing on the corner with a group of barefoot girls in long skirts dancing joyfully in front of them. Even if the volunteer she talked to at the meeting signed up for her class by default, she recognized Lee, and there's no denying it's a thrill to think that others here might, too.

Off in the distance is a huge white tent, so sprawling and tall against the brown of the mountains, it almost looks like a Quonset hut. 'I heard that tent holds about three hundred people,' David says. 'I'm not sure how I'd deal with a class that size. It seems more like a performance than teaching.'

Three people dressed in Renaissance fair outfits walk past them, leaving in their wake the tinkle of bells and a strong smell of pot. One of them is twirling a hula hoop with ribbons tied around it on a wrist held high above her head. No, not David's scene, and not hers, either.

'I just found out I'm going to be teaching there,' she says. 'I'm not happy about it. It looks like a stadium.'

'Someone has faith in you,' David says. 'Enjoy it. Pretend you're Kyra Monroe.'

'Have you taken classes with her?' Lee asks.

'Not really my style. A little flashy for my tastes.'

'She and my ex-husband are seeing each other,' she says. Did she say this to get his sympathy, or to make sure

David doesn't change his mind and go running off to become one of Priestess Kyra's groupies?

'Your ex is coming down in the world,' he says.

'I just talked with her. She's nicer than I remembered, even if she did say I look like hell.'

David laughs at this, too. 'What you don't understand,' he says, 'is that people are intimidated by you. You have this decency that comes off you in waves.' He steps in and hugs her, but only briefly and in a friendly way. 'It's like holding up a mirror to someone's phoniness. Kyra Monroe probably thinks you see through her, and she hates the way it makes her feel.'

'Is that how you think of me?' she asks. 'You think I'm judging you?'

'Of course not. I wouldn't be here if I did.'

Of all the ways she hates feeling, confused is probably at the top of her list. But that's how she feels with David right now. He's being kind to her and flattering her, but it's not clear what any of that means to him. He has an appealing boyish quality, but it makes a lot of his behavior seem as if he's just playing.

'Why *are* you here, David?'

He links his arm with hers and says, 'I told you. I wanted to come take your class. If you want, we can walk over to the tent so you can get the lay of the land.'

Lee is beginning to think she'll never get a direct answer from David, and it might be simplest to stop asking questions.

They walk along a path through a field of yellow grass and wildflowers until they get to the tent. It's partly open on all sides and the wind from the mountain is blowing through. As for the size, it's even more daunting up close, the roof soaring up to at least fifty feet. She doesn't know what frightens her more – the idea of teaching here with thirty-seven people dwarfed by the massive canopy, or the idea of standing in front of a full house.

Someone on the stage is doing a sound check, and in the background, she can hear the drone of a harmonium and guitars being tuned. 'It's not me,' someone says into the mike. 'This guy's G is flat, and I'm not rehearsing until we get it right.'

One of the more excruciating aspects of watching Alan perform with other musicians was that he was always blaming other people for being out of tune. Apparently, some things never change. He's standing at the side of the stage dressed all in white, a costume that makes him look like a cross between a guru and an ER nurse.

'Let's do one more check,' a voice says.

'No. 'Fraid not,' Alan says. 'Kyra, get up here.'

From somewhere behind the stage, Kyra appears, and Lee realizes that they're in matching costumes. 'If Alan says he's in tune, he's in tune, guys. Deal with it.'

David pulls Lee against him and says quietly, 'Cute couple.'

That moment, for better or worse, is when Kyra spots them from the stage and gives a big wave. She goes over to one of the microphones and says, 'How do you like this tent, Lee? Pretty nice, isn't it?'

'Beautiful,' Lee shouts out. 'I'm not sure I'll need all the space, but we'll see.'

Alan gives a halfhearted salute from the stage and then goes off, no doubt to discreetly retune his flat G.

'You'll love it,' Kyra says into the mike. 'They were going to put you in a smaller venue for your last class, but I insisted they give you this one. I have the class right after, so Alan and I are planning to attend. Or, if it's too crowded, at least watch from the back.' She shades her eyes with her hand. 'Alan didn't tell me you were seeing someone. Come on up here so I can meet your boyfriend. He looks cute. That's not David Todd, is it?'

'Sorry about that,' Lee says quietly.

'I've had a lot worse things said about me,' David replies. 'Let's go so I can at least tell my grandchildren I met her.'

Katherine's first class the next morning is a sunrise flow on the top of the mountain. She gets up before five so she can have time to read the book Renay gave her last week for the prescribed amount of time. Since this is a vacation of sorts, she could probably skip the routine, but she's become attached to it. She's decided that reading is like going to yoga classes: you enter into another world with its own set of characters and problems and challenges; while you're there, you're taken away from the concerns of your daily life, and when you emerge, you have pieces – scraps, really – of new information that start to inform your thinking, even if you didn't realize you were picking them up along the way.

Renay has been canny with her book selections, choosing for her novels that aren't too difficult and manage to touch on some of her own problems and experiences – recovering from addiction, the pitfalls of real estate, even one about a massage therapist. She's not sure about the current book, though, a novel about a young woman who finds an abandoned dog outside the supermarket two days after her husband leaves her for someone else. The woman is one of those sad characters who are always putting themselves down, and the pathetic dog is so traumatized, Katherine cringes every time she reads about him.

When she gets up, she has the queasy feeling in her stomach that she's been having for the past few weeks. Morning sickness, she supposes, but nothing as severe as a lot of women report. She's been tempted to go online and do a little research about what, if anything, this means, but she's resisted thus far. She doesn't want to make this any more real and emotional than it has to be. She abused drugs and alcohol for so many years in that dark, grim period of her life, it doesn't seem possible that her body could actually produce a healthy baby. 'They can test for all kinds of things,' Lee told her. But in many cases, not until it's too late, and by that point, she will have inflicted her own bad choices on another person. But even thinking that concretely about the 'other person' makes her uneasy.

She grabs her mat, her water bottle, and a bag with a few T-shirts, towels, and the book. She's going to be practicing all day, a thought that cheers her up right away. For almost six hours, she won't be thinking about anything but balance and breath.

The sky is beginning to light up in the east, but outside, it's still freezing. The narrow streets of the village are jammed with happy, sleepy people dressed in a weird combination of skimpy yoga outfits, mittens, and big furry hats that look like bears' heads. It's circus time, and she loves a good high-wire act.

At the base of the gondola, she gets in line with a crowd waiting to board. She casts a quick glance around, just to make sure her eager friend from yesterday isn't here. Jake. The last thing she needs in her life right now is a cowboy ski bum named Jake.

Once everyone is packed into the gondola so tightly they're nearly shoulder to shoulder, mats bumping against each other, a thin, pimply boy announces that he's Robert and will be their 'driver'. It's not a reassuring thought. But the car begins to move, silently and swiftly, and Katherine is swept away by the scenery as the ground falls off beneath them. Within seconds, the clutter of the village is insignificantly small, and they are floating in the crisp, thin air.

The talk around her is all about which famous yoga teacher someone spotted the night before.

'I swear it was Baron Baptiste at the table next to me last night, and it looked like he was eating a hamburger.'

'I heard from someone Shiva Rhea was out on the balcony of her room dancing right before dawn.'

'Do you think Duncan Wong wears eye makeup? I was two feet from him last night. He's so sexy.'

Katherine's standing at the very back of the car, looking out toward the lake, which has suddenly become visible in the distance, like a shimmering emerald. Conor, she thinks, would love this.

'Hey folks,' she hears. 'Can we have a moment of silence?'

The voice is unquestionably Alan's. She'd know that

obnoxious nasal tone straining for melodic masculinity anywhere. She turns and there he is, standing in the front, almost ruthlessly handsome, his arm around Kyra. They're both draped in white cotton, and Kyra has a gauzy shawl over her hair. What next, a nun's habit?

'There are maybe sixty or seventy people here,' he says. 'How about we all breathe in together and let out a collective om?'

It's amazing what people will do when they're confined in a small space with someone who seizes the role of leader. Within seconds, the car is filled with the voices of all seventy people chanting in unison. Katherine can feel the vibration deep within her. And just because she doesn't want to feel completely left out, she joins in.

There are a few nervous giggles afterward, and then Alan says, 'Thank you, yogis and yoginis. I needed that.'

Well, yes, and of course it *is* all about him.

'And can we have a round of applause for my beautiful friend, Priestess Kyra Monroe? If anyone isn't signed up for her classes, I've got the schedule here. Except they're all sold out anyway, folks, so good luck with trying to get in.'

Kyra is one of those smug, pretty women who look at you with a glow of beneficence, as if they're doing you a favor by letting you see their beauty. She's standing beside Alan with a vague look in her eyes, and what Katherine wonders is how it's possible that so many people can't see through her. Priestess? Why not goddess?

Alan is handing out flyers at the exit of the gondola, and when he spots Katherine, he frowns and shakes his head. 'You and Lee still travel as a pair, I see. Though from what I saw yesterday, she threw you over for that weasel David Todd. Sorry, Kat.'

So David Todd is here after all. Funny that Lee didn't mention it to her.

'Nice om, Alan,' she says. 'First time I've ever heard you on key.'

There's a swimming pool and an ice skating rink on top of the mountain, giving the whole chilly world up here an air of over-the-top decadence. Her class is on a deck overlooking the lake and the white specks of the buildings below. The teacher is from San Francisco, no one Katherine has heard of, but Lee recommended her as a solid, serious practitioner. There are only about twenty people spread out on their mats on the deck, and it looks a little skimpy. She can see hundreds of people streaming into a tent behind the swimming pool for a class with Taylor Kendall, a celebrity teacher famous for his sexual metaphors and amazing pectorals.

Katherine's teacher looks at her class and smiles.

'A small group,' she says, 'but a select group.'

Katherine feels a little lightheaded from the altitude. At the summit, they're at almost nine thousand feet. She can feel her heart beating more rapidly as they do their sun salutations, but along with it, she feels more clear. Not about her own life, but about the fact that she isn't going to let Alan and Kyra lead Lee into a trap. She can't cough up two million to save her own house, but she can make sure that Lee has a full class so she gets to stay in hers.

*

As Stephanie was driving the minivan to the festival grounds, she spotted the river beside the road, a wide stretch of rushing water dotted with people in kayaks, bobbing with the current. Then she did a double take and realized that the banks of the river were lined with people in bathing suits doing yoga poses on the rocks, backs arched, limbs extended.

'We're headed in the right direction,' she said. 'Check it out.'

'Should we stop and watch?' Renay asked.

'Let's hurry,' Becky said. 'I don't want to miss anything.'

Now they're strolling along the streets of the Alpine village with half an hour to kill before their first classes. There are so many people crowded into the narrow, shadowy passageways, the scene brings Stephanie back to a family trip she took as a kid to Morocco. She and her brother and parents spent days wandering through the medinas of Marrakech and Fez, buying blankets, djellabas, leather slippers with curled, pointy toes, capes, and other things they realized, as soon as they unpacked them, they would never use.

Marrakech has nothing on this place. The vendors here are at least as aggressive, and the goods are even more impractical. And irresistible. And come to think of it, not so different from what she remembers of Morocco: long capes, whimsical floppy hats, leather belts with studs and buckles and hardware covering every inch, and an infinite variety of skirts and dresses made of shredded jersey and chiffon with wildly irregular hemlines.

There's a whole subset of apparel and accoutrements that fall into the 'fairy princess' category: Mylar capes, wings covered in paillettes and fake fur, feather boas, and a range of wands, halos, crowns, and bejeweled hula hoops. A cadre of young women is parading around the village in these princess getups, skipping and blowing bubbles and casting spells on each other with wands. Somehow or other, Stephanie's going to get this into her next script. Assuming she has the discipline to get back to it.

'Pretty ladies,' one of the vendors calls out, 'you've got to check out these dresses.'

It's funny how you can know you're being reeled in and at the same time find the bait irresistible. Imani checks her watch, and they wander into the Matra-Mia tent.

'These clothes are so amazing,' the salesgirl says. 'All designed by a woman in Bolinas, and every one is a little bit different. The designs are incredible, because depending on how you wrap them, they can be casual or formal or flirty. You'll see a lot of people practicing in them, too.'

Becky holds a dress against her flawless body. Stephanie can't decide if it looks sexy or as if her cats took their claws to it.

'Stevie Nicks lives,' Becky says.

She's wearing sunglasses and a bandanna she's tied around her head in a complicated way to disguise her famous hair. As they were driving in, she pulled out a lipstick and applied it in a way that did a subtle but effective job of changing the look of her mouth and, to some extent, her whole face. She's not unrecognizable, but she blends in with the other gorgeous women wandering around the festival.

Even so, once she opens her mouth, the salesclerk gives her a sly, suspicious look.

'Somehow,' she says, 'I can't see myself in this.'

'Oh come on,' Stephanie says. 'You can get away with anything.'

The salesclerk has wandered off to the side of the tent and is in deep conversation with a girl who looks like her blond twin.

'And don't look now, but I think they saw through your lipstick.'

'I didn't really want this, anyway,' Becky says. 'Renay and Imani, let's go.'

By the time they've put back the dress, a small crowd has gathered outside the tent, trying to look casual, if you can look casual with your iPhone perched at the ready for a photo op. Becky throws her arm around Stephanie in a way that's a hybrid of friendly and lascivious.

'Send me a copy of the picture,' Becky says.

'You'll be able to see it on TMZ,' someone calls out.

'It's the best way to start generating some press for your movie,' Becky says. 'It's so easy to manipulate the press once you get used to it. And so fun!'

They're headed to a class inside one of the lodges, taught by a guy named Lenny Hogan, who famously overcame a wide range of drug and alcohol problems through yoga. He's not young, and although an amazing practitioner, he's not someone you'd peg as an athlete, with his gray hair and his lumpy, middle-aged body. Stephanie has been hearing about him for years and found his story inspiring, given her own struggle with alcohol.

The class is packed, and the room, with its soaring ceiling and wall of glass looking out to the mountains, is warm. She and Becky take a spot toward the front, near an open door where a breeze is blowing in, while Imani and Renay find places in the back.

Becky spreads out her mat and then nods toward the door, winks, and disappears. Leave it to Becky to get stoned before a class taught by a recovering addict. Lenny is at the front of the room testing out the sound system with a couple of assistants. Occasionally some snippet of classic rock comes blasting out of the speakers. Are they really going to practice yoga to Jefferson Starship? She spots Katherine on the far side of the room and waves her over.

'I didn't know you were taking this class,' Stephanie says.

'With my backstory,' Katherine says, 'you didn't think I'd miss out on this guy's routine, did you? We should talk after class. We have to figure out a way to help out Lee.'

By the time Becky comes back in, looking more adorable than ever with a loopy grin on her face, the speakers are blasting Crosby, Stills, Nash and Young, and Katherine is back on her mat.

Lenny is making his opening comments.

'So this is the music I listened to in my youth, huddled over a hash pipe or cutting up lines of coke and worse. It used to be that every time I heard this music, I'd flash back to those days and start to cringe. You want to know why we're doing yoga to rock and roll today? It's to reclaim the music and turn it into a soundtrack of this celebration of life, instead of triggering memories of an attempt to shut off life. Are you ready to get moving?'

Rock and roll has never been Stephanie's music. She always found the electric guitars and driving bass too loud and jarring. But she heard it growing up because it was her father's favorite. Her crew-cut, military-man dad, straight as an arrow in every way possible, used to listen to the loudest and most blaring rock he could find. And so when she hears the opening chords of 'Purple Haze' as she's trying to lift herself up into the first crow pose she's done in about four months, she's overcome with a nostalgic ache and a longing for her childhood. She falls down on her butt with an embarrassing crash. Why is she so damned secretive about everything, whether it's good or bad? Maybe Roberta is right about her being too closeted. She hitches her knees into her armpits again and tries to press up into the pose. This time she falls forward and nearly lands on her nose. Becky, she notices, is practically levitating. That's what she wants, that feeling of weightless freedom.

She's getting into position once again when Lenny comes over to her, puts his hands on her shoulders, and bends down so he can talk to her softly.

'Don't try so hard,' he says. 'Just relax and enjoy the music and let it happen. It's only work until you realize the lock is on the inside of the cage.'

He gives her shoulders a squeeze and a little massage with his thumbs, and then walks on. The music shifts, and suddenly Joni Mitchell is singing 'California' from *Blue*, Stephanie's favorite album of all time.

The lock is on the inside of the cage? What the hell is that supposed to mean? She struggles up once more, but this time, as she's about to try and power into the pose, she gets it. Maybe the weightless freedom she's looking for isn't in the pose itself but in freeing herself from the desire to do it. If she's locked into trying to do this, it's within her power to open the cage. No matter how much Rusty Branson is judging her, it's nothing compared with the extent to which she's judging herself.

Joni is singing the perfect accompaniment: *Will you take me as I am? Will you, will you . . .*

And then, maybe for the first time ever, she feels a tremendous surge of power in deciding that she isn't even going to *try* this particular pose again today. She's opening the big, fat, metaphoric cage.

She lies down in child's pose, and her spirits start to levitate as her body sinks into the floor.

Imani was planning to check in on Daniel between classes. She wasn't so sure about the day-care center where they dropped him off. A few too many eager costumed girls, and she wasn't convinced the baby hammocks they had hanging between the trees were secure. But she hates the idea of looking like a neurotic mother, so she swallows her worry and goes with everyone else to sit in the makeshift food court and try to concoct a plan to help Lee.

'She's a great teacher,' Becky says. 'She'll get good word of mouth, and her classes will start growing.'

'True,' Katherine says. 'But they can't grow fast enough to fill a huge tent by Sunday.'

Becky seems to be mulling this over as she chews her way through lunch, a plate of 'lasagne' from the raw food truck. The dish has something to do with thin-sliced squash and, as far as Imani can tell, absolutely nothing to do with lasagne.

'Any ideas?' Imani asks. She reaches over and grabs from Becky's plate a piece of kale that's trying to pass itself off as a chip. Surprisingly delicious. Deep-fry it and it would be really good.

'Alan was passing out flyers for Kyra's class this morning,' Katherine tells them. 'We could go into town and have some printed up.'

'I'm not sure; it sounds too efficient,' Stephanie says. 'If someone was handing out a flyer, it wouldn't necessarily make me want to go to a class.'

Imani checks her watch. She has fifteen minutes to get to her next class. Rock and roll wasn't what she was expecting at a yoga festival, but the music got her energy spiking, and she's ready for more.

It's Renay who speaks up next, a surprise, since she's been so quiet all morning. 'What would make me want to go is if I knew Imani Lang and Becky Antrim were going to be in the class. It's like a celebrity endorsement.'

'Anybody got a bullhorn?' Imani asks. 'I've always wanted to be a barker.'

'I've got a Twitter account,' Becky says. 'That could be a start.'

'How many followers?' Renay asks.

'I'm bad with numbers. Unless it's my salary. I guess it's something like two million.'

'I'd say that's a great start,' Katherine says. 'Just keep it quiet around Lee.'

'Oh, right,' Becky says. 'She has that thing. What's it called? Integrity?'

*

266

Ever since she got the phone messages, Graciela has been going out. Not exactly big excursions, but leaving her mother's house every day and driving to a store or a park. Yesterday, she went for a short jog. Not quite successful, but she felt better at the end than she had at the start. It was a beginning. She expected to feel abandoned by Jacob, but instead, the messages made her feel strangely liberated. She doesn't have that to wonder about and wait for anymore. It is finished.

When she got into her car today, she had no idea where she was going, and so it was almost a surprise when she found herself driving to downtown L.A. and pulling over across the street from the building where she had lived for two years. With him. With Daryl. She hasn't been back here in so many months it's almost hard to realize it was ever home. She looks up to the top floor of the building and picks out the windows of the loft. The shades are down, those ridiculously expensive wooden blinds she got as soon as she passed the audition for the Beyoncé video.

She parks the car and walks down the hot sidewalk, barely aware of the people brushing against her. In the lobby of the building, she's awakened by the familiar smell of varnish and the cleaner the superintendant uses on the tile floors. Her heart was racing outside, but an unexpected calm comes over her as she walks up the big metal staircase that hangs in the middle of the building. Daryl would have left the loft in a hurry. He would have left his clothes scattered all over the floor and the bed, towels in the bathroom, dishes and glasses everywhere, and food rotting in the refrigerator. It will look as if he's just stepped out for a few minutes. He was there alone for all those months she was on the road. It will smell of his clothes and his soap. She has to prepare herself. Maybe it would be better if someone were with her, but she's here now, and she needs to do this.

The hallway upstairs is hot and reeks of the floor cleaner. She turns her key in the lock, and as if she's in a dream, she walks into the loft. The blinds are slanted in such a way that sunlight is streaming in and making a dazzling glare on the polished floor. For a moment, she's blinded. She goes to the window and cranks the blinds closed, and the big open space becomes darker. When her eyes adjust and she turns to look, she sees that the room is spotless. Everything is so clean and tidy, it almost looks like one of those many hotel rooms she stayed in all those months. Or like the rooms in Jacob's spotless apartment. Except she isn't going to think of that. Is it even remotely possible that Daryl cleaned everything like this before he left? As far as she knew, he didn't have a clue how to use a vacuum cleaner.

She goes over to the bed. It's made up with freshly laundered sheets that are stretched tight. The pillows are plumped and arranged against the headboard. She sits on the edge of the mattress and presses her fingers against her eyelids. Maybe she *is* dreaming this. The loft smells of furniture polish and some kind of minty air freshener.

She opens the bottom drawer of the dresser, the one Daryl kept his clothes in. It's empty. In the closet, her clothes are hanging tidily, and her shoes are lined up on the floor. Otherwise it, too, is empty.

In the bathroom, she pulls open the medicine cabinet

and sees that only her things are there. The white porcelain of the sink, tub and toilet is sparkling.

The kitchen is all glistening counters and stainless steel. No dishes in the sink, the faucet occasionally leaking a loud drip into the drain.

Or maybe, she thinks, she dreamt her whole relationship with Daryl. Maybe it was all a bad dream.

She goes to the refrigerator, knowing that it, too, is going to be clean and empty. Stuck to the door with a daisy magnet is an envelope addressed to her in unfamiliar handwriting. She takes it down and goes back out to the living room.

Dear Graciela,

Thank you for having Daryl's ashes sent to us. It means a lot, and we will have him buried with his grandparents and his brother Berto. I want to apologize to you for everything that Daryl did to you. Your friend Stephanie sent us a letter to tell us everything. He was never bad but he had trouble all the time ever since he was a baby. It was just how he was made. He loved you but he could never be at peace about anything. That isn't your fault. Nothing is your fault. Don't ever blame yourself for anything. We knew how hard it would be to be reminded, so we came and cleaned for you. If there is anything you want of his to remind you of the good times you had, you write to me, and I will send you what you want. But if you don't ever write, I will understand, and I will always love you.

The note was signed by Daryl's mother.

Graciela folds it and puts it back into the envelope carefully. She opens the blinds and lets the sun in. It's all her furniture, arranged just the way she left it. She touches her hair. One day soon, she knows, this will feel like home again. But now, she needs to be around people who aren't going to ask her anything or expect more from her than she can give. She walks out of the loft, carefully locking the door behind her, and drives directly to Edendale Yoga.

'My first class had thirty-five people,' Lee says. 'In the second class, I had almost fifty.'

'People are catching on to what a good teacher you are,' David says. 'That's what you're here for, right? To build a following.'

'Sometimes I wish I were like you,' she says. 'No studio, no big bills to pay. You get to do what you love and set your own terms.'

'It's a choice I made,' he says. 'We all choose our lives, Lee.'

The afternoon has turned unexpectedly hot, and at the end of her last class, David showed up and asked her if she wanted to go for a walk along the river. She loved the idea of getting away from the teeming crowds and the blaring sun, the music and the commerce. At least she's trying to convince herself that that's why the offer thrilled her so much. Now they're walking along a shady path with the river on their right and the noise of the festival being drowned out by the water rushing past.

'Unfortunately,' she says, 'at this point, every choice I make affects about ten people, including my kids.' And then she's struck by an idea that seems perfect. 'Why don't you come and co-teach a class with me tomorrow? We'd have a great time. We can work out a flow tonight. Don't you think it would be fun?'

He laughs at this. He has a deep laugh that surprises her, somehow; despite his high spirits in front of students, he seems like the kind of person who doesn't laugh easily or often. 'I'm not sure that would be a great idea. I'm not into the festival scene, and besides, this is your show.'

She's put off by the word 'show,' but she lets it go for now. She's too exhausted.

He puts his arm around her waist and pulls her to him. 'If you want,' he says, 'we can go swimming. The river is freezing, but it feels great when it's hot like this. A lot better, anyway, than it did this morning when I bathed in it and it was still about thirty degrees out.'

Maybe it's the heat of the day, or the fact that this leafy path feels so private, or the sound of the river beside them, or the distant strains of music, but Lee lets herself relax against David's body. She wants to believe that suggesting this walk was more than a friendly gesture on his part, but she's learned that David is impossible to read, and she's trying to go along without any assumptions.

'Tell me the truth,' she says. 'You don't think I'm selling out by doing this, do you?'

He stops and turns to her so they're facing each other, inches apart. He slips his hands behind her head and gently pulls her to him. *Okay*, she thinks. *No assumptions.* When he kisses her, it's with an intensity and passion that, like his laughter, catches Lee by surprise. For a moment, she's still not sure how to interpret his kiss, and then she stops trying to guess and begins kissing him back.

'I've wanted to do this for so long,' she says.

He pulls her body in even tighter against his, almost as if he's trying to crush her. Finally, he looks into her eyes and says, 'I've been trying *not* to do this since we met.'

They don't stop until they hear the crunch of footsteps along the path, and then they break apart as if they're kids who've been caught doing something forbidden.

David takes her by the hand and leads her off the track and deeper into the woods, until they come to a clearing with a cluster of tents set up at a distance from each other. He tells her he got the last available spot and leads her to a low, asymmetrical tent set off in the woods. Lee has been camping only a few times, but she was always struck by the combination of pristine nature, tents made out of garish synthetic fabrics, and all the smoke and refuse of campfires and food. But right now, she doesn't care what any of it looks like. She wants to feel his skin pressed against hers so badly that before they've even stooped and entered the low tent, she is clutching at him and trying to lift off his T-shirt. The inside of the tent is airless and stifling, but there's something about the way the green nylon is lit by the sunlight slanting through the trees that makes it all look beautiful. David's light hair is falling around his face, slightly damp in the heat, and when he takes off his T-shirt, Lee kisses his shoulder and his neck and runs her hands along the smooth muscles of his torso.

'Your body is perfect,' she says softly.

She tries to take off his glasses, but he stops her. 'I don't want to miss anything.'

In the past few days, she has been practicing so much, her body feels both tight and relaxed. But it's been so long since she's been with anyone other than Alan, it feels strange to be here with him and she finds herself almost blushing at the thought of getting undressed in front of him.

'Let me help you,' he says.

And then, with tenderness and urgency, he takes off her clothes until they're kneeling in front of each other, naked, while the river rushes past outside and the heat inside the tent builds.

'I'm sorry it's so hot in here,' he whispers into her ear.

'It's perfect.'

'You're sweating,' he whispers and bends down to blow on the sweat trickling between her breasts while circling his hands around her thighs. She winds her legs around his waist so she's sitting in his lap and starts to kiss his face, shuddering as she feels him rubbing against her stomach.

'Let's go out to the river to cool down,' he whispers.

'No. Please,' she says. 'Don't move. Stay here. Like this. Please. Stay.'

Forever is what she means. But she doesn't say that, because even if it's just for right now, for one hour this afternoon, it will be enough.

Katherine could easily get used to this climate. High desert, it's called. Dry air, and week after week of uninterrupted sunshine in the summer. The days are warm and intensely bright, but as soon as the sun begins to go down, it starts getting chilly, in the most benign and pleasant way possible.

She took three classes today, meaning about six hours of yoga, and now, at eight o'clock, she feels blissfully flexible and stretched. Too bad she didn't know about ten years ago that this is the best physical high you can get. A little more work than what she was doing then, but so much more satisfying. After her last class, she decided to wait at the top of the mountain and sit in the outdoor café with the killer view of the mountains and the lake. It's a little hard to believe that in a matter of months, everything she's looking at will be covered in – buried under, in fact – snow. But there it is.

Below her, people are swimming in the heated pool, and one ridiculous guy in a yellow bikini is doing some kind of choreographed yoga routine, just in case no one noticed how perfectly lean and muscled his body is while he was standing there or parading around the pool's perimeter. She's sure he came for the yoga, but for someone like this, admiration is a big part of the yoga experience. To each his own.

Based on today's observations, the men at the festival come in three varieties.

There are the young hippie/surfer types with dreadlocks and bandannas. They all wear calf-length cotton pants and no shirts, and practice on mats that look like they haven't been cleaned in a few years. From what she's seen in classes, these guys have amazing practices, but they treat the whole thing with the rapt, slightly masochistic risk-taking she's seen in surfers. The more likely they are to injure themselves with an impossible backbend or complicated arm balance, the better. They float, they fly, they soar. Unfortunately, they don't wear deodorant.

Then there are the men like Conor, nice guys who could take it or leave it but are along for the ride because they're trying to stay in a girlfriend's good graces. Usually, they're joyfully clumsy, taking a lot of spills with good humor and making fun of themselves whenever possible. Preferred yoga costume is baggy gym shorts and a ratty T-shirt. On the whole, pleasant, jovial guys who, if they keep at it, might one day be able to do a forward fold.

And then there are the guys like Yellow Bikini and, well, Alan: handsome and flawlessly fit, well-groomed and arrogant in their narcissism. They practice with an intensity that Katherine finds a little creepy, almost as if executing a perfect handstand is a moral imperative. Stern, chiseled faces and laser gazes. Nice suntans. The most astonishing thing about them is how little fun they seem to be having while practicing. Or, come to think of it, doing just about anything else. Nothing they do is ever good enough for them, but they let you know by their glances that *you* damned well better be impressed.

She sips at her juice and takes out her novel. She read another couple of chapters between classes, and she's starting to care more about the heroine. There's not exactly a plot to the book, just details of the woman's daily life, which isn't even all that interesting. But Katherine hates putting the book down, mostly because she's beginning to get terrified that the woman is going to bring the dog to the animal shelter. It's not that she cares so much about the dog; it's just that it seems like it would be the absolutely wrong decision for the woman.

The waiter, a tall, fleshy guy with a bored expression, brings her a martini in a sweating glass.

'Sorry,' Katherine says, 'but I didn't order this.'

He points to the doorway to the restaurant, where Jake is leaning against the doorjamb, arms folded across his chest. He gives her a little wave and makes his way over.

'Nice of you,' Katherine says, holding up the glass. 'Unfortunately, I don't drink.'

She points to the chair at her table, and he turns it around and sits on it backward.

'I forgot,' he says. 'Health nut.'

'You could say that. Or you could say drug addict in recovery.'

'Okay. That's blunt.'

'It saves a lot of time,' Katherine says. 'I'm sorry for wasting the drink.'

He shrugs. 'The bartender's a friend of mine. Let's say I got a good deal.'

'Okay,' Katherine says. 'Blunt. I like it.'

What is it, she wonders, about this kind of pointless banter with men she doesn't totally like or trust that she's missed so much in the past year? The attention? The little back-and-forth power play?

'Having a good time so far?' he asks.

'I haven't pulled any muscles yet, and I don't think I got a sunburn. So that's good. This is my second trip up on the gondola without catastrophe. Thank you for that.'

'I thought you'd appreciate it.' He takes off his mirrored sunglasses, revealing a pair of clear eyes that are light amber in color. Even with the weathered skin and the slightly gone-to-seed appearance, he's a handsome man. She can see the inside of his apartment already: a lot of tossed-around clothes and ski equipment, a partly squalid kitchen without much food. The home of a man who's most at home outdoors.

He slides the martini glass back and forth on the table, almost as if he's contemplating drinking it. 'You should let me take you on a private gondola ride. The view is the best just after sunset, when it's officially closed.'

Katherine watches the glass sliding across the slick surface of the table. It's all fun, but it's probably gone far enough. 'My boyfriend in L.A. might object.'

'Oh yeah? Lucky guy. Serious relationship?'

'We're about to move in together.'

He smiles at this and raises the glass, as if he's toasting her. 'Congratulations. A big step.'

'It's been coming for a while.'

'I'm glad you told me,' he says, and downs half the martini. 'I was beginning to worry you were single. Now I feel like my chances are a whole lot better.'

You can get away with a line like that as long as you know it's ridiculous, and judging from Jake's grin, he does. 'Sorry, cowboy. I gave up making bad decisions a while ago.'

'We'll see about that. I have a few things to finish up. The gondola shuts down in twenty minutes. Meet me there in forty-five.'

Stephanie is sitting at her computer in her bedroom. Her room is one of the few on the front of the house instead of facing the lake. She's not sure why she chose this one, since there were a couple of empty bedrooms on the water, but it probably has something to do with feeling a little bit like the outsider in this group, not exactly worthy of the best view. If she ever told that to Imani or Becky they'd probably physically move her across the hall, belongings and all. It was easier to say she liked the color of the walls in here (a pale, chilly blue) and the coziness of sleeping in the single bed under the eaves.

Becky started her Twitter campaign for Lee's class, and Stephanie made up a flyer on her computer, which they can distribute as soon as they get it printed up tomorrow. Through the open windows across the hall, she can hear Becky out on the dock, trying to teach Renay to sing. The real question is: Who's going to teach Becky?

'Moon River, wider than your smile . . .'

At least the sentiment is right. The moon is coming up, and probably shining gold on the water.

For the past half hour, Stephanie has been trying to write an e-mail to Roberta. Trying to explain. Billie had told her daughter that she'd seen Stephanie going out dressed up, and when Roberta pressed her for details, Stephanie had to confess that it was for the wrap party. 'I didn't think you'd want to come down all the way from San Francisco,' Stephanie said.

'You didn't *think*, but you couldn't *know* because you didn't *ask*.'

And that was the last time they talked.

Stephanie misses her. Roberta would be the first one out shilling for Lee's class, passing out flyers and, if needed, strong-arming people into class. Becky would undoubtedly get a kick out of her and would most likely flirt since, as she said last night, 'The most manly men I know are butch women.' And here in this setting, after a day of yoga, Stephanie craves her physically. But every time she starts writing, she gets tangled up in the language.

I'm ready to do this differently.

A lot has happened in the last couple of weeks.

If I'd known you wanted to come, I would have asked.

None of it, strictly speaking, is true. The only thing she can say for sure is that she misses her. So she should probably just write that and see where it all goes.

She signs in to her e-mail account. She has thirty-two new messages. She scans the list quickly, but opens only one: Bob Trent, the agent from ICM.

'I'm not trying to pressure you, but I've been talking you up to producers, and I have three who are ready to look at your next script. No pressure. Just saying.'

Whether or not this is true – and how much in the world of agents and producers is true? – he hasn't lost interest.

She starts writing the e-mail to Roberta, but she can feel a little buzz of excitement about the message from Trent gnawing at her. Her next script. Somewhere on this laptop are the pages she started months ago, before the shoot began.

'Oh dream chaser, you old faker . . .'

Maybe it would be fun to begin this way, with her hapless main character singing all the wrong lyrics to a song. Or maybe this is the hook she needs to make the whole character come together – someone who thinks she's a great singer but can't remember a lyric.

She closes out the e-mail account, opens a new file, and starts typing. It's best to go with the little burst of inspiration. She can write to Roberta later. Or get in touch with her once she gets back to L.A.

Unlike a lot of people she's known with substance abuse issues, Katherine has never blamed anyone else. Yes, she had a horrible childhood and an irresponsible mother, and yes, she had a lot of tough breaks. But she knew what she was doing when she took drugs, and she had a good understanding of the consequences. Being able to say 'I was a fuckup and I fucked up' is a matter of pride for her.

When she shows up at the gondola at the time Jake suggested, she knows what she's in for. She knows she's going to regret it and knows that if Conor finds out, it's going to hurt him and possibly ruin their relationship. But there's something irresistible about it. She's been acting like an adult for too long.

Jake is leaning on the handrail with a smug expression, but not an unkind one.

'I was beginning to wonder if you'd turn up,' he says.

'Disappointed?'

'Not at all. I hope *you're* not. In yourself, I mean.'

'Oh, a little bit,' she says. 'But I figure I would have been equally disappointed in myself if I hadn't come.'

Oddly, the gondola is less appealing empty than it is crowded. The metal floor is noisy, and the wear and tear is more obvious. She takes a seat on the bench at the back, and very slowly, they begin their descent. The lights down below have a magical twinkling quality, and there's a spill of yellow moonlight on the dark lake far off in the distance.

'So how do you get into a job like this?' Katherine asks.

'It's a tough training period,' Jake says, coming to sit beside her on the bench. 'You have to spend way too much time on the slopes for most of your youth and then have your Olympic dreams dashed by a major back injury. It helps if you're the kind of person who doesn't let go of things easily. You stay too long at the fair, and next thing you know, you're Mr. Gondola. Which is actually more satisfying and interesting than it probably seems. Most things in life are, as long as you throw yourself into them.'

'I'll keep that in mind. I'll tell you something really stupid. Somehow, I thought we were magically going to go down the back side of the mountain, off the grid. I just realized that even Mr. Gondola can only take this thing on its one route.'

He laughs at this. 'Very true.' He walks over to the control panel and says, 'But don't forget, I can hit the "pause" button.' The gondola comes to a stop and begins to sway from side to side. Katherine feels her stomach drop the way it did earlier in the day. She estimates they're about halfway down the mountain and suspended somewhere above a steep drop where the mountain seems to fall away in a sheer cliff. She has a moment of panic, and then Jake kills the lights and the illumination from the village and the festival below leaps into clear, sharp focus. In the silence, she can hear the wind and a thumping, booming bass from the music venue echoing against the granite.

'That pink way off is Reno,' Jake says. 'Fondly referred to around here as Las Vegas's trashy little sister.'

'I've heard that before,' Katherine says.

Jake comes and sits beside her again. He puts his arm

around her and pulls her in close to him. 'It's more dramatic and severe in winter. Colder, but more beautiful. You'll have to come back.'

Katherine pulls away from him and lies down on the bench with her head resting against her rolled-up sweater. 'This is definitely going to work best if we don't pretend there's anything romantic about it,' she says.

'How are the boys?' Lee asks her mother.

'The way you ask that,' Elaine says, 'it almost sounds like you think I'm letting them run wild.'

'Of course not. I'm just wondering how they're doing.'

'Oh, Lee, honey. Do you really think I'd forget to make them dinner last night and let them starve? Please give me more credit than that.'

'It never crossed my mind, Mom.'

'I know that's not true, honey. But as a matter of fact, as soon as they reminded me that we hadn't eaten, I got right to work, and I had food on the table for them before nine o'clock.'

The important thing is that the kids ate. If Lee raises any objections, she knows her mother will only get more defensive, and then everything will get more complicated and take more time. It's toward the end of her second day, and she's still on a high from the way her classes have been going. In the last class of the day, she had students spilling outside the little tent, practicing in the sun. In an hour, she's meeting David at his campsite for a communal dinner, although she's hoping they can skip the meal altogether.

'Can you put them on, Mom?'

'In other words, you want to make sure I'm telling you the truth?'

'I want to say hi, that's all. I miss them. What's that noise?'

'I'm sorry, honey. I'm just getting around to cleaning up the dinner dishes from last night and these pizza boxes are hard to break down. Someone ought to tell Domino's to get their act together.'

It's only one meal, Lee reminds herself. In the long run, one Domino's pizza isn't going to matter a bit.

'Anyway, the boys aren't here,' her mother says.

Lee checks her watch. She tries to think of the least controversial way to ask her mother where they are. 'They love visiting friends on Saturdays?' she says hopefully.

'Not friends. Earlier in the afternoon, that Lainey person who works at your studio made a surprise visit at the house with Graham. Apparently she's been phoning the kids to check up on them, which means she's checking up on me. I find her very hard to follow, Lee. I think she smokes pot. She had me sign some petition. I put down Bob's name. If anyone's going to get arrested, I'd rather it be him.'

'Do you know where they went?'

'He offered to take them all on an outing. The kids said they wanted to go to a miniature railroad. Thank God no one invited me.'

'They love that place,' Lee says wistfully. 'Or they used to. Do you know what time they're coming back?'

'They're coming back here, and then we're all going to Graham's house and he's making dinner. I did not tell him to have dinner for us, by the way. I just said that *if* he invited us, I wouldn't turn it down. I'm dying to see what his house looks like. I'll give you a full report.'

All things considered, she would prefer that Graham not start getting involved with the boys. On the other hand, it's a huge relief to know they're with a responsible adult. The opening of the studio will be shortly after she gets back to L.A. Once they're past that, Graham will have fewer reasons to visit; David, hopefully, will be in the picture then, and they'll all become friends. Graham is a reasonable man. He won't take it personally.

'I'm glad you're going out tonight, Mom. You deserve a little break.'

'Oh, Lee, don't make it sound like I have a hangover or something and am going to take a nap as soon as I can.'

'I appreciate you coming out. It's a big help to me.'

'You haven't even told me about the festival, honey. Is it fun? Are you a big star? They must love you. Tell me *everything*.'

'Well, I –'

'I'm sorry to cut you off, Lee, but I have to get in a quick call to Lawrence. I'm so worried about him. He rented a house down on Cape Cod this week, and it's been raining there for two days. The poor dear can't get a break.'

'I won't keep you on. Give the boys my love. And don't get too involved with Graham, Mom.' She starts to go on about why that would be a bad idea but quickly realizes that her mother has hung up.

For the past few days, Graciela has been driving to Edendale Yoga each morning and taking as many classes as she can. She's amazed at how quickly she was able to get back into her routine and start to feel at home. The people she meets here and practices beside know her by what she does in class physically. If she falls, they grin with understanding; they've been there. If she executes a posture with special grace, they nod appreciatively, or talk with her after class about her technique. No one asks her about her hair. No one gazes at her with pity. It's not what they're here for.

Maybe more than the interactions with other people is what happens to her inside when she's taking the classes. She's so focused on the placement of her feet or the balance in her arms or the depth of her twist, she doesn't think about anything else. And when she does, she takes a deep breath and lets the thoughts disappear. She was never a great believer in all the talk of toxins being wrung and twisted and sweated out of your body, but little by little, she feels as if she's clearing out the pockets of fear and grief that have been weighing her down. Maybe it is all true. Or maybe it's easiest and best to believe it's true and see what happens.

She's been taking a lot of classes with Chloe. She's one of those high-spirited teachers who, in a different generation, would have been leading an aerobics workout. She teaches with a breathless, excited quality in her voice, as if she's really, *really* happy to be here. And *really*, Graciela believes she is. Unlike Lee and some of the more adventurous instructors Graciela has taken classes from in the past year, Chloe almost always teaches the same poses in the exact same sequence, accompanied by the same instructions and prompts. At first, this annoyed Graciela – didn't Chloe herself get bored with her routine? But once she was able to give herself over to it, she found that she was sinking into a meditative state more quickly and easily. She always knew what was coming next, so there was no anxiety and nothing to anticipate. It was just movement and breath.

It is now the end of class, and Chloe has them all lying on their backs with a towel over their eyes. Instead of talking them into deep relaxation, Chloe falls silent, and for the first time in a few days, Graciela finds herself thinking about Daryl. Not with the anger and horror and guilt that she's experienced recently, but with an unexpectedly sweet fondness. She remembers the day he moved into the loft, how he arrived with one big bag of clothes and a few boxes of personal items. No furniture, no appliances, no food. He reminded her of a little boy who'd run away from home and had shown up on her doorstep. And throughout her relationship with him, he seemed like a lost, runaway boy. *He was never bad but he had trouble all the time ever since he was a baby.*

'Your practice is as strong as ever,' Chloe says to her after class. 'In some ways, it's even more amazing.'

'I don't know,' Graciela says. 'I'm just putting one foot in front of the other.'

Chloe laughs at this and says, 'That's how we do it around here. But the way you put that foot, it's beautiful.'

Graciela knows that in all likelihood, Chloe has heard the story of what happened to her in New York and that she, like everyone else who knows, is trying to be as kind as possible.

They're standing near the front desk of the studio, and Chloe, with her long curly hair, suddenly grabs Graciela by the hand and starts leading her down the hallway. 'I want to show you something. Lee doesn't want anyone to see until opening day, but I know she wouldn't mind in your case.'

It's probably the way people treat you when they find out you have cancer, Graciela thinks. You get taken behind the curtain to meet the wizard and have all your wishes granted.

Chloe unlocks a set of huge French doors and leads her into the new studio space. It's a bright afternoon, and the studio is sparkling with light and the smells of new wood and plaster.

'It's beautiful,' Graciela says.

'It's going to be an amazing place to practice,' Chloe tells her. 'And to teach.'

She sits on the floor in a patch of sunlight and pulls Graciela down so they're sitting beside each other, gazing through a long window that looks out onto the courtyard in back, which has been planted with flowering bushes and huge pots of geraniums.

'Your hair is starting to grow in,' Chloe says.

'The funny thing is, I'm getting used to it being short. I never realized how much my whole image of myself was tied up in it. I feel freer without it.'

After a few minutes, Chloe says, 'What are you going to do now?'

'How do you mean?'

'With your life. Are you going to keep dancing?'

'To be honest,' Graciela says, 'I hadn't thought very far ahead. One step at a time, remember?'

'You should be teaching,' Chloe says.

'There are a million and one dance teachers in L.A. Anyway, I'm not sure I'm ready to dance again.'

'I meant teach here. Lee needs to start doing some teacher training. She's against the idea, but it's almost impossible to pay the bills without offering training. For some studios, it's thirty or forty percent of their income.'

'I'm not sure L.A. needs another yoga teacher, either.'

'I don't know about L.A., but Lee does. Think of it as doing her a favor.'

Graciela looks around the new studio, glowing in the afternoon light. She knows that Chloe is being kind. The fatal-disease syndrome again. Graciela has been shy throughout her life. Growing up, she was always told that she should be quiet so the adults could talk, and if not the adults, then her brothers. It's one of the reasons she started to dance – a way to express herself without words. The idea of standing in front of a room filled with students waiting for her to say something makes her heart race with panic.

'I promise I'll think it over,' she says. 'When is Lee getting back?'

'Day after tomorrow.'

'Is she having a good time?'

'According to Lainey, it's complicated.' Chloe bounces up off the floor. 'In my next life,' she says, twirling, 'I want to be a dancer. I wish we could trade lives.'

Graciela bursts out laughing at this. 'Sorry, Chloe, but I wouldn't wish that on anyone.'

'I've got a great idea,' Chloe says. 'My boyfriend has tickets to a Dodgers game tomorrow night. We've got an extra one, and I know he'd love it if you came. They're playing New York. It should be a great game.'

Graciela is about to turn it down when she realizes that

she's never been to a baseball game before, which isn't the real reason she says, 'I'd love to, if you're sure it's okay with your boyfriend.'

Katherine wakes up at sunrise, wraps herself in a blanket, and goes out to the end of the dock. It's so cold, she can see her breath in the morning air. She knows that by noon she'll be sweating. This feels like the one moment in the day when she will have a little quiet and solitude, and she can finish reading her novel.

She and Renay went to the concert last night on the festival grounds, and when she drove Renay back to the house, she was talked into spending the night. It didn't take a lot of convincing. The whole of the Alpine village was throbbing with music when they left, and after a few hours of dancing with Renay to all that deep bass and strangely beautiful electronic music, surrounded by people dressed in wings and capes and dusted with glitter, she was ready for a little quiet. Not that she'd admit it, but she was also worried that if she stayed in the suite she's sharing with Lee, she might bump into David Todd coming out of Lee's bedroom in the morning. She had been trying to get Lee to start dating again as soon as Alan was finally out of the picture, so in theory, she should be happy about David. He's kind, he's handsome, his interests make sense for Lee, but she's always been a little suspicious of the loner types like David, who are usually hiding some kind of crippling insecurity under their vaunted independence.

The lounge chair at the end of the dock is as good a place as any to finish reading this book. That way if the heroine doesn't keep the dog in the final pages, she can toss the book into the lake.

It doesn't look hopeful. The last chapter begins with her loading the poor mutt into the passenger seat, the dog's preferred place to ride, paws up on the dashboard. Ed, the dog, is a twenty-pound hybrid of shaggy breeds and, from the description, sounds like one of those Dr Seuss creatures with the mismatched ears and scraggly fur. It's true that Katherine hasn't read all that many novels, but she's read enough to suspect that the outcome of this one is going to be happy. But how? She flips ahead and sees that there are only three more pages.

On the second-to-last page, she actually starts pleading with the heroine. 'Don't fuck it up. Please don't fuck it up.' She's waiting for an intervention of some kind, even an accident. In the last paragraph, the woman hands Ed over to the attendant at the animal shelter, and they put him on a leash and start to lead him away. She doesn't save him. She doesn't try.

It's Ed who saves himself. The woman watches as he's led away, but he doesn't look back at her, doesn't whimper, doesn't stall. That's when she realizes that whether she deserves the dog or not, she needs him a lot more than he needs her.

'Wait,' she says. The book ends there.

She feels footsteps on the dock behind her and quickly tries her best to mop up her face. It's Renay, barefoot and wrapped in a quilt. She sits beside Katherine and lays her head on her shoulder.

'So early,' she says, her voice rough with sleep. 'I loved dancing last night. You're so much fun to be with.'

Katherine is afraid that if she says anything, she's going to start crying again. So she waits a minute and says, 'Why did you give me this book?'

'I thought you'd like it.'

'That's not the only reason, is it? You think I should have the baby.'

Renay doesn't say anything, just burrows her head more deeply into Katherine's shoulder.

'I know that what you did was hard,' Katherine says, 'but my decision isn't going to change any of that for you, Renay. I'm sorry.'

'I know that. I'm not stupid.'

'I didn't think you were.'

'Anyway, it isn't about that at all,' Renay says. 'It's because you'd be a good mother.'

'I'm barely able to take care of myself,' Katherine says. 'I don't know why you think I could take care of a baby.'

'Because of how you took care of me,' Renay says.

The sun is coming up over the rim of the mountains in the distance and already the icy nighttime chill has dissipated. Katherine can hear the clatter of dishes in the house behind them. Everyone is waking up.

'It's something else, too,' Renay says. 'I think you want to have the baby. You just don't think you deserve to because of stuff you did a long time ago. But you're a different person now.'

Two nights ago, as the gondola was swaying above the cliff, she also began to think that maybe she's a different person.

After five minutes of making out on the uncomfortable bench, Katherine told Jake she thought it might be a good idea if they changed plans. He was a gentleman about it; her hesitation didn't come as a total surprise. He'd made peace with disappointment a long time ago, and he wasn't going to take this one personally.

'Not feeling it?' he asked.

'Not exactly that,' she said. 'Just worried about what I'll be feeling when the sun comes up.'

'Yeah, well, I'm pretty much an expert on morning-after regret. There are better feelings in the world.' And with that, he handed her her sweater.

'You know what I've always loved about bad boys?' Katherine said. 'They so often turn out to be really good guys. Take your shirt off.'

'I think that's called a mixed message,' he said.

'I'm a pro,' she said. 'I've worked with a lot of people who've had back surgery. And believe me, this is going to make you feel much better than Plan A ever would have.'

And then, as the wind picked up and the gondola swayed more, she worked on his back for a good thirty minutes. By the time they were back at the bottom of the mountain, they had a history together, just not the one they'd thought it would be.

Becky is calling them from the house, telling them that coffee is ready. 'You'll see,' Renay says. 'You'll see I was right.'

Chloe and Brian stop by Graciela's loft on their way to Dodger Stadium and pick her up. So far, Graciela has spent two nights at the loft, and although she was barely able to close her eyes the first night, she had a surprisingly good sleep the second. Things are headed in the right direction. As Graciela is settling into the backseat, Chloe turns around and nods toward Brian with a look that clearly means: 'Can you believe how hot my boyfriend is?'

Brian is a guy Chloe met in college and, according to her report, 'never even realized how sexy he was!'. Her breakthrough came a couple of months ago when they reconnected on Facebook. Brian is pretty much the opposite of lithe and energetic Chloe. He's a pear-shaped guy who seems to be going bald, although he's probably not even twenty-five. He has blotchy facial hair that is either the cause of or camouflage for a lot of acne along his jawline, and he's wearing a Dodgers T-shirt that looks as if it hasn't been laundered in about six months. Maybe it's one of those lucky charm items. The strange (or maybe wonderful) thing is that Chloe is so much in love with him, she views him as a total hunk.

After commenting on how much beer he drank the night before, Brian asks Graciela to reach into a cooler in the backseat and hand him a can of Heineken. As he's turning to take it from her, he looks at her and says, 'What's with the haircut?'

'I *told* you,' Chloe says between clenched teeth and then turns and shrugs apologetically to Graciela.

When they drive in to the stadium, Graciela starts to feel butterflies in her stomach, but as soon as she looks up and sees it looming there in front of her, she realizes that the chances of any sort of encounter with Jacob are so slim, they might as well be in different countries.

Brian parks the car, grumbling about how far they have

to walk. 'He has bunions,' Chloe whispers as they're walking across the miles of asphalt to the stadium.

'Really?' Graciela says.

'I know. It's unusual in someone his age. Especially since he doesn't move very much.' They walk along, looking at Brian's body in front of them, slumping ahead. 'He's so adorable, isn't he?' she says, leaning into Graciela and swooning. 'I'm so lucky.'

'I think you're both lucky.'

It's easy to imagine Brian as one of those guys whose friends are constantly ribbing him about having scored with Chloe and how undeserving he is of her. He probably has a great personality, Graciela thinks, but what she means is he probably has a better personality than what she's seen thus far. Or maybe he's an incredible lover, but that is one place she truly does not want to let her imagination wander.

'I know you're going to find someone else,' Chloe says. 'When the time is right, you will.'

I already did, Graciela thinks. *But the timing was wrong.*

The stadium is more beautiful inside than Graciela imagined. The startling green of the field with the grass cut in neat, perfect lines fills her with a nostalgia she doesn't understand. The seats are arranged in colorful stripes, one section stacked on top of the other, so the whole inside of the stadium feels like a colorful painting.

'I got you girls great seats,' Brian says. 'Just past first base. Yellow.'

'You're amazing!' Chloe says. Too bad Chloe already told her that Brian was given the tickets by his boss for being Employee of the Month at the chain restaurant where he works.

Looking out past the outfield from their seat, Graciela can see a line of towering palm trees, and beyond them, the brown hills in the distance. As the stadium begins to fill up, it feels more and more like a Roman coliseum, teeming with bodies and sounds, a moderately sized city's worth of people gathering here to watch the spectacle. Does Jacob get nervous before these events? It doesn't seem likely. He has that razor-sharp concentration that lets him tune out everything else.

The roar of the crowd is almost deafening when the teams start to run onto the field. When Jacob is announced, there's more jeering and shouting than for most of the other players, an indication that he's more valuable to his team and thus unpopular with the Dodgers fans.

Chloe nudges her, fans herself, and whispers to Graciela a rumor she's heard about Jacob Landers. If only she knew.

What's surprising to Graciela is that she finds herself forgetting Jacob and getting caught up in the game, in the beauty of it and the unexpected poetry, the sun on the grass, the swell she feels when the whole stadium becomes one living organism as the crowd goes wild in unison. She's transported back to the moments in her childhood when she heard her father watching the game on television in another room.

All of that changes when Jacob gets up to bat and suddenly the huge screens ringing the stadium are filled with his face. He's as intensely focused as she'd expect, and when he looks toward the camera directly, he almost seems to be looking at her. She can feel the anticipation building around her, the crowd waiting for the New York superstar to fall on his face. After his first strike, there's a huge roar of laughter and applause, and Graciela realizes that she's clutching the edges of her seat. A few seconds later, he swings and sends the ball sailing up and out so far, it's out of reach of the outfielder, and she watches on the giant screens as the camera follows him past first and then second base. His face appears on-screen again, and she can see the excitement and joy in his eyes and she knows then for certain that he is not thinking of her, that he has moved on, that he's past all of the anger he expressed in the messages he left for her, and all the love as well. She is just a fan sitting in a stadium filled with more than fifty thousand people, and he is a star.

A few minutes later, when one of his teammates hits a double, Graciela leaps to her feet as he's coming in to home plate.

'Jesus,' Brian says. 'You don't even know what you're applauding for. He's playing for the other team.'

'I know that,' Graciela says. 'But he has such a nice smile.'

Lee is in her hotel room, reviewing her notes and making a few last-minute adjustments to the sequence of her poses. Her final class, the big one, is in two hours. No matter how many people show up, she's committed to making it fun, to making it a journey that begins with vigor and sweat and movement and ends with a meditation that somehow wraps up the experience of the past several days of the festival.

She talked with Stephanie earlier in the day and asked

her to write a few jokes she could toss in. Who says yoga has to be dour to be serious? David puts a lot of humor into his classes, and he's one of the best teachers she's ever had. Delivery is what matters most. She's trying to decide if she can pull off the joke about pigeons when she gets a text message from David.

Come down to campsite? Here waiting for you.

She checks her watch. It should take her twenty minutes to walk there and twenty to get back to the yoga tent. Even if she spends forty-five minutes with him, she'll still have time to spare. And if she spends only ten minutes with him, it will make her more relaxed and prepared to teach than sitting in this room could. She tosses everything she'll need into a pack, grabs her mat, and heads out.

The festival is winding down, but the enthusiasm of the crowds on the streets of the Alpine village is growing, nurtured by four days of music and sun and movement. As she walks through the mass of people, she can see a few heads turning. Maybe they're students who've taken her classes or seen her on the posters. She thinks back to the first day she arrived here, when she was crushed by the weight of her caffeine-withdrawal headache and felt lost sitting in the back of the tent for the welcome talks. Now she feels as if she belongs, as if she's earned her right to be here, no matter what happens this afternoon.

She's so hemmed in by the people rushing off to their classes and playing music on the corners of the narrow passageways, it feels as if it's taking forever to get to the path by the river. Once she does reach it, she starts to sprint through the cool shade. It doesn't cross her mind until she's almost at the campgrounds that David could have come to the hotel and saved her all this time. He is coming to her class, after all.

She goes to his site in the trees, but his tent is down, and all of his belongings are packed into a few tidy bundles, neatly stacked on the ground. It's not her style to travel so light, but she'll get used to it. For him, she could probably get used to anything. He's sitting on the bank of the river, and as soon as he sees her, he leaps up and hugs her.

'It took you a while,' he says. 'I was worrying.'

'It's so crowded up there, I could barely move. We should leave plenty of time to get back, just so I don't worry about being late.'

'Are you looking forward to the class?'

'I'm not dreading it as much as I was,' she says. 'A lot has happened in the past few days.' Maybe she should keep her mouth shut, should not make herself vulnerable by telling him too much, but isn't life better when you just put your feelings out there on the line? 'Do you want me to tell you what's happened? What a wonderful thing happened to me?'

He smiles but says nothing.

'You, mainly. Not that you couldn't have guessed. It's been a rough year, but as long as it was leading up to this, it was all worth it. Just knowing you'll be in the class makes me feel a lot more confident.'

He kisses her eyes gently and says, 'Lee, I'm not going to be in class.'

She steps back from him. He said it softly, but it's hard to read his tone. 'What do you mean?'

'I was walking around the village today, pretty much all

298

day. I took a couple of classes, and I looked in on a bunch more. This is bullshit, Lee. The whole thing. It's commercialism and consumerism and corporate sponsors and celebrity culture and everything I've tried to get away from in my teaching and my life. The whole thing is wrapped up in a big moneymaking bundle with the word "yoga" slapped on top, not because anyone cares, but because that's what sells. I don't want to be a part of this, and I don't want you to be a part of this. I don't want this to be what we're about, what we stand for.'

Lee has a slightly panicked feeling, as if now she's going to be made to pay for the fun she's had with him the past few days.

'It's a festival,' she says. 'Thousands of people getting together to romp around in nature and have fun and celebrate something they love. Some of it's over-the-top and ridiculous. I don't deny that. But there are probably hundreds of people here who had their lives changed in a small way that's going to stay with them forever. What's wrong with that?'

'Don't you see you've fallen for it? You took the bait.'

'I took an opportunity, and I'm trying to make the best of it.'

'Why get into a competition with Kyra Monroe to see who can bring in the most people? Just step away. If you go into that big tent and get wired with a microphone and put on a big, showy performance, how are you any different? Once you're in, you're in, and there's no turning back.'

Is he suggesting she not show up for her class after everything that's gone into getting ready for this? 'I signed a contract,' she says. 'My friends have been helping get people to my classes. I can't just not show up.'

'The thing is,' he says, 'you *can*. They'll have fifty teachers in the wings waiting to fill in for you. You *can* just not show up.'

'It's not that simple, David. I've got a studio. I've got kids and employees. I can't just walk away from all that.'

'I'll help you. I'll help you make it work without all this bullshit.'

'You'll come work at Edendale with me?'

'If that's what you want, we can talk about it.'

Except it sounds as if this is really about what he wants, and it doesn't have much to do with her desires at all. She can cancel the class and have him, exactly what she's been hoping for since she met him. And if she doesn't? He hasn't said anything about that, but she has a strong suspicion that if she goes ahead with the class, she won't see him again for a long time. She's never cared about being a 'star', and the truth is, if it hadn't been for Lainey, she never would have thought about trying to teach here at all. Why should she give up David for something she's not sure she even wants?

'You can drive back to L.A. with me,' David says and pulls her into him. 'We can camp out along the way. The only thing I'm asking is that we leave right now.'

'Before the class.'

'Yes, before the class.'

Katherine was supposed to meet Lee behind the stage at the tent half an hour before the class began. As of now, Lee is running fifteen minutes late, and Katherine's starting to worry. What could have happened that would make her this late? She's called the hotel a few times, but there's no answer in her room, and she's not responding to her text messages, either.

The sound guy comes over to her and says, 'She was told to check in twenty minutes ago. We need to get her mike on and make sure everything's working. At this point, if there's a fuckup, it's not on me.'

'I know her,' Katherine says. 'She'll be here.'

'Well, tell that to Krishna O'Reilly. He's having a fit. We've got four hundred people in this tent, and if she's not here in five minutes, he's putting in a substitute. Which would look pretty crappy for her.'

Katherine looks out into the tent. The mats are lined up so closely, their edges are practically touching. There's music playing on the sound system, but you can barely hear it over the laughter and conversation of the students.

Please, Lee, she thinks, *don't screw this up. He's not worth it.*

Stephanie and the others are in the front row, chatting in a little circle. She can see that Imani and Becky are thrilled by the attention they're drawing, even if they're doing their best not to show it. She walks down to them, and Stephanie says, 'You don't look like you're having fun yet, Kat.'

'Lee's running a little late. I'm starting to get worried.'

'She's a pro. What could have happened to her?'

'If she doesn't show,' Becky says, 'Renay and I will get up and entertain the troops. We do awesome covers of "Moon River" and "Blue Skies". Relax.'

The sound guy is talking to Krishna O'Reilly and pointing at Katherine. The two of them wave her over.

'Be right back,' she says. 'Don't give away my spot.'

Krishna is a large, jovial guy, and since he's the one responsible for booking Lee, Stephanie can't blame him for being bent out of shape. 'Unacceptable,' he says. 'All weekend long, dozens of teachers, not one of them started a class late. What does she think she's doing?'

She thinks she's in love, Katherine feels like saying. Of course, she doesn't. In the end, it's her life and her decision. If she decides to throw it all over for David, it's up to her.

'I'm done with this,' Krishna says. 'I'm putting in Taylor Kendall or Baron. I should have stuck with a bigger name anyway.'

Katherine's made enough of her own mistakes to know that sometimes you just have to fall down. In one way or another, Lee will eventually pick herself up.

'Do what you have to do,' she tells them. 'I'm just here as a friend.'

'Well, as a friend, you can tell her she just ruined her chances of having a career in L.A. The word that she screwed over four hundred people is going to spread fast. Who's going to want to come to her studio after that happens?'

Katherine takes one last look out at the field behind the tent, at the broad, open expanse of green. She can see mountains in the distance and that open, startling blue of the sky. This is what she'll remember of the experience years from now, the beauty of the colors and the soft, warm breeze blowing down from the mountain. She'll go down into the front row with her friends and take the class, whoever ends up teaching it. That's when she sees something in the distance, a spot at the end of the field, slowly getting bigger. She steps outside and tries to focus her eyes. Hopefully, she waves. And then she sees clearly that it's Lee, jogging along the path toward the tent. She waves back at Katherine in a crazy, happy way. Unless Katherine's mistaken, she's laughing, too.

She rushes back inside and grabs the sound guy. 'Tell him she's here,' she says, pointing. 'And tell him it's going to be an incredible class.'

Lainey turns on the fan in the new bathroom. Silent, but so powerful, it practically sucks the paper towels up to the ceiling. Graham is a good man. It took a little coaxing for him to see things her way, but he came around. No immovable ego on this guy, a rarity among architects and among men in general. Imagine a glass bathroom door with only a light frosting people could practically see through. A nutty idea. You need two things in a bathroom: privacy and a good exhaust fan. Everyone knows that. She rummages around the bottom of her bag until she finds her lighter.

Then again, this whole yoga world is full of nutty ideas. If someone had told her a few years ago that she'd be spending her days surrounded by a bunch of people in leotards with their heels above their heads, she wouldn't have believed it. All the crazy names for the crazy poses, as if calling something by an allegedly Sanskrit word is going to change the fact that you're basically jumping around and turning yourself into a living Gumby. She read a book a couple of weeks ago that claims the yoga postures were adapted from calisthenic routines Danish soldiers were doing in India in the 1920s. She tossed out the book after she finished it. Not a theory that's likely to help bring in more business. She chews on the image of a bunch of green, gummy Gumbies doing yoga, exhales, and starts chuckling. There are so many people gathered for the opening party in the studio tonight, no one's going to hear her in here, so she lets herself have a really good laugh.

She flushes the toilet, just in case someone's waiting outside wondering what she's doing in here, washes her hands, splashes on some body wash that smells like a freshly cut lawn, pops in a Juicy Fruit, and she's good to go.

Everything is glowing in the studio, mostly because Graham insisted they use only candlelight. It's amazing how beautiful rooms and people look in this soft, flickering light. She probably looks halfway respectable herself. She steps into the crowd of people and feels a sudden rush of happiness. Getting fired from UCLA was probably the best thing that ever happened to her. Good salary and great benefits, but basically a velvet-lined rut. No one needed her there. As soon as she walked into Edendale for her interview, she knew that wasn't going to be a problem here. A lot of loose ends needed to be tied up. Mission accomplished. Or partly.

Lee is standing at the front of the studio, talking with her friends. They got back from the festival just under two weeks ago, but they're still going over their adventures. Who knows what really happened with the skinny guy with glasses – but whatever it was, at least he's out of the picture. The minute he walked into the studio, Lainey knew he wasn't right for Lee. What Lee hasn't caught on to yet is that Graham *is* right for her. Lainey is not going to rush that, just nudge things along gently.

She talked Graham out of his more elaborate plans for the party. It's easy to get people to do what you want if you can figure out their motives. He wanted to impress Lee. Best way to do it, she convinced him, was to scale the party back by a lot and instead of having a ton of wine and fancy food, turn it into a goofy kind of yoga class.

Graciela comes over to Lainey and says, 'It's mobbed!' in that sweet, wide-eyed way of hers. 'Were you expecting so many?'

'Lee got so much great press at the festival, we had an idea it was going to be crowded. Although maybe not this jammed.'

'I hope I'm able to get into her classes now.'

'Come see me if you have any problems. I've got a ton of pull around here.'

Lainey hasn't told Lee yet that Graciela is going to be her first trainee. Not that she thinks she'll object, just that it's best to let her settle back into her life and the new studio before filling her in on her next step.

Graham is at the back of the studio, huddled with Glenn and Conor and the contractor who did most of the work. He's got on his trademark white shirt and black pants, but tonight he went all out and added a black tie. No doubt Glenn and the contractor are reassuring Conor that having a baby isn't going to end his life as he knows it. Translation: they're trying to convince themselves that they're happy about being fathers. For her money, Graham is the best looking of the bunch, but she's going to have to talk to him about adding a little color to his wardrobe every now and then. Who wants to go out with a guy who looks like a newspaper?

Lainey has no idea how Lee is going to conduct a class in this place with so many people, but she obviously has a plan. She tells everyone to gather in the studio, and when they do, they're so packed in, it's hard to imagine them moving at all. Lainey hangs back.

At home a few nights ago, while she was watching another one of those reality shows about obese people eating salads and hitting punching bags, she got up and tried doing one of the warrior things. Nothing to it, really, and probably she would have been even more successful if she hadn't been wearing a skirt. She liked the way it made her feel – a little silly, but a little strong, too – so she did it on the other side. She went online the next day and found a site that sells yoga pants for people her size, which is to say, normal people with real bodies. She got close to ordering a pair but backed down at the last minute. Too expensive, and too exposing. It's always best to keep your vulnerabilities well hidden.

She can hear Lee starting to talk to the people gathered in the studio. Funny to think that after working at Eden-dale for months now, she's never heard Lee teach a class. She stands in the doorway, neither in nor out of the room. Lee has them all breathing in unison, in and out, slower and slower. Lainey closes her eyes and listens to the sound of all those lungs working together like a giant bellows, and she has a weird moment of feeling as if she's losing control and melting into this group.

She feels a hand on her arm, and when she opens her eyes, Lee is standing beside her. 'Come in,' she says. 'I want you to take the class.'

'Not a chance,' Lainey says. 'I didn't wear my yoga bra tonight.'

Lee smiles at her in her kind way. 'Whatever you decide to do, even if it's just stand there, is exactly what you're supposed to be doing.'

'It's going to take me a minute to process that comment,' Lainey says.

Lee has led her into the room and placed her between two skinny girls in T-shirts and tights. 'All you have to do is breathe,' Lee says quietly. 'Just start breathing, and the rest will happen on its own.'

It would be more embarrassing to leave than it is to stay, so Lainey closes her eyes and takes a breath in. She doesn't need special pants for this, or someone else's body. She doesn't even have to open her eyes. All she has to do is breathe. Lee said so herself. She can do that.

ELIZABETH NOBLE

THE WAY WE WERE

Susannah and Rob were childhood sweethearts. But as with most early love affairs, they broke up, moved on and now find themselves in very different places. And not entirely happy – who is?

A chance meeting between them sends shockwaves through their lives. What happens when your first love makes a surprise reappearance? Is fate telling you it's time for a second chance . . . or should you simply walk away and let the past become ancient history?

But Susannah and Rob just aren't able to forget the way they were . . . and the world is about to realize the consequences of their reunion.

Elizabeth Noble, the Queen of the Heartbreaking Bestseller, returns with a wonderful novel about love and second chances.

'Wonderfully well written . . . full of emotion' *Daily Mail*

AVAILABLE NOW IN HARDBACK

JANE GREEN

GIRL FRIDAY

When Kit and Adam separated after almost fifteen years of marriage, Kit felt like she had lost her lover, her best friend and her identity all in one fell swoop. But now, a year on, Kit's life is back on track.She has the perfect job – working for a famous novelist – two wonderful children, a good relationship with her ex-husband and time to enjoy yoga. Then her friend, Tracy, introduces her to Steve – attentive, charming, the perfect gentleman – and Kit thinks she may have found the right one. But is Steve really as perfect as he seems? And why does it bother Kit when Tracy starts dating Kit's reclusive boss?

What no one knows is that Tracy is hiding a secret – one that threatens to ruin her new-found happiness with Robert and her friendship with Kit. And now Tracy must decide whether to keep her past hidden for ever or whether she should reveal the truth before it's too late …

A densely plotted brew of love and mistakes' *The Times*

Lucinda Riley

HOTHOUSE FLOWER

As a child, concert pianist Julia Forrester would linger in the hothouse of Wharton Park estate, where exotic flowers tended by her grandfather blossomed and faded with the seasons. Now, recovering from a family tragedy, she once more seeks comfort at Wharton Park, newly inherited by Kit Crawford, a charismatic man with a sad story of his own. But when a years-old diary is found during renovation work, the pair turn to Julia's grandmother to hear the truth about the love affair that turned Wharton Park's fortunes sour . . .

And so Julia is plunged back in time, to the world of Olivia and Harry Crawford, a young couple torn apart by the Second World War - and whose fragile marriage is destined to affect the happiness of generations to come, including Julia's own.

Lucinda Riley's heart-rending storytelling embraces war-torn Europe and the exoticism of Thailand as she examines the messy tangles of love.

JULIA LLEWELLYN

LOVE NEST

Roll the dice

Grace's childhood home, Chadlicote Manor, is being sold to settle family debts. Will losing her home break her heart or is it the chance for a new life?

... move two spaces

Karen's husband has the Manor in his sights as a chance to start over in rural paradise. But Karen prefers city living and, when a new flame turns up the heat, starting again might just mean the end of the road.

... climb the ladder

Gemma is longing for a baby and, unlike her own loft apartment, Karen's house is an ideal family home. But the dream house can only have its dream baby if Gemma can convince her flakey sister to help out.

... to land on

Up-and-coming rockstar Nick has designs on Gemma's flat. He's also taken a shine to classy estate agent, Lucinda, but she's not all she seems - and neither is he, since he's hiding a girlfriend he's looking to ditch when the sale goes through.

. . . the Love Nest
where all their troubles come home to roost!

Psst

want the latest
gossip on all your
favourite writers?

Then come and join us in . . .

THE
BOOKBOUTIQUE

. . . the **exclusive club** for anyone who loves to curl
up with the latest reads in women's fiction.

- All the latest news on the best authors.
- Early copies of the latest reads months before they're out.
- Chat with like-minded readers as well as bestselling writers.
- Excellent recommendations for new books to read.
- Exclusive competitions to get your hands on stylish prizes.

SIGN UP for our regular newsletter by emailing
thebookboutique@uk.penguingroup.com
or if you really can't wait, get over to
www.facebook.com/TheBookBoutique

He just wanted a decent book to read ...

Not too much to ask, is it? It was in 1935 when Allen Lane, Managing Director of Bodley Head Publishers, stood on a platform at Exeter railway station looking for something good to read on his journey back to London. His choice was limited to popular magazines and poor-quality paperbacks – the same choice faced every day by the vast majority of readers, few of whom could afford hardbacks. Lane's disappointment and subsequent anger at the range of books generally available led him to found a company – and change the world.

'We believed in the existence in this country of a vast reading public for intelligent books at a low price, and staked everything on it'
Sir Allen Lane, 1902–1970, founder of Penguin Books

The quality paperback had arrived – and not just in bookshops. Lane was adamant that his Penguins should appear in chain stores and tobacconists, and should cost no more than a packet of cigarettes.

Reading habits (and cigarette prices) have changed since 1935, but Penguin still believes in publishing the best books for everybody to enjoy. We still believe that good design costs no more than bad design, and we still believe that quality books published passionately and responsibly make the world a better place.

So wherever you see the little bird – whether it's on a piece of prize-winning literary fiction or a celebrity autobiography, political tour de force or historical masterpiece, a serial-killer thriller, reference book, world classic or a piece of pure escapism – you can bet that it represents the very best that the genre has to offer.

Whatever you like to read – trust Penguin.